Cover Art by Stephen Cooney

James Ward Kirk
PUBLISHING
2 0 1 3

Copyright James Ward Kirk Publishing 2013

Web: jwkfiction.com
Twitter: @jwkirk
Facebook: James-Ward-Kirk-Fiction

Cover art by Stephen Cooney
Ugly Baby Clip Art Collection by Jeff Swenson
Compiled by Sydney Leigh
Before Collapse © font courtesy of Galdino Otten
Monster Vector Art courtesy of clipartsfree.net
Excerpt from The Fifth Child by Doris Lessing, First Vintage
International Edition, May 1989.
The Tyger © William Blake, 1794

ISBN-13: 978-0615898308 (James Ward Kirk Publishing)

ISBN-10: 0615898300

All rights reserved. No part of this book may be reproduced in
any form or by any electronic or mechanical means, including
information storage and retrieval systems, without written
permission from the publisher or author, except in the case of a
reviewer, who may quote brief passages embodied in critical
articles or in a review.

"She was at the end of a long ward, which had any number of cots and beds along the walls. In the cots were—monsters. When she strode rapidly through the door at the other end, she was able to see that every bed or cot held an infant or small child in whom the human template had been wrenched out of pattern, sometimes horribly, sometimes slightly. A baby like a comma, great lolling head on a stalk of a body...then something like a stick insect, enormous bulging eyes among stiff fragilities that were limbs...a small girl all blurred, her flesh guttering and melting—a doll with chalky swollen limbs, its eyes wide and blank, like blue ponds, and its mouth open, showing a swollen little tongue. A lanky boy was skewed, one half of his body sliding from the other. A child seemed at first glance normal, but then Harriet saw there was no back to its head; it was all face, which seemed to scream at her. Rows of freaks, nearly all asleep, and all silent...Well, nearly silent..."

—from Doris Lessing's Fifth Child

THIS BOOK IS DEDICATED TO THE WRITERS BOTH IN AND
OUTSIDE OF THESE PAGES...

MAY YOU FOREVER FIND INSPIRATION IN THE MOST
UNIQUE AND UNORTHODOX THEMES.

☡☻☡

Contents

POETRY

Dona Fox
Orphan Ship

We gave new meaning to the term.
A giant orphanage,
we roamed from galaxy to galaxy--
harvesting the homeless children,
the undesirable toddlers,
the horrendous infants--
the ugly babies of every type.
We tried to find them families
among other species who might not realize
they were dreadful amongst their own kind.
Unfortunately, ugly appears to be universal
and our ship got more crowded
at every stop.

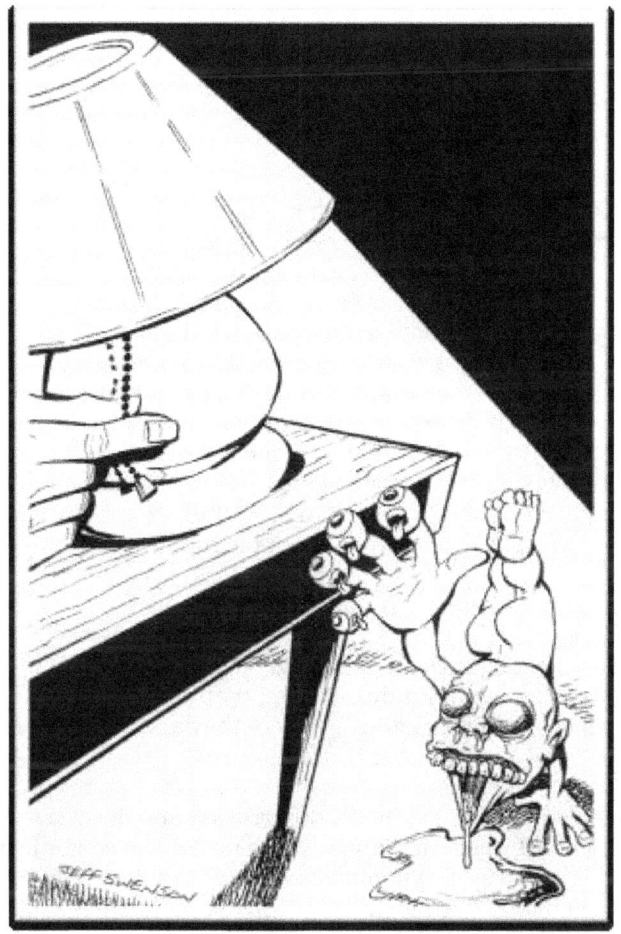

Baby No Name by Jeff Swenson

Stephanie M. Wytovich
Baby No Name

It wasn't a child.
To call it that would be *wrong*.
A child doesn't eat like that. Doesn't
drink from its eyes, smell from its mouth.
It walks on its hands—yes, its—I can't tell
the gender because there's nothing *there*. But
it sees with its fingers, and tastes all the sounds. It tells
me when I'm wrong—when I don't spend enough
time with it. Lectures me like an adult
with a voice that cracks and wheezes as if the
thing had smoked four packs a day for 20-something years
when it only crawled out of me three days ago.

I don't know where it's at now. It comes and goes as it pleases,
hates being in the light. It's probably under the couch
again, laughing like it does. It giggles at shadows, thinks
it's funny how they move. When I try to turn on the lamp,
it screams, so I don't. Better to stay in the dark. That way I don't
have to see it move.

One time, I tried to hold it. It burrowed into my cleavage,
cooing like the child it definitely was not. It looked at me with
its big green eyes and touched my face. It threw up water,
sneezed blood. Then it smiled a 200-toothed grin and kissed
my hand. I haven't held it since.

Matthew Wilson
The Witch's Lover

For the sake of revenge, I
have sold my soul.
Mark refused my love, so I have
chosen another who showed me things.

How to read forgotten words and make
those who hurt me suffer. Die.
I hoped my child did not have her
father's eyes.

Despite my wishing, the midwife
screamed and all my hoping
is for nothing.
They say motherhood is a beautiful thing,

but I lost a little of my flesh as my child
locked its teeth into my thigh.
A baby has to eat, I suppose.
Such an ugly child. Her father said she would

look better when her first skin molted
off like a rattlesnake.
Newborn spiders eat their mothers and I dislike
how she looks at me. Hungrily.

Her father has her for the weekend, in a place
too hot for me to survive.
I can breathe a little easier here, alone.
And think how better things would have been

if Mark had loved me.

Maria Mitchell
The Last Son of Circe

Circe
trusted his treachery.
Aeetes
fleshed her philosophy.
He sliced her iris with a jagged wing
she ate his flesh to the tune of spring.
A cradle coiled from a solemn tomb
when her stomach opened
her ageless womb.
Tranquil Circe
holds squalling blood,
a brother made a son by cannibal lust.

Maria Mitchell

David S. Pointer
Long Term Care

Space infant airway
management was serious
as the toddler brain tumors
that returned heavy as a
mortician's typewriter, but
eventually it was learned
that congenital anomalies
fruit or cabbage division
could utilize the tumor slices
and improve oxygen flow to
the smaller diameter tracheas
of the space babies being
groomed to guide Martian
spawn to the geriatric welcoming
center refurbishing old flesh
with incoming graftable new

Mathias Jansson
Forbidden Pleasure

Between her legs,
she saw the white hood.
The head of her child,
a reward of a long, hard labor.

She pushed and screamed
until the thing slipped out.
From her exhausted body
came a long white capsule,
blank, shining, and moist.
With a twist, the maggot turned
where it lay on the floor
and started crawling toward its mother.

Never more, she thought,
will I seek my pleasure
among the rotten corpses,
the fly-infested cadavers,
lying in the cemetery.

Envy's Child

J.D. Isip

It wasn't that they didn't care—
they were angels, caring
was their means—just
staying on, weeping and gawking
over a muted reflection
seemed insincere
like praying he had lived...

They took flight, a glory
on the wing like his father
who had descended holding
sunlight in his hair, at his hands and his feet
and her by the trance of him
revealed, like the son
here in and of the cold earth

He was no Christ, but his coming
was told in his father's eye
on the free-willed vessels
which he watched like scurry mice
unaware of the hunger
that spreads, swoops, seizes
and squeezes out life

She bore the first winged human
dying in an empty embrace
of his imagined father
who she waited for, and prayed
that he would return the sun
that came with him, blinding her
with the white holy heat...

And as the last seraphim lifted
above the broken body
cupped in his own young wings
a serpent heaved heavily forward, eyeing
vacant heaven, and resting at the feet
of the winged Halfling

---

pausing to remember...

Her kind he had shamed; his
kind shamed him here
to crawl, creep and cry
cradled, now, at the chest of his own
fallen image, his only son
too human for heaven,
too angel for the earth

That sent up its sons against
"The Demon" they called him
and let fly their weapons
proficient at cutting down heaven's
questionable, misunderstood, half-
winged creatures—
To bring them back to earth.

David S. Pointer
Kiddie Labor Camps

The surgeon excised the
enormous forehead flap
before succumbing to noxious
odors as the abdominal cavity
kids arrived held by next-gen
robot corps celebrating the
arrival of more child labor
as button repair pushers
or an extra pair of kiddie
eyes to detect ice cream
false front stores holding
green embalming fluid to
nourish the dead ahead

Daniel Ari Warts and All

At the marketplace, my eggs sell themselves.
My basil's gone by nine, and my rhubarb
pies fetch a creamy price, so my walk back's
weightless. It's just me and my empty cart.
You see? It doesn't matter that my face

scares bats. By day, my visage stays downward
on dirt, scales and coins, but my nose lifts up
ambling back with a jingle as the stars
glint like tavern lamplights off raised ale cups.
If I can jingle, who could say I'm cursed?

I was foul and fourteen when my pop-pop
pulled me bodily out to the garden,
bent my stubborn knees beside the turnips,
gave me a trowel, looked in me and said: "Start.
Warts and all. Start." My body sprouted warm.

That day I became apprentice to dirt.
It never kills me that their comments hurt.

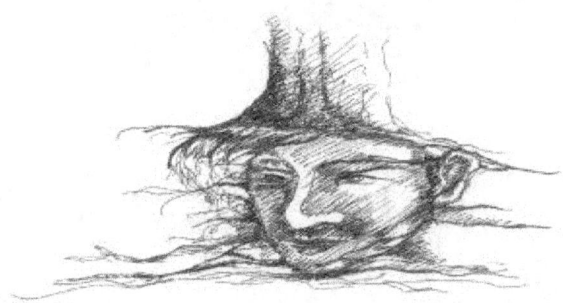

Matthew Wilson
The Nursery in the Cellar

I don't like taking my friend's
children to the fair.
It reminds me of my ugly babies
sleeping in jars down in the cellar.

I have loved many women,
but had no wish to be a father.
Their small faces are torn with the instruments
I used for their abortions, to rip them

from their mother's bodies.
Hitchhikers that have appeared
as missing on milk cartons. Some slim
celebrity before next week's disappearance

knocks them off the news.
My ugly babies sleep in embalming fluid
from my days working as a mortician.
I suppose some make-up might make them pretty.

But what would be the point when only their
mothers see them? And their screams of madness
force me to go to the highway
and find another woman who has broken down.

FLASH FICTION

Joseph J. Patchen
Infested Candy

A low cackling wakes me at exactly at 3:23 am. The laughing swells, surrounding the room, and yet at the same time can be heard moving slowly about the rest of the house. It is not many voices, but one: the sound neither male nor female; different, deeper, edgier, caustic.

A biting cold mist rises from the floor and washes over me, first caressing my skin and then slowly saturating my bones. My limbs, neck, and jaw are immobile; only my eyelids can flutter.

Once deep inside, the cold congeals into a wet mass that travels up and down my spine before finally breaking apart into smaller fluid pieces that skitter along every inch and curve of my ribs.

Steam billows from my mouth and nose. I shiver as it swirls about, on and in itself, just a foot or so above me. As if held in place, the steam seems to form a thick ceiling of vapor that sporadically spits back droplets of hot stinging blood.

The cackling stops, only to be replaced by a low and constant moan I can hear before me and traveling throughout the house. As the mist dissipates, I still can't move or even scream...but I can taste the blood stuck to my teeth and tongue. Despite the pain I feel, all I can do is sleep.

But for how long, I do not know. I wake to find I'm still drowsy and achy as the sun pours in through my windows. I find my shades and curtains are torn down and lie twisted in heaps on the floor with broken furniture and clothes that are strewn about. My bookcase is smashed and my books are all torn into slippery heaps. My digital clock is debris on a wire. There is blood splatter everywhere—on every wall, the ceiling, the floor—all over me and my bed. Even my damaged property is sprinkled in crimson. The sight leaves me nauseous.

Lightheaded, my balance elusive, I stumble toward the bathroom in search of a mirror I hope is still on the wall. Part of it is in long jagged pieces and stabs and slices my feet from the floor. The pain is numbing, but the shock of what remains of my face, bloated with erupting lesions, is even more alarming.

My gut is sore as though I've been pummeled. I can feel a pressure from within building in my intestines and against my chest. I'm exhausted and mutilated without a clue as to who attacked me during the night.

My toilet and sink are in ruins, sharp shards of porcelain barely standing. I want to throw up but I can't—everything I try to summon from my stomach only stops and chokes off in my throat. Coughing, sweating, bleeding, swirling in panic, I wonder what has happened in the hours since night...what has happened to me and to my home—my family home—the home of my birth...the home I inherited after caring for my parents.

As an only child this house has always been my anchor and the violation I feel tonight on my body is magnified by the vandalism done to my home. Why they didn't kill me is a mystery. I will leave for the police station as soon as I can get myself together.

Covered in blood and sweat, I rise and make my way out to the kitchen phone to call for help. My feet flush in glass, stinging and ripping with each step on a carpet shredded with tacks and nails sticking up through the hardwood.

Each room I pass is equally trashed until I reach the doorway to my kitchen. There before me is a pristine arrangement: a room much cleaner than I had left it, with a breakfast table neatly set for three, and next to it, a cradle I have never seen.
Flickering shadows and a swirling, colorless mist surrounds me and gently pushes me into the room. I am coddled by voices, low and many; but whispering voices, all in soft tones saturating my ears in unintelligible conversation. I'm disoriented. My eyes begin burn and the nausea I have carried causes me to walk directly into the chairs and drop to my knees. I fight the urge to curl up into fetal position on the floor. Instead I steady myself with one hand on the table and the other on the cradle.

Inside the cradle, a cold, light touch caresses my knuckles. I try to pull my hand away but am held there, stuck in the same coldness I felt in bed the night before.

Looking in, my heart stops for a moment...the longest moment of my life. Seven bony fingers are clamped on my hand and squeezing. Seven bony fingers, gnarled and sharp, encased in grey peeling flesh and poised on a long, withered arm that curls back into blackness are holding me in place.

As I gasp for air, the thing in the cradle stirs, showing its face and causing my heart to pause yet again. My face—the thing in the cradle is wearing my face—smaller, though, and clearer. Like it was when I was an infant.

The more I pull away, the tighter the grip on my hand. Our eyes—the thing in the cradle and mine—are now locked. Its mouth opens slightly, revealing more darkness as a shadow swallows me from behind. I can't divert my gaze; I can't turn around to see what is behind me. But I know whatever is behind me is more horrifying than what's in front. The shrill voice makes a final proclamation, and I feel the cold words on the back of my neck.

"Child, you may now eat your placenta."

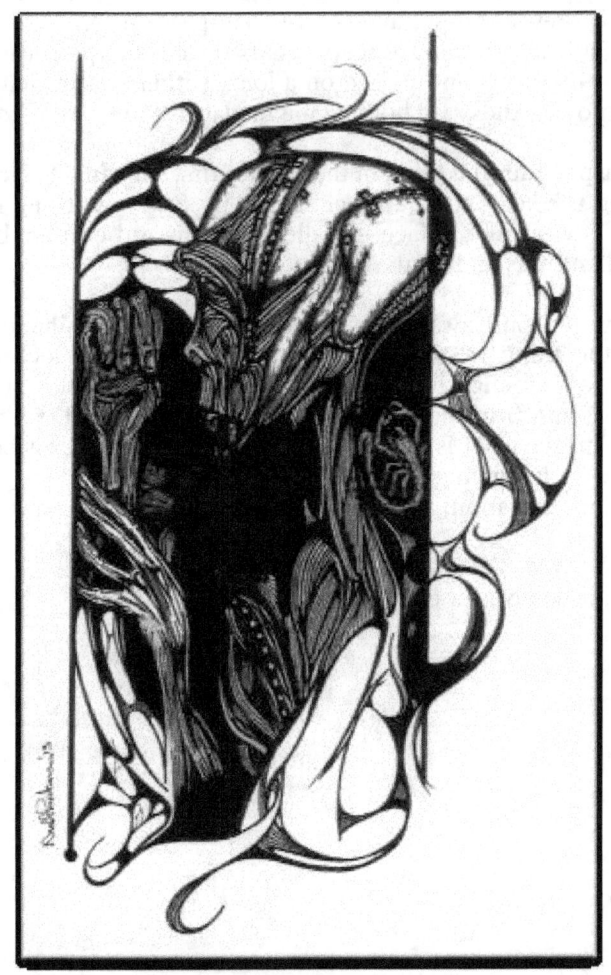

Ad Finem Ultimum by Niall Parkinson

K.Z. Morano
The Other Child

My name is Lila. Not that I expect anyone to recognize my name. I am after all, just the "other child". But I do have a story to tell. And though it may not seem as magical as the candy-colored versions they tell about my brother and sister, it is nonetheless the truth.

I was ten when Hans and Greta came into our lives. They were no more than suckling infants, children of Mr. Higgs whose wife had died of childbirth. I pitied the woman; the babies'—if you could call them that—enormous heads must've ripped her apart. Her single reprieve was that she did not live long enough to see what they looked like.

Ugly creatures they were, with limbs gnarled like the branches of an ancient tree and pink eyes that poked out from their massive skulls. Shameful scandals of nature. To have brought them into this world was a sin in itself.

Still, there could be no greater love than that of a mother's. And it was for my recently widowed mother's love for me and my baby brother that she had agreed to nurse them. Money was money, after all. And I'd like to think that it was for Mama's love for us that she had agreed to share Mr. Higgs' bed as well.

Since they were always suckled first, the creatures grew stout and strong while my little brother grew thin and sickly on whatever that was left. I shall never forget that one afternoon when I came home from the forest with my palms full of berries. I saw Mama staring out the window, a twin's mouth latched on each of her nipples. They wriggled in horrific delight as they greedily sucked the life from her. Their plump cheeks and snub-noses were smeared with crimson that dripped toward the floor in a rhythmic tap, tap, tap...

"Mama!" She started and looked down at her bloody breasts.

"Goodness," she murmured absently. "They must've been very hungry."

It baffled me how they were already able to grow a complete set of teeth—they were yellow and needle-like—while my brother still hadn't any. But then they were always different. The boy's reddish gaze followed me everywhere while the girl's stare seemed frighteningly intelligent, as though she had an understanding of the hatred and fear that her presence stirred from within me and enjoyed it immensely.

Great was my relief when Mama declared that she'll stop feeding them. But the news soon eclipsed my happiness. Mr. Higgs, now impoverished, was to live with us in our tiny cottage. It was hardly surprising. Famine was upon us and Mama was a woman with conscience. What did surprise us all was the sudden death of Mr. Higgs. He was found in the thickets—dismembered, disemboweled and drained of blood.

Mama was inconsolable. It didn't help that we grew hungrier and poorer with each passing day. Left with nothing but a few crumbs of stale bread, I finally convinced Mama to get rid of the twins. Fewer mouths to feed, I said. And they were always insatiable. And so one night, we took them deep into the woods. The wind stabbed at flesh like icy knives and the barren trees reared like frozen giants. They didn't cry. The twins simply sagged against the tree like a pair of hideous puppets, holding hands, framed against the background of silver mist.

Whatever Mama did, she did out of love for me and my brother. Not that it helped him much. My brother died anyway, consumed by a sickness. It was too late to save him; the monstrous twins had already stolen what they could from him. It wasn't long before Mama's guilt caught up her with her and slowly, she began to lose her grasp on reality...

For me, it was years of struggling with famine, years of caring for my ailing Mama...People were afraid to venture into the woods for fear of the strange beast that lurked there. Though it had never been caught or seen, it always left a trail of blood, bones and bowels.

So grave were my troubles that I was close to forgetting that the twins ever existed. But then they came back, as Mama said they will. We pay for the sins we commit, she said. One day, the tangle of bushes parted and out they came, five years older but no less repulsive. Mama begged me to let them stay. She said we could afford to feed them now and she wanted their forgiveness.

The twins never spoke a word. I suppose there had been no one in the woods to teach them. The fact that they had managed to survive on their own was disturbingly peculiar. Then I looked at them and thought: *How utterly silly; they're so tiny.*

Then one afternoon when I came home from the market, a delicious aroma wafted from the kitchen, insinuating its way into my nostrils.

"Surprise" said a voice, soft and spidery. It was the first time that I heard Greta speak.

Something hissed and crackled in the oven.

"Where's Mama?" I asked.

And Hans spoke; his voice was deep and hoarse: "Yummy, Yummy."

He rubbed his bloated belly and pointed into the rustling inferno: "Tummy, Tummy."

It was then that I saw the blood-stained pieces of Mama's clothing on the floor.

I think I went mad then.

I ran out of the cottage screaming and went as far away as I could, never to return again. News from the old village would still reach me as troubadours sang their versions of the tale, adding candy and gingerbread—distorting the story, syllable by syllable, until the truth lies buried beneath the fantastical lies.

Mama said we pay for the sins we commit. But I think we pay more dearly for the sins we fail to commit. I look at my infant step-daughter, her unfamiliar eyes dark and beady, and I place the pillow on her face.

Carly Berg
Deer Season

The church people are right. Halloween is no joke. Normal people might listen to them better if they weren't such biddies, though. My neighbor, Sara, is born again and now I believe her. In this season where everything dies, a veil is lifted between this world and the next. Anything can happen.

Allen and I loaded the shopping cart with stuff for his deer hunting trip; three cases of beer, a twenty pound hamburger roll, and a giant bag of peanuts. I tossed in some cute pumpkin suckers for the trick-or-treaters although not many come anymore. I considered putting the pumpkin suckers back because of what they reminded me of. But no, the best way to weaken a bad memory is to make new associations with the hated thing. We went to the bedspread aisle next.

If he gets to spend on his stinky hunting pals, I'm getting something for the house.

Here she came again. This witch was large vertically and horizontally. She had one of those ridiculous basset hound ear haircuts where the front is longer than the back. She seemed so frumpy and tired I almost forgot to be jealous. Allen's last witch had red hair. My neighbor, Sara, is a nurse when she's not at church, and she said redheads naturally smell between the legs, but this one had dark hair.

I heard the witch before I saw her . . . Her baby in an ancient carriage with the song playing, all sing-songy and creepy about dead deer. The kid was malformed. Sara says deformities often happen with babies conceived in sin when the veil between worlds is open. The baby sported a pumpkinish head. Too big, too round. The skin was orangey. I don't get close, but I swear indented vertical lines ran down the face. In a twisted way, it cracked me up. Sara says sick jokes are Satan's favorite.

The song might have been meant to threaten me, to mock the deer-in-the-headlights look Allen got whenever she appeared, or for no reason at all. Trying to figure out crazies will make you crazy for sure. The song went "The deer, the fear, and the shot rang out! Dah-doopy-doopy-dah! Get out the knife, you big Boy Scout. Dah. Doop!"

I stroked the red satin comforter. Let the witch think about our marital bed. She could be a home wrecker literally, with those thunder thighs. That made me feel a little better or maybe even worse. I hugged Allen for her to see. I whispered, "Did you fuck her at the deer camp, you stupid idiot?"

Allen shook his head. He always denied everything. I kissed his mouth. Ha, move along, witch.

She moved along. I double checked the aisle, then slapped Allen's face. "Idiot." I'd love to put a stop to the witch, but I'd probably get stuck with her ugly baby.

"I didn't do it. This is a dream, dammit!" Allen faded out and I woke up.

Of course, the bag of pumpkin suckers was right there on the kitchen table. The nightmare doesn't end so neatly. That's not how Halloween works.

M. E. VonBindig
Letter to a Young Selkie

You were conceived from a brutal concept; a night of drunken debauchery with a handsome Orkney man whose name I cannot recall. My legs were spread wide as the slippery sea slithered inwards, spilling you into my womb. One month later, I didn't bleed and took the piss-test. When I saw the dreaded line turn pink, I dreamt of coat hangers and back ally doctors whose offices reeked of rubbing alcohol and cigarettes.

Mother said I had to keep you. I said *where, in a cage?* She smiled and backhanded me full across the face, then told my father there was shopping to be done. We went to the bedding aisle and she asked me what theme I preferred, but it appears that Carcharodon Carcharias is not too popular amongst the younger moms these days.

At twenty weeks, the technician told me not to be concerned that you were earless and web-fingered—that your evolution was still pending. She said you wouldn't stop squirming long enough to see your sex, but I knew the truth when I saw the vulgar nose overlap the rest of your face that you would be born a male.

You were a lumbering slick pink mass with grey speckled spots across your back. You propelled yourself into this world as if you were heading off to sea, all fin-footed, with your black eyes—tiny abysmal buttons staring blankly back up at me. I thought of white-furred baby seals and how they deserved the life you now had; but there was no club to be found in the delivery room with which to make the exchange.

When I took you home, you cried and wailed till I blended the smelt with your baby food...only to have you vomit up their spines. You grew only four teeth, like an outcropping of rocks within your mouth, jagged yellow broken things which pierced my flesh when you fed till my breast was spitting pus and blood instead of milk. I tried to be careful when I would tweeze away the whiskers on your stubbly cheeks to make you look more natural. Perhaps I yanked too hard in the process, for you always seemed to bleed. But who could blame me when your nose was always in the way, a quivering snotty mass of a thing that produced loud barking tantrums.

My mother made me give away our cat away to keep *it* from killing *you*. I told her it was not the cat's fault for mistaking you as prey, the way you flopped and scooted on your abdomen, your massive belly all rug-burned; a helpless tumor crawling across the carpet spilling the contents of your diaper in the process; a chum trail on the floor for it to follow. It's true that I may have left the door open just a crack at night hoping the cat would slink inside and make its way into your crib. I might have watched, fascinated, as it sat on your chest and licked away the tuna-fish taste from your lips, and hoped desperately that it would suck your soul away on more than one occasion.

Mother always said there were no ugly babies, and that at least you did not have a Yeti-scalp like all those others who were suctioned out or scrunched from the tips of metal forceps, and that all one had to do when you cried was put you in the bathtub and watch you float on your back; short webbed hands folded inward, your legs merged into one another; a fleshy rudder. You were such a buoyant pup, a wriggling little sea cow birthed from a disappointed parent who left the room hoping each time that you would drown.

By one and two you mimicked in horrific repetition a few bleating words, and soon I began to loathe the sound of my own name. For Christmas that year, Papa made you a chair with a sling with one hole. The insurance wouldn't cover the separation of your limbs and you screamed when you couldn't maneuver around to follow us in and out of each room. By three and four you molted, and your skin became the color of bruised fruit. You scribbled pictures with the crayons you held in your mouth, of those cold distant islands where I had become infected with you.

By five you were the length of a fully grown man and almost four hundred pounds of meat that had to be rolled over so each wrinkled part, the only parts that resembled me, could be wiped down with a cloth. A small crane and hospital bed became your constant companions till the day when you and mother were left all alone and you crushed her beneath you till parts of her became indistinguishable from your own and the firemen had to scrape her remains from the folds of your blubbery skin.

You became famous that day, and the lawn trolls wept as reporters filled our yard. Child Protective Services and Sea World both came, but PETA declined because you weren't animal enough. And now here you are, one year later, as I watch you through the glass enclosure that once housed a polar bear, in your element as you press your face against the glass and the make the little children scream.

Monster by John Stanton

Gary Hewitt
Manikin

Her hands darted to and fro across the lump of peach wood. She carved. The hour turned to midnight. A dog in the street howled and fled from the unnatural darkness it sensed on this wretched night. Mitzy dismissed the sound and continued her work.

The wood took on human shape. A nose, a pair of ears, a mouth, eyes, neck, feet, and hands all came to life in perfect detail. Mitzy's brow bled sweat. She did not stop. Time was precious.

She smoothed away imperfections on the face. The skin was smooth under her touch. She felt the piece come alive under her gaze.

Mitzy deposited the carving into a bundle of rags. She intoned ancient Xiamense words and the room swirled about her. The smell of incense became ever stronger. She did not pause. Her words became a mantra.

She cuddled the unholy bundle and remembered the death of her baby all those years ago. The figure in her arms stared back with unseeing eyes. Mitzy continued her spell. The figure sighed.

Mitzy brushed away tears of joy. She placed her wooden baby onto the floor and held her arms aloft. The infant cried out in deciduous protest before snapping open pus filled eyes which beheld her new mother.

Below, Mitzy's employer let out a scream upon discovering her lifeless son. The doctors would say it was a cot death. She felt sad for Mrs. Reid, but she could have another baby. Mitzy had long passed the time of child bearing. She gathered up her daughter and urged her to sleep.

They would leave at first light.

Bruce L. Priddy
Only Dimly

Your child is not deformed, Hadiya. He is quite perfect, every bit as beautiful as Our Lord intended.

I can tell by the look on your face you recognize me. I bet if you had a list of all the people you expected to walk into your home today, or any day for that matter, I would not be anywhere on that list. Please, pardon my intrusion during such a trying time. I'm here as a friend. And I am here on the behalf of other friends you never knew you had. People like me. People with money, power, fame, position or some combination thereof. We want to help you.

You keep looking at the door, wondering how I got in, or if your father and brother will be next. Don't worry, Hadiya. You are safe. A bolted door is no barrier to someone like me. As for your family, they will not hurt you. Though I can't say the same for the unfortunate boy they think fathered your son. As we speak, your father and brother are being arrested for his murder. I am sorry the boy had to be sacrificed, but it was a necessity. Your father and brother would've had to be dealt with, and it is much easier to let them do it for us themselves.

Oh, Hadiya, please don't cry! I am bringing you good news. This is a time for rejoicing.

See, I know the truth. The pregnancy was not your fault and whatever they may think, your family has not been dishonored. The virginity that your culture so values is still intact. Our Lord has bestowed upon you His blessing. Why He chose a poor immigrant girl ignorant of His ways, even His name, is not for me to question. I am but his faithful servant.

How do I know all these things about you? We have shared a dream, Hadiya. Do you recall? The immense door beneath the sea, yawning open revealing even greater depths. The hand that brought you unto Him. How He...well, you remember. I was witness to it all. As He planted His seed in you, I saw. In that moment, He whispered all of you to me.

May I hold your baby, Hadiya? Ah, yes. Your child smells of thunder.

What a grip he has! You would think such boneless limbs would be useless but he is quite strong.

And his eyes, all six of them, so bright; Oh, what wonders they can see! Why do you make such a face, Hadiya? I know, being ignorant of His ways, it is a struggle to care for an infant that rest of the equally ignorant human herd tells you is an abomination. A strong maternal instinct compels you, however repulsed you may be, doesn't it? You can't help but to bring his mouths to your breast. I suspect His will does play some role. He would not let His fruit wither. I can tell you, Hadiya, your child is no abomination of any sort. This child was made in the image of Our Lord. His true image.

The Seven Cryptical Books of Hsan tell us how in the war with the Starfish-Headed-Things, Our Lord was robbed of the four eyes that allow him to see and commune with the Old Ones. Thus, He could not direct them against His enemies. The oldest depictions of Our Lord show him with six eyes. Those dreamers who brush against Him in their sleep know His true face. That is how you separate the fakers from His true prophets. Take for example, sculptor Henry Anthony Wilcox's magnificent 1925 masterpiece.

You are not familiar with his work? Oh, I suppose you would be. You have so much to learn. But I digress.

"He is Their Cousin, yet He can spy Them only dimly," says the Prophet al'Hazred, Knowledge Be Upon Him. But your baby, Hadiya, your baby can see Them, resplendent and glorious. They speak with him now, though he cannot understand. One day, he could, yes, if allowed to mature, in five or six years as a man.

But that is not Our Lord's plan, I am afraid. The midwife was right, your child will not survive past infancy. Though, they are right for being wrong. Your child is but a means for His followers to see and commune with Them. Then, the world will be returned to its rightful state, serene and primal.

His eyes will taste divine.

Wait, Hadiya, wait. I said I would not harm you and that is true. Our Lord will continue to bestow Himself upon you. Even now, the next child is blossoming inside your belly. The mother of a new age, you will have a place of honor among us. Wealth unimaginable will be yours. You must only continue to bear the fruit of His blessing.

Dave Dormer
Tangled Nursery

The park was humming with visitors when they rolled in. A caravan of RVs accumulated behind, anxious to select their ideal site. The couple paid their entrance fee and crawled tentatively through myriad of trails. The aroma of cook fires seeped into the truck as they passed campsite after campsite of curious stares. The sounds of kids playing echoed throughout the grounds.

"We're looking for row *H*," Debbie said, vigilantly watching for a stray kid to bolt from the foliage at any moment.

Ever since she was a young girl, she'd come to this park and she knew each trail well. If someone needed directions, she could point out every one-way trail, washroom and shower facility, or fresh-water outlet within the mammoth campground. Until this season, all she'd known about camping involved tents. Now, they owned an RV and this meant new sites to inhabit, complete with all the luxuries.

"Just think how comfortable we'll be when the baby comes...we'd never be able to camp with a newborn in a tent," she reasoned, caressing her ballooning belly.

Rob smiled, nodding in agreement, as he marshaled the twenty-seven-foot camper into its temporary home. He went to work, leveling the unit and making sure all of its systems were functioning while admiring his very pregnant wife. He couldn't help but grin watching her waddle about the site, doing what she could to help.

If there was one good thing about a pregnant woman, he decided, *were considerably larger breasts*. It was only a week or two before her due-date, but she insisted to go camping. She'd always been a strong woman, he determined, and didn't know too many women willing to go camping in similar condition.

"Are you sure you want to do this?" he'd asked her several days beforehand.

He wanted to postpone the trip for a while until things settled down. Less than a week before their trip, Rob read an article in the local paper about a man and his dog who were apparently mauled by a black bear. Unusual behavior for a black bear, he knew, but the newspaper headline read: *Local man missing*.

They found and examined the dog's body and experts quickly determined from its wounds that a bear was in fact the culprit

Ugly Babies

and warned citizens about the potential threat. Rob kept a close watch on his wife, rarely leaving her side. He kept a hand ax within reach.

"There are too many people around for anything to happen, Rob," she reasoned. "Besides, look at the number of wardens patrolling the park now."

Ice cream pails in hand, they walked the nature trails relaxed. Each trail, uniquely mapped, geared to various levels of difficulty and endurance. They had hiked them all, but she quickly realized she'd been in better condition before.

"We need fresh blueberries for desert," she said.

The boarded path led them through the "Novice" portion of the trail, cutting a swath through forest and foliage. It skirted the edges of a swamp and every so often, a billboard posted detailing surrounding habitat. Each sign described indigenous animals, plants, and aviary native to the area. The boarded walkway seemed a floating dock through the swamp.

"I never get used to this part." Rob grabbed her hand, hurrying her through the unsteady sections. "Here. This is usually a good spot," she said, leading Rob from the manufactured trail.

They ascended the rocky outcropping, moss-covered and slippery. He jumped ahead and turned to help her at each elevation. Rob could see it winded her when they crested the rocky terrain. The air was stifling, and mosquitoes swarmed the patch. It was a sea of blue, so wouldn't take long to fill two ice cream pails. Rob knew they couldn't linger in this heat in her condition.

As Rob and Debbie crouched to pick the berries, they were watched by the eight simple eyes of something stalking them from above. Its fangs supported a large, white sac while its legs furiously worked silk strands from its spinnerets. Patiently, it descended from its perch on a branch.

"Oh my god!" Debbie cried, dropping her pail of berries. "Is that what I think it is?"

Rob rushed to her side, pulling her back as they both tried to comprehend the macabre assembly of rotting bones. Last year's leaves and needles littered the form. Thousands of tiny spiders scurried, emerging from gaping holes in the remaining flesh.

"Holy shit! That's the guy they're looking for." Rob gaped at the gnawed limbs. It was obvious that the damage had been inflicted by more than raven or rodent. He ushered Debbie away, gently caressing her shoulder. "Let's go...I'll go and get the rangers."

Debbie couldn't tear herself away. Among the army of spiders blanketing the corpse were white egg sacs suspended and protected in a nursery of webs with thousands of hungry little pedipalps carrying away their share of flesh. Rob pulled at her again.

"Let's go. *Now!*"

After escorting her back to the camper, he demanded she stay behind while he led the ranger to the body.

"And do *not* leave the camper until I come back."

She laid her backpack down and sat at the table, hands trembling. Her stomach heaved, and she vomited on the table. Tears welled and gentle sobs set in when it struck her—she knew what she'd seen was a product of nature. The bear attack, the spider and the eggs were all part of a cycle. She appreciated the mother's instinct in creating the nursery within the corpse; the need for food, the need for protection.

The female dolomede emerged from the backpack on the floor toting the egg sac in her jaw.

She crawled to Debbie, to the nursery.

Ben Arzate
Little Jimmy's Secret

Little Jimmy's parents were reading in the living room when Jimmy came in. Jimmy tugged on his father's sleeve.

"Dad?"

"What is it, Jimmy? You're supposed to be in...HOLY SHIT!" he said, and froze when he saw Jimmy.

"What's the matter hon...OH MY GOD!" Jimmy's mother said as she looked up.

Jimmy's skin was rotting all over. Green and black discoloration covered his entire body and large chunks of it seemed to be peeling off. Jimmy's dad stood up. He held out his hands but was afraid to touch his son.

"Dad," Jimmy said. "I had a secret."

Jimmy reached up and tore the skin off his head in strips. Underneath, Jimmy's head was still there. It looked like it was back to normal, other than the fact it was transparent.

"I died while I was inside Mom," Jimmy said. "I didn't want to make you sad, so I put my skin over my ghost."

Jimmy's mother gasped and held her hands over her mouth.

"It's going bad. The skin went bad," Jimmy said. His head became more transparent. "My ghost is going away. I'm sorry I didn't tell you."

Jimmy's father moved closer to his son as he started fading. "Jimmy..."

"I'm sorry. I love you both," Jimmy said.

As Jimmy's father went to hug his son, he disappeared, leaving nothing but an armful of decaying flesh. Jimmy's father threw the skin to the ground in disgust and despair.

He looked at his wife, who was clutching her stomach. She stood up and walked toward the bathroom. He saw there was blood running down the insides of her legs.

"What's wrong, dear?"

"I feel like I'm having contractions."

"What!? Should I call 911?"

"Help me into the bathroom first."

He took her by the arm and rushed her into the bathroom. She took off her bloodstained underwear and pulled up her dress. She sat in the tub with her legs spread.

"Something's coming out! Hold my hand."

She felt a sharp pain.

A rancid soup of blood, pus, muscle tissue, and bone splinters poured out of her vagina. A rotten smell filled the bathroom.

She screamed.

Her husband retched, turned away, and covered his mouth and nose with his hand.

The soup flowed across the tub and into the drain.

Mark Slade
Jah Wobbly

Jah wobbly crawled out of his mother's womb every night to suck the blood from his sister.

She was always lost in a sequence of filthy dreams that caused her epileptic state. Her nose bled red goo that covered her naked breasts, where her husband's hand rested firmly. Jah would slither out from between mother's legs, the umbilical cord still attached. Jah would pull himself across the dirty wood floor by his short stubby arms. The further he went, the longer the umbilical cord stretched.

Jah was not supposed to do such things. He knew this. But Jah wasn't even supposed to be alive, and he knew this as well. He also knew he wasn't supposed to drain blood from his sister. Mother's husband said so. The tall, stick thin man had beaten Jah savagely with his gnarly hands for it. Jah took the punishment, often hypnotized by the man's flabby skin whisking in the air like a flag in a great wind. Sometimes Jah would cry and the man would stop beating him for a moment. Jah's saucer shaped black eyes were transfixed on the many holes caused by needles up and down the man's bony arms.

Tonight would be different, he promised himself. Sister would meet her demise and he would feast upon her. No more taking *heres* and *theres*. He was going to take her very essence from her. He was going sink those two long spikes he grew a year ago into her jugular and drink the pretty red. He didn't care if mother's husband caught him. If Jah drank enough of sister's essence, he would become strong enough to break him in half, drink *his* essence. Then it would just be Jah and mother. Jah would be happy forever. Just he and mother. And if he was hungry again, he would crawl out of her womb and drink someone *else's* essence.

Jah crawled toward sister who slept a few feet from the bed where mother and her husband slept. Sister was still chained to the leg of the bed frame. *Oh,* Jah thought, *sister was bad again.* The frail little girl was wrapped in a dirty sheet, sucking her thumb, dreaming of a better life, a better family. Jah *so* hated sister. She got to stay out of womb all the time. He could only come out at night. Jah's fat round body found itself next to sister.

At first, he laid his head on her grimy pillow. Only for a moment, though. No time to waste. He was tired. His body was tired.

When Jah regrouped, he raised his head. He opened his mouth to let the two little spikes protrude from fleshy blackened gums. He let out a small hiss. He lunged at sister's jugular.

Jah felt incredible pain in his navel that ran amok through the rest of his body. He felt more tired....as if...as if the very essence had left him. He fell to the floor, his over-sized head bouncing off the wood floor. Darkness came over his eyes slowly like a veil. He saw mother standing over top of him, holding a butcher knife in one hand and the severed umbilical cord in the other.

"I caught you at last, you little monster," mother said.

That hurt more than taking his essence from him.

SHORT FICTION

Neil Baker
Latch

Finally the screaming stopped.

Trevor Turner crushed his cigarette butt into the crown of the god-awful child hanging next to the back door: a gray concrete cherub pointing an arrow at Trevor's shed and its ass at the kitchen. Why she wasted her money on this kind of crap, he would never understand.

Trevor hadn't really needed this smoke, having feigned his fainting spell just to get out of the damned bedroom where Josie was pushing their first child out of her tattered snatch, and his callousness had shocked even himself, but the quiet outside was intoxicating; the fresh air, delicious. *Oh well, back to the trenches*, he thought, opening the back door and recoiling as the cloying stench of blood, shit and baby powder wafted out. He grimaced and strode toward the stairs, pausing momentarily as the first cries from the parasite they had made together pierced the air. *That's it, then.* He took his time on the stairs, and slowly made his way into the guest room, which was now a temporary birthing pit complete with mountains of diapers, fresh towels and a midwife who rivaled a dead sheep for charm and attractiveness. Naturally this miserable woman could see right through him, and she gave Trevor a look that would sour cream as he meekly took his wife's side, holding her hand, trying not to look at the bed sheets that had been turned into a tie-dyed mess. Three cheers for the red, brown and yellow!

"Congratulations, Mr. Turner," the old hag croaked, syringing gore and mucus out of the baby's nose and throat, swaddling it tightly in the standard striped blanket. "You have a beautiful baby boy."

Fuck. Fucking fuck. Trevor feigned delight as he stared at the mewling face enveloped in terry cloth, his insides churning as he knew he would have to find a job. Not for the money mind you, Josie's inheritance and a joint bank account had lessened his need to do an honest day's work. Nope, a job would get him out of the house, away from the little bastard that was even now being placed in its mother's arms.

Josie, ruddy-faced and near exhaustion, cradled her baby joyfully, oblivious to the snipping and popping sounds coming from below as the midwife stitched up the rips between her thighs.

"Look, honey, he has your eyes."

Trevor looked into his son's puffy eyes, the lids gummed shut with rapidly crusting gunk. *Is that what she thinks I look like?*

"I don't see it."

"Oh, come now, Mr. Turner," the ugly woman mumbled from between Josie's legs. "He's the spitting image."

As if on cue, the wrinkled heap in his wife's arms coughed up a slimy globule of muddy phlegm directly into her face, spattering her soft features with sticky bubbles. The midwife rose from her repairs and reached for the child, loosening the cloth around its torso and pushing him into Josie's chest.

"Good, his tubes are clear, now let's see if we can get some food into him, shall we?"

Trevor watched as his tired wife tugged at the neck of her flimsy gown, and noted with some disdain that nothing stirred in his pants as her breasts plopped out, full and inviting. It was official then. His wife had become a mother, and those glorious tits now belonged to somebody else. Standing uselessly by the door, he thought back to the moment when he had stopped loving her, that night in Bali when she had proclaimed, out of the blue, that she wanted a family. Trevor's mind had immediately shut down as images of seven-seat vans and diaper bags drifted through his rum-addled consciousness, blotting out all future possibility of Josie's wealth going toward the things *he* desired; a home theater, a wet bar, a sleeker model from Honda with at least five less seats. Of course, it hadn't taken much for her to get her way due to his complete and utter lack of willpower when it came to dipping his wick, and he had cursed himself relentlessly for the past seven months as Josie had grown bigger while the bank account had diminished as fast as his affection.

"Come and watch, Mr. Turner," rasped the old woman as she manhandled his son, forcing the baby's face into Josie's left breast. "You may have to help your wife for the first few feedings."

Trevor took a few steps into the room and craned his neck to peer over the woman's shoulder.

"There now, we need a good latch, my dear." The midwife guided the baby's head until its pursed lips brushed Josie's swollen nipple. The old woman rubbed the end of the nipple between the infant's lower lip and chin, and the tiny mouth opened wider. "You see, you can stimulate the little man into opening wide by tickling his chin," she brushed the baby's mouth across the nipple one more time, and Trevor could see beads of fluid, yellow like an old man's hair, oozing from the tip. "Lovely," murmured the midwife. "The colostrum is in and ready to go." She pushed the rose bud lips onto the nipple and the hungry mouth took it all. Josie inhaled sharply through gritted teeth and closed her eyes.

The midwife stroked Josie's hair. "You will soon get used to it, my dear; you're just a little sensitive at the moment."

"Christ, I hope so," hissed Josie, her brow knitted, fresh sweat running down her cheek to join the dampness pooling above her collar bone. The baby made several smacking sounds at it greedily gulped down its first meal, and Trevor recognized those noises; sounds of contentment, of taking with no intent of giving back.

The old woman took her hand from the back of the baby's head and placed Josie's free hand there, tucking the child deeper into the crook of her other arm. The baby did not pause for a second; its rhythm remained constant as it drew on the fleshy peg with increased fervor.

"It's really starting to hurt," groaned Josie, opening her eyes and fixing them on Trevor. "Can we stop now?"

"When the little man has had his fill, he will detach," the old crone whispered as she made her way to the end of the bed and began to gather in the filth-covered sheets.

"Trevor?" Josie said, her voice stronger now. "Tell her I need to stop."

Trevor stretched out one hand as if to touch the old woman on the shoulder, then thought better of it. "She needs to stop."

"When the child is finished;" The midwife's reply was curt and any semblance of her former gentleness was swiftly smothered.

Josie suddenly cried out, and Trevor rushed to her side as his wife roughly grabbed her child by the torso with both hands and tried to pull him off.

"Help me!" she screamed, tugging at the baby which refused to budge. Trevor tentatively took hold of his son's arms and pulled back on them, softly at first, then with some force.

"Get it off!"

As his wife arched her back in agony, Trevor turned for advice, but the old midwife was gone.

"Get in here! She needs help!" There was no response.

A louder scream from Josie snapped his head around, and he looked down just as his wife's breast, her beautiful, doughy bosom, collapsed in on itself, shriveling like a salted slug. He felt a splash of bile lurch up his throat and swallowed it quickly, dropping the sucking child and reaching for a clean towel.

"What the fuck are you doing?" screamed his wife. "Pull it off!"

"I don't..." He pulled at the swaddling until his new son was naked and wriggling, still clamped to the ruined breast. "I don't know what to do!" He grabbed the baby's legs and pulled, harder, harder still, until the child was near horizontal and Josie's withered bosom was stretched to its limit. Josie had her fingers around the child's mouth, trying to pry a finger between lip and skin to no avail, and then she began to convulse; her hands dropping to the mattress.

"Where the hell are you?" shouted Trevor at the open doorway as he continued to pull on the tiny pink thing attached to the woman he once loved.

A noise, deep and foul, resonated from Josie's chest and Trevor watched, horrified, as her right breast suddenly puckered and caved in, deflating faster than a dollar store balloon and disappearing into her shuddering form. Josie's eyes had rolled back, and she no longer screamed. Instead, a sad, wheezing sob escaped her bluing lips as the baby feasted on, and Trevor dropped its legs as he searched the room for something, anything, he might use to pry the infant off.

The room was entirely baby-safe, not a sharp edge to be found. Finally he grabbed a hand pump, twisting off the plastic handle which resembled a tiny shoe horn. This would have to do. He rushed back to the bed and drew up quickly, skidding into a heap on the floor as he took in the newly evolved scene. Josie's eyes were now pure white orbs in a mottled bed of burst capillaries and her head hung limply back against the bedframe. Her arms had not moved from her sides, but her shoulders twitched sporadically with each heaving gulp from the thing drinking eagerly at her breast. Her entire torso seemed to have shrunk and Trevor could clearly see her ribs and sternum through the fading skin. Their baby, on the other hand, was the polar opposite of its mother. It had swollen to twice its original size and glowed with rude health, its plump limbs straddling her torso as they swelled larger with each deep draw. Trevor tried to grab the infant by its distended waist, but waves of repulsion swept over him as his fingers sunk into the gelatinous skin, the contents warm and undulating. He felt his mouth moisten and then the bile rushed up followed by his lunch as he sunk to the floor, vomiting wildly.

By the time his stomach was empty, and he had regained his footing, the sucking noises had stopped. The child was finished.

Trevor recalled a time, a little over three years ago, when Josie had paid for them both to take a couple of weeks' vacation in San Francisco. They had taken a trip to Muir Woods, marveling at the majesty of the redwoods, the cathedrals of leaf and bark. Trevor had somehow managed to acquire a tick, and the little bastard had feasted on his blood, hidden behind his right ear until Josie had noticed it that evening. In her usual, no-nonsense manner, she had plucked off the swollen, pea-sized insect and crushed it underfoot, staining the hotel floor with Trevor's stolen blood. This memory had reared its head, somewhat perversely, as he took in the final tableau.

By all accounts, his wife was dead. Her translucent skin was drawn tightly upon her frame giving the appearance that she had been freeze-dried. Her eyes had sunk back into their sockets to the point that Trevor could only see dark shadows beneath the lids and her lips had drawn back exposing long teeth and ashen gums. Her nightgown hung awkwardly on her bones and fluttered in the breeze caused by her baby as it flapped its fat arms and legs in a futile swimming motion, rocking on its enormous, quivering belly. The child was bright red and the size of a hockey bag. It was still attached to Josie's withered breast but it was no longer sucking and its eyes were still gummed shut. Trevor stared, unable to move.

A sound to his left: He slowly turned his head and saw the midwife standing in the door frame, her bag in one hand and her coat in the other. She smiled.

"He's finished then."

Trevor wanted to speak, but his bile-burned throat could only emit a dry croak.

The old woman bundled herself into her coat and started to turn. "I'll see myself out."

Trevor staggered to the doorway and watched as she descended the stairs, his mind trying to process the recent events. A dry noise escaped his lips, then he repeated it, and this time his words were clear.

"It sucked her dry..."

The midwife turned and smiled once more, meeting his gaze with cut-glass eyes.

"Like father like son, Mr. Turner." She chuckled. "Like father like son." She turned and opened the front door, stepping out into the fresh air, and then she was gone.

Trevor slumped to the floor, gripping the bannister. He wanted to cry, but no tears would come. Then, a new sound, an unearthly wailing, came from the bedroom. Trevor tried to block his ears but the screeching cry still wormed its way in.

It was the cry of his son...

A son still hungry.

Latch by Neil Baker

Erik Gustafson
Switched After Birth

Shadows disguised everything in the dark hallway, causing ordinary objects to appear unknown, mysterious and frightening. Amanda fumbled for the light switch outside her bedroom door, wishing her husband wasn't out of town—yet at the same time, she was frantic to respond to her baby's cries in the room at the far end of the hall. She hated the dark her entire life, but was embarrassed to admit this to anyone. So she slept without nightlights, without leaving the bathroom light on, or even a door cracked. She just toughed it out and quietly sighed with relief as the darkness was smothered by light come morning. She made her way to her children's bedroom, but jerked to a stop.

Her six-month-old daughter was sprawled out on the floor, arms and legs swinging above her tender body in tiny arcs.

"Julie!" she shrieked, dropping to her knees and sliding up to her child like a baseball player stealing home plate. "How did you get out here?"

She scooped up the infant into her arms and calmed the baby girl. They made their way back to the bedroom where she turned on the light and stepped in. Her mind reeled with both alarm and confusion as to how her daughter had made an escape. She hurried over to Julie's twin Jake's crib and looked in. He was sound asleep on his stomach, legs tucked under his hips. She exhaled loudly and held Julie up.

"It looks like everyone is okay."

Julie's crib hadn't fallen apart and all looked as it should. She placed Julie onto the mattress. Amanda watched her for a few minutes and then decided to doze off in the chair to keep an eye on things. It would be time to nurse them both again soon anyway.

Amanda awoke with a jolt. It was daylight, and it took a moment for her to realize where she was. Her eyes darted to her children. Both were standing up in Julie's crib, staring at her—at least her daughter was. Jake's face was turned in her direction, and Amanda knew he was aware of things around him—even at his young age. Jake was basically born without eyes. In their place were two deep, shriveled pockets of dark pink flesh.

Jake's sclera, the white parts of his eyes, were the only parts that had formed. However, the sclera had developed outside of his eye cavities like grayish-purple bibs. The masses were fused to his checks. Doctors were hopeful that they may be able to surgically remove them when he was older, but for now the nerves within the flattened mass made surgery prohibitive.

Amanda would never admit it—she loved both her children equally—but the site of Jake made her shiver and slightly nauseous. She was ashamed of herself for feeling that way.

"What are you doing in your sister's crib, Jake?" Amanda asked, yawning. She stood and shuffled in her socks toward her babies. *How is a better question.* She shivered a bit at the idea of an answer to that. Someone had to be playing a joke on her.

Her mother must have let herself in and be somewhere in the house. She stepped back to the hallway. Warm, comforting sunlight filled the narrow space.

"Mom, this isn't funny!"

She turned back to her children. They were both in their own cribs and neither was standing. *Six month old babies can't stand on their own, Amanda,* she assured herself. Jake was lying on his back kicking his feet in the air. Julie was sitting up staring at her, reaching out and smiling.

"Get a grip, Amanda." She dismissed her experience as a trick of her mind, some hormonal hallucination, or exhaustion. "Let's get you guys changed and have some breakfast!"

Jake was fussing as she pulled his little blue night shirt up and changed his heavy diaper. Amanda's eyes kept returning to her son's disfigured eyes; the deep grooves, which she had to keep clean, the puffy puddles of flesh under each eye that looked like birthmarks. It was almost too much some days. She was glad he couldn't see her staring.

She switched cribs and began cleaning up Julie, who giggled while Amanda changed her. Julie's little blue eyes sparkled so perfectly. Amanda brushed Julie's fuzzy hair and pinned on a strawberry clip.

"Beep!" Amanda playfully pushed on the small birthmark on Julie's forearm as if it were a button; A happy button.

"Jake needs your eyes."

"What?" Amanda dropped the soiled diaper and looked around the room. Her heart dropped into her stomach. She wasn't sure who was talking, and she was less certain of what she had heard. At least, she was telling herself she didn't hear the actual words. Babies don't talk, either. Amanda felt her pulse quicken.

She looked at Jake. He was grabbing the rails of the crib in his tiny hands, sightless face fixed on her—like he was using sonar or something to track her. The indentations where his eyes should have been were bright red, sunken. It made his nose look oblong and too large for his face.

"You're six months old. How are you doing that?" Jake rattled the wooden slats.

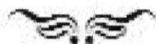

The twins sat in the playpen watching Amanda while she folded laundry. Julie with her eyes, of course, and Jake tracking sounds. Amanda talked to her children while she matched socks and rolled them. The babies cooed and laughed. By the time she finished organizing all the clothes, she attributed all the odd occurrences of the morning to her overactive imagination and dismissed her worries. She even felt a twinge of pride, because if her children were already so advanced for their age, she could only imagine how gifted they must be. How talented. When her husband called to see how she was getting along, Amanda didn't even bring it up.

She phoned her mother next, and spent most of that conversation listening to her mother" rants about Amanda's sister and the parade of boyfriends in and out of her life. Her mother's chattering became a steady drone as Amanda shifted her eyes to the twins to see if they were still sleeping. They were not.

"Mom, I gotta call you back," she mumbled, and let the phone slip from her hand to the couch. Julie and Jake were standing up in the center of the living room, staring at her. Amanda had no words to express what she was witnessing.

Amanda was no longer basking in the glow of a proud parent. She was freaked out. She felt the blood drain and her skin grow cold.

"What the hell? Julie? Jake?" Taking a deep breath, she approached her children. "How did you...?"

Her precious twins only stood, unmoving and silent as angel statues in a cemetery.

"What are you guys doing out of your playpen?"

It was a stupid question, and sounded even dumber when she said it out loud. There were more pressing questions to ask. Three steps from the twins, her hand snapped over her gaping mouth. She froze.

They had switched clothes. Jake was even wearing the strawberry hair clip.

"How did—?" Her eyes darted around the room. Someone had to be in the house. "Who is in here?" Fear channeled into protecting her children and she scooped them up. The twins safely bundled in her arms, she began searching for her cell phone and found it lying on the couch. Juggling the kids, she picked it up and marched for the front door.

Jake starting fussing, causing Amanda to look down at them. His arms were swinging in protest to being dragged around the house, but she clearly saw the birthmark on his forearm. That was Julie's birthmark. Her eyes crinkled down and she frowned. She double checked at the baby's face to make sure she hadn't just got the two confused.

No mistake. The baby in pink clothes, with the forearm birthmark, was missing eyes. The baby dressed in blue had perfect hazel eyes and no birthmark. She crashed to the floor.

"No one has green eyes!" she shrieked.

As she sat on the carpet legs splayed open like a child playing in the sand, the twins crawled away from her. They moved fast, like serpents gliding across the carpet. She watched them slither until the duo vanished underneath the couch.

"Jesus," she called out, gasping for breath.

Amanda maneuvered around the coffee table and retreated until she was up against the brick mantle. She looked down at the fire poker and considered picking it up. She shook her head. Those were her kids under there...what was she thinking? She pressed her hands tight against her chest, as if stopping them from grabbing the weapon.

"Julie?" The blood in her head pounded. "Jake? Honey?"

A tuft of blond hair poked out. The head turned up, revealing the eyeless face of her son. The eye cavities were swollen and the skin was engorged with blood. Jake hissed.

Amanda sat on the bricks hard as she collapsed from fright. She snatched the poker and aimed it at her children. At the things under the couch...whatever they had become.

"Stop it!" She cried, waving the thin metal saber. Jake ducked back under the couch.

Amanda stood and moved closer, crouching in hopes to see under the dark space. She inhaled deeply. Tears ran from her eyes as she exhaled. *What was happening?* She looked at the fire poker, her fingers bright red from squeezing it so hard. Ashamed of herself, she threw the poker aside. Kneeling, she patted her knees.

"Just come out!"

She was full blown crying now. Wailing. Her mind was spinning like the broken reels of a slot machine. Leaning forward, as if in deep prayer, she buried her face into her hands and sobbed.

"Mommy?" Sniffing, Amanda raised her face. The tiny infants loomed over Amanda from atop the coffee table. Jake spoke clearly.

"Julie needs your eyes, Mommy." Amanda stared through bloodshot eyes, but did not comprehend.

Julie stood there, forehead flattened, two dark red pits where her eyes should have been. She was grinning. Horrified, Amanda crawled backward toward the kitchen. As she inched away from her children, she screamed.

Jake's face twisted and compressed, his sclera drooled from the sockets like glue and dried, while at the same time Julie's blue eyes *grew* back. It was like watching a time-lapse video of plants developing from seed to flower.

Julie cackled, "Jake needs your fucking eyes, Mom!" The twins leapt from the glass table and pounced on Amanda, tiny fingers clawing at her eyes. She screamed, batting at her own flesh and blood like a mad woman.

The last thing she heard was a tiny, excited voice, barely above a whisper, promise, "Now it will be dark forever."

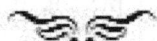

The next morning, when Nick returned from his business trip, he let himself in the house and set his suitcase on the hardwood floor. The infants stood in the hallway holding hands. *Both* were grinning and so thrilled to *see* their daddy.

James Suriano
The Alcombery Waystation

I cradled the window, afraid if I drew one breath or moved in any direction even a centimeter I might lose sight of what was happening. It was through the window on the adjacent building to mine a floor or two below where I could see the blank space on the floor in the apartment. The whole floor was not empty, just a piece of the avocado green linoleum shrinking between the three heads that had appeared in the last two days. Three perfectly sized little melons of fine wispy hair, blunted, rounded features and big innocent eyes. I couldn't hear their cries from their gummy little mouths, but if the windows were open and the winds pulsing through the valley of Market Street, I am damn sure they might come along and ask me for a teat.

Ms. Alcomb was in the unit next to it. I could see her burgeoning herb garden overtook every window flowerbox her apartment had. I knew her because she used to be my neighbor. She never invited me over and I never took offense. She was my favorite neighbor because she baked me cookies, casseroles and coddled eggs whenever she could get me to open my door. I could see her excitement when I came stumbling back from a bar, drunk with passion and celebration. She'd jump out of bed and be rapping on my door with a big tall glass of some syrupy drink and two white dusty pills that would get lost in that fold of her hand. She didn't want to flatten out her palm because she was cautious of anything falling to the floor in the hallway between our two doors. This wasn't the Ritz Carlton. It wasn't even the damn Holiday Inn. I was a poor student, grinding away toward a degree I wasn't sure I wanted anymore and she was unemployed. It was always a miracle and while I protested at the beginning, one gulping of her helping of what can only be described as sweet celery meets gasoline and smoke, I woke up the next morning feeling better than I did the sober one before. And how she got the small porcelain jars on to my table with the piping hot eggs inside the minute I woke up, but without a trace of her presence was a mystery I didn't want solved.

Oh, I'm Eric, and sometimes things come up in my life that I can't explain. But when you get to the end of the story you might understand a little better about why it's hard to keep asking questions, when the answers provided don't make a whole lot of sense.

The babies were being well taken care of now. Remember Ms. Alcomb was their neighbor. I caught a glimpse of her red corkscrew hair in their unit moving them around, waving her hands over them and soothing their crying. She never picked them up though, not for a cuddle a cradle or a coo. From my view they touched the floor at all times.

She looked left and right out of the apartment window, oblivious to my gaze and pulled the shades down. For not being her apartment, I thought it was pretty damn rude. Maybe the baby's parents wanted some sunlight. Yes, yes, it did cross my mind that she was the one taking care of them. But I couldn't be sure and I wanted to be. My first class was approaching and Professor Eliak was waiting for my paper to use as the last piece in his puzzle for his research article due to be released in a week. My second cup of coffee was stone cold and I threw on a sweater huddling in the corner of my bedroom and made my way into the rickety, creaking elevator at the end of my hall.

The front door in my building was from the last century and it soared to the ceiling in the foyer. I couldn't help stopping on the sidewalk when I got to the front door of the building Ms. Alcomb was in. *The Saint Claire* was announced with rusted metal letters above the stubby entrance with a muted, dented and scratched metal door. The whole building appeared ominous and uninviting. I just stood there looking at it, wondering if Professor Eliak could wait to allow me time to figure out why the tiny tots were holed up in this urban decay. I decided he couldn't.

I found myself in front of that door again, basking in the glow of the mercury streetlamp. It was pulled open and a piece of concrete from the crumbling sidewalk was lodged in the seam to hold it open. A pea green truck was parked out front. The kind you see groceries or flowers delivered from. I heard Ms. Alcomb's voice, the cackle which was her laugh and then hushed tones as she discussed serious things with the driver. My key was in the slot of the paneled oak door of my building unlatching the handle when I saw him duck under the cover of night into the driver's seat and speed off. The metal door slammed shut behind him. It was a familiar sound I heard through the night from my window seat. I tried not to fall asleep in the window seat with my head propped against the scratchy block pattern burlap my grandmother who still lived on the reservation sewed, but the nostalgia of the decade that had passed between now and when I was home to see her last, beckoned me with guilt to use it. So I heard this door often, a fixture of my neighborhood and a contrast to the serene, insulated buildings I hoped to live in some day.

I stood over that pillow now with my hand on the cord to raise the shade. Goddamn, I was still hesitating and couldn't figure out where the apprehension was bubbling up from. When Professor Eliak was yapping away about the merits of my "scholarly research," as he liked to say, I could see a set of eyes from one of the babies looking at me blankly. Not for help, no pleading, nothing akin to that. It was staring off in the distance like we adults do when the sun is hitting the side of our face perfectly in a long car ride through the countryside. Those eyes called to me to find the reason they were there.

I pulled the shade and my eyes swept past Ms. Alcomb's kitchen where she was dutifully brewing something on the stove. Her white freckled hand reached out the kitchen window and grabbed a snippet of herb leaf for whatever it was she was cooking. When my eyes arrived at the window where the babies were, my heart jumped. The babies were still there, alright. The orange glow from behind them was something from the campfires I had told stories around as a child. But the floor was covered. The eyes which had captured my mind during Professor Eliak's rant were still there in spades. An arm hung over his mouth and his arm over another mouth. It was legs and arms and big eyes and tiny toes everywhere. They covered the floor in a thick layer of baby soft skin. Where one body began and one body ended was indiscernible from my vantage point. The glass between us threatened to obscure my view. I pushed the window up into the ceiling, the cloth ropes clopped along on the rusty old wheel in the window jam.

I pushed my legs through the window and out onto the fire escape clutching tightly to the thin black iron railing which guided me safely between the fear of certain death ten stories below and the grounding certainty of a brick wall. Suddenly, the orange glow, I had come to feel comfortable with extinguished. The room filled with a white liquid that covered the mass of infant's bodies and refracted the alley light like fresh snow under a full moon. It flowed over them, their protests causing ripples in what would have been a steady stream and within the half minute, the gummy mouths were suckling the air like my fancy goldfish Gimko does when I drop little flakes of food on the surface of his world. Their heads turned, their arms flailed in delight, searching, with uncoordinated zeal for any remaining leftovers. It occurred to me it was milk. What else do infants eat?

I don't know I conceded quietly, but milk seemed to be a plausible explanation.

My fingers were digging into the crumbling mortar between the bricks of my building when it occurred to me. I don't have to be a casual observer and no sooner than I settled the decision against my warring intellect to investigate I was at the metal door looking into the small window squarely in the top half of it with chicken wire running through the glass. It wasn't propped open any longer. What I could see through the glass was a hallway which ran the length of the building. The plastic coverings to the long fluorescent tubes were filled with dead insects and grease which if you didn't look up made it look like the building supervisor had gone fancy and installed dimmers on the light switches. I twisted the knob, but the damn thing was locked. I just gave it a yank with all the strength a noodle eating, poor grad student could provide. The door plate must have been either worn thin or not installed correctly, because the door came flying at me with the little effort I had put into it.

Once I was on the seventh floor, winded from the climb, I crept quietly through the corridor. There were only five doors on each side of the hallway and I knew the apartment I could see into was not on the end. I also knew Ms. Alcomb's wasn't either, so I was looking at a fifty-fifty chance of getting this right. I knocked on my best guess and crossed my fingers Ms. Alcomb wouldn't come out of her apartment or so I hoped. I knocked again, faced my head to the ground and waited for a shuffle or a rumble from behind the door to tell me someone was on their way. But it was only silence which greeted me, until, a sputtering of orange light trickled out over my toe and stopped, then another, out over my over toe. The darkness between my two feet now seemed profane.

There was a thump and a quiet whimper. I pushed my ear against the door, waiting to hear more: A second thump, followed by a roll and multiple gurgling and coos. This must be the right place. The orange light retreated from my toes and I pushed on the door to follow it. What had gotten into me was anyone's guess. The door gave way and on the other side I could not have imagined.

Baby cribs lined the walls of the otherwise barren main room of the apartment. I could see arms and legs poking out of the rails, each of them filled to capacity. The satellite mobile which hung from the ceiling orbited a massive orange ball in the center. It looked more like a fifth grade science project of the solar system than it did a baby mobile or a chandelier. There were too many planets to be any of those things, though. Hundreds of different sized orbs circled the massive orange light.

They began to whiz into motion, around and around, a crackling sound filled my ears and ozone filled my nose. The orange ball in the center glowed brighter and brighter until it opened and a baby fell from it. My eyes followed him down to the ground where he landed with a thump on a soft pile of cardboard egg cartons which had been assembled neatly on the floor.

"Eric, dear...what on earth?" Ms. Alcomb was exasperated as she came out of the bedroom. She rushed over to the wriggling lump of adorableness on the floor scooped him up and disappeared into the other room. She came back without him with her hands on her hips blowing one of her rogue corkscrews out of her face with an extended bottom lip. "Is this normal behavior for you? Just barging into other people's homes without knocking?"

"I knocked." I wasn't going to get called out for something I had done.

"Ugh, shut the door." She walked over to me and grabbed my arm. "Now you don't tell anybody about this! You hear me?" She was wagging her finger hard at me, like I was a puppy who had just messed the carpet.

"What is it?" I pointed at the first occupied crib.

"Never mind!" she threw my arm down and stormed off into the bathroom. I could hear long sobs coming from behind the hollow door. I followed her tilting my head toward the door. "Ms. Alcomb, are you okay?"

"Eric!" she screamed, and then mumbled something else, but it was unintelligible.

I made my way into the bedroom, cautious not to walk under the mobile, though the planets had stopped rotating and it was holding position with a steady and low hum.

I heard several breaths, leisurely inhaling and exhaling, quiet movements, squeaks and peeps. I stood over a sea full of sleeping babies. Wall to wall, every corner, every space, every square of avocado linoleum, the legs and arms and tiny torsos intertwined. Their chests rose and fell in sync, their dreams woven together through the fabric of the room. I couldn't help myself. I reached down and picked up the closest face next to the entrance. I might have guessed he was the same one who I witnessed fall from the mobile but it was too hard to tell. Their small naked bodies all looked the same when put together. He was serene and calm and he rested his head in the nook of my elbow and reached around to my shirt to hold on. The mobile started buzzing, the planets whirring into action. The bathroom door flew open and Ms. Alcomb's heavy footsteps made their way to where I was standing. I could see the yell working its way to the front of her mouth. With my free hand I reached to my mouth and nose with my index finger to shush her. How could she wake all of these perfect souls just to scold me?

I set the baby boy down amongst his brothers and sisters. He wriggled his way in with them like a puzzle. I followed Ms. Alcomb back into the main room where the mobile was in full motion. The crackling sound was louder than last time and the orange globe looked like it was going to go supernova. The babies in the cribs were starting to whine and writhe.

"We have to leave now." She looked at me with serious commitment.

Apparently, she was waiting for me to take the first steps toward the door—but I stood there fixing my gaze on the growing spectacle in the center of the room. She mumbled a few words and made a wild gesture with her hand. I felt something sprinkling over my head and brushed at it realizing I was standing in the hallway outside the apartment. The flash from inside lit up every unsealed crack in the door and projected to the blank hallway wall opposite it—the image of dancing ants.

"What is it?" I was bewildered.

"I don't know. But it comes for them and I am hell bent on staying out of its way."

"Every day?" I said.

"There is no schedule. I could use your help." She gestured to her apartment door.

There was a stark contrast from the apartment next door. She had made her living space up nice and cozy with soft fabrics, warm colors and comfortable furniture. The kitchen at the far end was full of steam and strange smells. The huge cauldron on the stove was boiling furiously.

"Can you help me carry this into the other apartment?" She wasn't really asking.

I grasped the loopy brass handle and heaved my side. I looked in and saw the white liquid I assumed was the same thing I had seen in the window. I followed her lead. We walked down the hall and back into the apartment, setting the cauldron next to an identical two other cauldrons cooling on the countertop of the kitchen. Every crib in the main room was empty. The orb a deep and wintery blue, the planets had frozen in space. A few had icicles hanging from them.

"Take one of these" she pointed to the other cauldron. She led us again carefully carrying the liquid to the bedroom. "On three, dump it over the children. *One. Two. Three.*" We hauled the massive pot of nutrients into the air, it splashed down on them. Ms. Alcomb chanted three lines of a language I did not understand and the thin covering which we had thrown began to fill in the crevices between the babies and on top of their bodies. The eyes, hundreds of eyes widened and those suckling mouths opened and drank. I looked over at her and for one stolen second I saw her smile at what she had done. Then it was back to the main room. We repeated this over and over...the babies fell from the mobile, drank the milk, and went on their way, never subsiding. Ms. Alcomb was tireless. I caught her drinking the milk from a ladle, lapping it up like a cat. She giggled when she saw me and patted her rotund hips.

"Yeah, I know condensed nutrition is not what I need." She pushed the ladle toward me, encouraging me to drink. "Go on, you deserve it after all of your hard work. A little milk spell never hurt anyone.

When I woke up face down on her kitchen floor with my cheek in a puddle of my saliva, I knew I could not keep this pace. Weeks had passed...I knew because at first I confused the orange glow from the globe with the orange light filtering through the sky at sunset. But how many was anyone's guess. Professor Eliak was blowing up my phone with questions, Gimko must have wondered where I was, and the rent was due. I couldn't afford to have my belongings in a pile on the sidewalk.

Ms. Alcomb was in the other apartment when I stopped outside of the door, not sure how I was going to tell her I was leaving. That apprehension was stronger than it had been the first time I was standing here wondering what was on the other side. We had become a well-oiled machine she provided the magic and I provided the manual strength to keep this going. But here I was, leaving.

I could hear the mobile in motion and my instinct led me to abandon my resolve. I rushed in and stood just below the mysterious machine I had come to respect as it worked through the cycle I had witnessed hundreds of times. The energy from the planets coursed through me. I held my arms out and waited. When the baby tumbled perfectly into them, I looked down to see. He was three breaths from crying. His small ribs strained against his skin, his burnt caramel skin scaly and dry. Clumps of curls were missing from the mop of black curls on his head.

But he was perfect, and I carried my son out the door.

David Greske
Hush Little Bebe

"You keep away from those matons before they turn you into a puta," Juanita's madre scolded.

"Momma, they are not hoodlums, they are my amigos."

"'Nita, they are no good. They are maleado."

A wet stench of blood and shit and urine saturated the crumbling interior of the decrepit apartment building where bums and addicts, too drunk or high to move, lay in crumpled heaps in the shadowed corners of the dim hallways. The heavy, acrid smell of burnt crack hung in the air like a gray cloud of death.

From behind closed doors came the muffled, baleful wails of the putas. All they wanted was enough money for a fix and maybe a carton of milk for their kids.

Children, naked and filthy, roamed the halls. Their ear-splitting screams bounced off the walls, mixed with the moans of the whores, and sounded like the devil's choir. They gave wide girth to those hidden in the shadows. They called them boogiemen and if they caught you they'd eat you.

Listening to the commotion from the relative safety of her locked apartment, Juanita Sanchez wondered how long ago she had had that conversation with her madre. Five years ago? Ten? Twenty? It didn't matter, really. Madre was dead now, but damn it, she was right.

Twenty-seven year-old Juanita Sanchez looked more like fifty-seven. Her skin hung from her wasted body like congealed molasses and cottage cheese-like fungus grew under her discolored fingernails. What hair she had left was a tangled mess that stank like an unclean toilet. Her eyes were sunk so deep into her skull they were hardly visible at all. Open sores covered her face and thick, yellowish pus oozed down her cheeks. Most of her teeth had rotten away and those she still had were black, brittle nubbins set in shriveled and bloody gums. Consequently, her breath smelled like dead fish left out in the hot afternoon sun.

Juanita paced about the room, rubbing her arms with her bony hands. Her last fix was yesterday, Memorial Day, and if she didn't get something soon, the bugs beneath her skin would drive her mad. But there wasn't much of a demand for a puta that was five months pregnant.

She thought about an abortion, but she'd been unable to raise the money. Everything she made she'd spend on a fix. She considered going to one of those backstreet butchers, but changed her mind, having no desire to be left bleeding to death in the gutter of some stinking alley. So she really had no other choice than to get rid of the thing herself.

Juanita stripped off her rags and rubbed her bloated stomach as she made her way across the tiny room. Like a cancer, her belly was hard and alien. Sometimes at night, once the drugging and whoring stopped for the evening, she was certain she could feel the thing as it grew, sucking the life from her. She felt its brain becoming bigger, its arms and legs growing longer. A wave of revulsion rippled through her and she fought back the urge to vomit.

The bi-fold door of the closet shuddered when she pulled it open. Reaching inside, she snatched an empty hanger from the rod. Untwisting it, she straightened the wire and fashioned a hook at one end. A crude instrument, but would get the job done.

On her way to the bed, she plucked the cracked mirror from the top of the scarred dresser.

The bed, which was just a mattress, but one of the finer mattresses the building had to offer, was covered with a sheet of plastic Juanita had stolen from a tenant the night before. The man she'd taken it from was too high to notice that it had gone missing and Juanita needed it more. Clean up, she suspected, may be messy and she didn't want to soil the mattress.

With the modified coat hanger in one hand and the mirror in the other, she flopped on the bed and rolled onto her back. She spread her legs and arranged the mirror so it reflected an unobstructed view of her crotch.

Sweat ran from her pores like water through a sieve. Her mouth felt full of cotton. She swallowed, but the dry, fibrous taste only increased. Sweating, she wondered if she was going through some kind of withdrawals or her nerves were just shot to hell. Juanita suspected it was a bit of both.

Using the mirror to guide her, Juanita poised the hooked end of the tool in front of her crotch. She took a deep breath, closed her eyes as she said a prayer, and shoved the hanger inside her. Then with a quick turn of her wrist, she twisted the instrument and yanked it out.

A piece of tissue, red, bloody and clotted dangled like wet yarn from the end of the hook. Cramps twisted her stomach into iron knots as her mind reeled from a ripple of nausea that thundered through her. The onslaught of blood came next. It covered the inside of her thighs like a red satin sheet and spattered the walls like paint. Gore ran off the edge of the mattress and pooled at the corners, soaking into the cotton stuffing.

Juanita panicked. She knew there'd be blood, but there shouldn't be so much of it. She struggled to her feet and doubled over as her gut turned inside out and a second torrent exploded from her. A stream of red peppered with chunks of meat splattered the floor and dabbled her feet. An unbearable pressure built up inside her and natural instinct told her to push. She did and as the baby moved through her birth canal, she screamed until she thought her lungs would explode. Given any stretch of the imagination, what Juanita expelled wasn't human. It had substance and form, but nothing else.

Blackish-red, it lay between her stained feet like a blob of melting gelatin. About the size of a dinner plate, its skin, if it could be called that, was smooth, slimy and reflective. Hundreds of tentacles the length of earthworms and lined with sharp golden barbs, squirmed around the circumference of the beast. Paddle-like hands attached to stumps that may have been arms protruded from what could've been the front of the creature. It didn't appear to breath, yet the erratic movement of its tentacles suggested life.

Juanita dropped to the mattress, her wide-eyes staring at the thing she'd birthed, then turned her head to one side and retched. She kicked it with the heel of her left foot. It skidded across the floor, leaving behind a trail of sticky, oily goo. With a watery splat, it hit the wall near the dresser and opened its eye.

Located near the top of the creature, a pale blue stock rose upward from a fire-red slit. Covered with a greenish-gray membrane, an orb about the size of a gold ball dangled from the twisted length of sinew and nerves. Like cold molasses the membrane rolled back to reveal a black, oblong pupil suspended in a jaundice iris.

The mess of tissue stiffened and swayed through the air. The eyeball flared. It looked like an animal sniffing its surroundings.

A second slit appeared just below the eye. As thin as a pencil line, it stretched across the diameter of the monster. It thickened until something that resembled a mouth formed. The lips peeled back and its mouth was lined with black gums. Although toothless, the gums had the hard, stony appearance of obsidian.

Ugly Babies

Then it cried and a horrible stink of spoiled meat and old vomit issued from its maw.

Juanita clapped her hands over her ears to block the piercing screeches. That was when the realization hit her: the writhing, screaming, stinking misshapen thing on the floor was part of her. She'd carried it in her belly and when she tried to abort it, birthed it instead. It cried because it was hungry.

Juanita uncovered her ears and shuffled across the room. She picked up her blouse and moved toward the child. Kneeling, she gently lifted the mass with her left hand and after clearing away the web of mucus-like threads from underneath it, wrapped it in the ragged cotton fabric.

Swaddling clothes . . . Wasn't the baby Jesus wrapped in swaddling clothing? Didn't someone write a spiritual about it? Juanita thought so, but her mind was too muddled to be sure. But could it be she'd given birth to the new Savior?

Juanita smiled and stroked the creature. Her palm came away slimy and sticky. She wiped it clean on her thigh.

The baby stopped crying and cooed. Its eye looked at its mother's face as its lips stretched into something that might've been a smile.

"Madre," it croaked, and waved its clawed hands in the air, wanting to be picked up. "Hambriento. Eat."

Juanita wiped a tear from her cheek and choked back a sob. She pushed her stringy hair away from her eyes. "Madre's here, my little bebe. Madre's here."

She picked up the baby and cradled it in her arms. Returning to the mattress, she sat down and raised the child to her breast. Juanita grimaced as the baby suckled. Those hard gums hurt her nipple, but she'd get used to the pain.

"Hush little baby, don't say a word," Juanita sang while she rocked her baby and watched it nurse, *"Momma's gonna buy you a mockingbird..."*

It was the same song her Madre sang to her when she was just a bebe.

Justin Hunter
The Third Try-mester

Karen heavily lowered herself onto the stained toilet of her third-floor tenement apartment. She held onto the small half-wall that made up the only privacy barrier allotted to the studio. The one-room apartment was so small that she could walk the length of it in ten steps. The fact that she had to defecate so openly didn't bother her. She was alone. Karen had moved to Tennessee from Wisconsin only a week ago. She was able to sell most of her meager belongings to afford enough gas to make the drive. She sold her car when she got to town. Karen didn't get much for it. An old Ford Fiesta, with high miles and rusted from harsh northern winters, wouldn't fetch much money. The cheap car she sold even cheaper, for cash and no questions asked. She got enough money to pay for a month at the apartment and for the procedure. Karen didn't have much of a plan after that.

She finished using the toilet and went around the half-wall to the small kitchen sink to wash her hands. She gazed at her swollen reflection in the cracked mirror above the sink. Karen hardly recognized herself. Her pregnancy had taken a severe toll on her physically. Anything youthful in her appearance had dulled under the stress her body was under while the child inside her grew. She looked far beyond her age of seventeen years.

Emotionally, she was dead. Her family didn't believe her about the pregnancy. She tried to tell them that she was still a virgin. She sobbed bitterly as she pleaded to her family that she didn't know how this could have happened to her. They called her a whore. They had gotten her boyfriend Chad arrested for statutory rape, which was laughable. Chad was so shy that he broke into a sweat just holding her hand. The thought of such intimacy as actual sex would probably have given him a stroke. Karen wondered where Chad was now. Bail would be out of the question for his family. They were too poor. Maybe he was released. Maybe he was in jail. Karen didn't know and it didn't much matter to her situation now anyway.

Karen left her apartment, locking the door behind her. It took her what seemed like an eternity to walk down the three flights of stairs to get to the street below. She had to take a few minutes to rest and get her breathing under control.

Karen had to walk most of the way to the clinic before she found a taxi that was willing to take her. The address she gave and her advanced pregnant state meant only one thing to the drivers. Most wouldn't take her. Karen wasn't surprised, Tennessee being solidly in the Bible belt. One driver, an obese African American, took pity on her. He got out of the Taxi and helped ease her into the backseat. Karen thanked him and wiped the copious sweat from her forehead with the back of her hand. The driver pulled away from the curb and regarded her in the rear view mirror.

"We're going to break the transaxle of this thing," he said. "I wish I could blame my weight on being with child. My problem is pizza. I can't get enough of that stuff. If I gave birth, it would be to a ten pound extra-large with double pepperoni."

"I'm not feeling very talkative."

"Sorry. Serves me right, talking about food. You're probably too nauseous to eat. My wife had the same problem. Are you feeling sick?"

"A little."

"Are we talking about physically sick or more of a something eating at your conscience sick?" the driver asked.

"You can stop and let me out if you want."

"I know. It's my cab. I know where you're going and what you're going to do when you get there. I don't agree with it, but the last thing you probably need right now is a hard time."

"Thank you for understanding." The taxi driver looked at Karen in the rear view mirror and seeing the defeated look on her face, stayed silent for the rest of the drive. Ten minutes later he pulled up to the grey painted brick clinic building. He got out of the taxi, went around to the passenger side and opened the door for Karen.

"How much do I owe you?"

"Nothing but a minute more of your time," the driver said. He took her hand and helped her out of the car. He put a ponderous hand on her shoulder and looked at her. The look in his eyes was one of sternness but genuine concern. "I find myself in the dubious position of being the last person who will try to talk you out of this. Your life is your business and I'm a stranger to you. I just want to make sure this is something you want to do. Some things you can't take back once they're done."

"I don't think I have much of a choice in the matter."

"Is your man making you do this?"

"There is no man," Karen said. "It's not like that. I just don't think I have an option. I'm trying to see if I do."

"You don't think the clinic will do this for you since you're so far along?"

"It isn't that either. I know this doesn't make sense. I just don't think I have an option. I need to see." The taxi driver shrugged his shoulders.

"I'm not sure I get it. Like I said, it's your life." He got back in the car and drove off.

Karen looked at the small gray-painted brick building of the health clinic. There were a couple cars parked in the lot, but otherwise the place was deserted. Karen was thankful for that. She was worried she would have to cross a line of pro-life picketers on her way into the building. She was well enough aware of her own sins. She didn't need anyone shouting them to her face. She had met with such resistance in her previous attempts. Nothing those people ever said swayed her decision. They didn't understand her situation. They weren't living it. Moreover, she saw no compassion or empathy in the people that reviled her. The attacks seemed to be of a personal nature and not about her decision to terminate her pregnancy. The sinner seemed to be just as hated as the sin. That wasn't how she remembered her Sunday school teacher saying things were supposed to be.

Karen entered the building and was shown directly to the operating room by the receptionist. The receptionist left. Less than a minute later a nurse entered the room and handed Karen a hospital gown. She was given a Valium and told the doctor would see her in about fifteen minutes. The nurse left. Karen took the pill and changed into the gown. She looked at the table where the procedure would take place and decided to sit in the room's only chair.

The doctor entered, an older man with thinning white hair and comically thick glasses. He was of below average height and bent from his years. He smiled at Karen and patted her hand. He gently coaxed her onto the examination table. Karen leaned back on the table, grateful for its soft padding. She had no idea how tired she was until she let herself relax. Karen thought that maybe her feelings may have more to do with the Valium then lying legs splayed in front of an old man. She giggled at the thought.

"Everything okay?" the doctor asked.

"I'm fine," Karen said, "Just a little nervous."

"Don't worry. Everything will be done in a moment. You'll feel a little pressure. Just try and lay still." The doctor took a pair of forceps and pushed them gently into Karen. She tensed at the intrusion. It felt alien and cold. She could see nothing but the hump of the doctors back from where she was laying. Karen turned her eyes toward the ceiling. Soon it would all be over.

She felt the cold tool turning inside her, searching for a hold on her baby. Suddenly, she felt a strong tugging sensation inside. She looked back at the doctor. His body was tense and shaking. All of a sudden he jerked backward as Karen felt herself fill with the hard cold metal of the forceps. Karen screamed. She knew it was happening again.

"What did you do?" she asked. Her body poured sweat. The forceps turned painfully inside her. The doctor gazed at her. His eyes, magnified by his large spectacles, were wide with disbelief.

"The forceps were pulled inside."

"All the way inside? The whole thing? Get them out!"

"I will," the doctor assured. He shook off his shock and leaned back toward Karen. He put his fingers inside her and felt for the tool. All of a sudden Karen felt the doctor's arm ripped into her up to the elbow. She felt hot pain as her vaginal walls tore. The doctor put his other hand on her thigh, braced his foot on the table and pulled hard to get himself loose. He yanked backward and Karen saw her baby. It was clinging to the doctor's hand. It looked unearthly. It's wet and wrinkled mass clung tenaciously to the doctor as he waved his arm frantically to free himself. The still-connected umbilical cord whipped up and down with his struggle. Karen thought she would tear asunder from the inside out. The doctor cursed vehemently as he tried to get free.

The baby launched from the doctor's hand onto his face. The violence of the lunge snapped the umbilical cord taught. It pulled Karen's feet out of the stirrups and almost off the examination table. The doctor screamed as the fetus clawed at his eyes. Karen saw the baby bite its gums down on the doctor's nose. The doctor flailed a hand toward the implement table, grabbing a scalpel. The fetus shoved backward off the doctor and landed on Karen's stomach. The doctor spun wildly with the blade and slipped on the wet pool of afterbirth on the floor. He hit the ground, impaling himself on the knife. Karen and the baby watched the doctor wretchedly twitch on the ground while he bled out.

When the doctor's body ceased to move the baby turned his small face toward Karen. His mouth was pursed closed and his eyes spelled cold hatred.

"I won't do that again. I promise," Karen assured. The baby didn't move. Seeing her child gave Karen an equal amount of love and fear. She wanted the child, but dreaded what it was at the same time. "I mean it," Karen said. "I won't try and hurt you again."

The baby pulled back Karen's gown and shoved himself feet-first back into his mother. Karen felt a sharp stinging pain as the forceps were pushed out of her. They clattered to the floor next to the body of the doctor. She felt the baby move and kick as he made himself comfortable in the womb. The baby quieted and Karen felt its peace. She put her hand on her stomach.

"Is there any way I can make this up to you?" Karen asked. She felt a sudden and intense craving for ice cream.

Randy Rubin
This Is a Troll Free Call

"Hello."

"Hey Cary, it's me..."

"Got ya. This Is Cary, I'm out right now so leave a message. I'll get back to you. Beep."

"You fucker, call me back when you get this, you prick—ass prankster. Love you, you little bastard—it's Grandma. Heh heh, YOU know who this is, bro."

The day was one of those freakish ones that pop up every summer. It's Seventh Realm of Hell hot for a fuckin' fortnight well into the mid-nineties with a humidity factor of somewhere between tropical rainforest moisture and breathing air the consistency of creamy peanut butter. Sticky, sweaty, shit weather that makes one a slave to air conditioning and cabin fever, is what you end up with; the kind of summer where you feel guilty taking your dog out for a shit. Then it rains sometime right between the time when you feel the necessity to wash the seven layers of bird shit off your automobile or your grass needs cutting or what little of your lawn still gasps for breath gets a merciful evening hose-down and soaking. Then the torrent drops out of the sky, pulling the aforementioned humidity back down into the ground and the temperature drops into the actual life supporting lower eighties and the human race is momentarily set free from the confines of conditioned air and claustrophobia. So I said to myself, "Self...let's go for a walk. Get the fuck up out of the 'cabin' and out into the 'summer woods' for a change of scenery."

I even tied my dog Eva out in the yard so she could get a breath of fresh air. She's a digger, that lovable little scamp, (fuckin' destructive mutt) so before long she had the weed-speckled fabric of my lawn torn open and was half- buried in her cool summer dirt hole. Thanks, Bitch! Daddy loves you. But I digress...

So, I grabbed my grabber and a large black trash bag and decided I would collect some aluminum cans for recycling while I got my daily well er, um, semi-annual exercise. I turned in some cans last month after holding them until I got four contractor bags full and that paid for my bottle of top shelf Canadian sipping whiskey.

I took off around ten thirty and walked the perimeter of the neighborhood for the better part of an hour. A beer can here and a soda can there and before I knew it, I had my trash bag full and decided to tie it off to keep the sour beer smell from making my gorge rise. I was headed back home with my grabber twirling like a drum major's baton and a big black bag in the other hand, swinging it like a suitcase. I decided to take a different route back and walked over to the draw bridge to see if I could catch a glimpse of a sailboat or a tug-in-tow. Maybe some lucky rich fucker's yacht would be there holding up traffic as it passed under the open draw. I could daydream or wish upon a star or whatever, that the lucky fucker was me in that mighty pleasure craft, ambling under the bridge, holding up all those hundreds of angry, sweaty, working stiffs who were seething pissed, in a hurry to either get home from work or get to work before their cars overheated. I got to the bridge and set my bag down, taking a hankie from my pocket to wipe the beads of sweat off my forehead and the lenses of my glasses. I put my hand up over my eyebrows to scope out the waterway. A single mast schooner had passed under the bridge right before I arrived and the counterweight was still lowering the bridge back into place.

That was when, amongst the cat tails and hovering dragonflies, past the tall pampas grass like unkempt river whiskers, and around a draw bridge where nothing but water and steel beams and dirty, graffiti-tainted concrete pylons littered with vagabond's rubbish slapped and waved, splashing rhythmically against the overgrown and polluted shoreline, I heard the faintly muffled cry of a newborn baby somewhere off in the distance.

"Tag, Randar, you're it! I'm returning your call, Bro. I had to go out and pay a bill but I'm home now for a few so if you want to Fucker, call me back. That shit, you sounding like Grandma, cracked my new girlfriend up, man. She really thought it WAS my Grandma from the way you had your voice disguised. She's like, 'Does she really talk to you like that, Cary?' and I fell the fuck out laughing. Good one Bro. You had her going there. Call me. Later."

So I'm listening to this barely audible crying sound and I'm starting to freak out. Where the hell is this kid? More importantly, why is there a baby crying near a river? What if she falls in before I can get to her? Where are the parents? This place is a filth trap so why would anyone have a baby down here unless they meant to drown it or abandon it and make a clean getaway? Who the fuck would be so cruel and callous and evil?

I left my grabber-gripper and plastic bag on the gravel shoulder of the road and stepped into the high weeds, trying to pinpoint the exact location of the baby. Bugs attacked. Bugs tried to escape my advance. Bugs loomed and lighted on me. They bit me, they stung me, and the chiggery little bastards that look like black pepper made me itch in places that soon became urticarian rashes and raised hive welts on my skin. Still I felt compelled as a card-carrying decent human being to find this distressed baby. Bugs of every shape and size took flight as I stomped down the tall grasses and weeds that stood taller than I am. I slipped on a discarded forty ounce beer bottle and fell into the mud on my ass, soaking it in muddy river water and green slime. My other leg slid into the river. Nice...and soaking wet! I had made it to the shoreline, evidently.

The crying noises were a bit clearer and seemed nearer to where I sat spread-fucking- eagle in a sort of painful man-splits position. I swung my leg around and stood up, being careful this time of where my feet stepped down. I moved toward the noise and the vicinity of the bridge pylons. What if the bugs were messing with baby the way they were chowing down on me? The litter that floated in the water was sickening and a bit depressing. Dead fish could be found floating in it, stinking up the air. I looked up as I followed the river's edge and the rounded contour of the shoreline was obscured by a patch of cat tails hiding an old refrigerator on its side and a gas stove with its lid flipped up. Herons or some other stork-like bird had obviously used this as a nest in bygone times. I heard the crying baby again, louder than before and at last I spotted what looked like a watermelon swaddled in dirty blanket cloths and a torn piece of a sleeping bag with a dingy plaid lining design. I saw it resting under the bridge support atop a concrete shelf. I tried to walk around the dead discarded appliances turned bird habitat then stopped abruptly and crouched down in the weeds letting the boxlike structures hide me. There, further under the bridge but sticking out of the darkness, was an enormous pair of dirty bare feet. Flies and the larger dragonflies circled them and they never moved.

I slowly advanced, trying to get a better look. I tossed a beer bottle at the foot, hitting it squarely on the heel but it didn't move. I bravely stood up then and trudged closer to the bundle of noise and was shocked to see a second set of feet obscured by the darkness of the bridge but equally as lifeless and unmoving. These humongous fuckin' feet belong to, dare I say it... Bridge Trolls! Do you believe this shit? Big-ass, ugly Bridge Trolls, too! I'm freakin' the fuck out here people! They make their homes under bridges, so the stories go, but in my entire half century of life I'd never seen one, let alone a whole family unit. They're supposed to be very rare and very moody and stand-offish so it's best if you steer clear of them and let them live out their quiet little, simple, shitty Troll lives unencumbered and unchallenged under whatever bridge they wish to call home.

Holy ship, Batman! A male and a female, obviously a couple, obviously the parents of this baby troll in swaddling clothes, who's obviously as hungry as a hostage, both fall asleep while the draw bridge is up and lay their weary heads down in the wrong place and as the bridge comes down...Squish! Both of their gigantic Troll heads crushed and squeezed like bulbs of roasted garlic, leaving newborn Baby Girl Troll to cry herself half to death.

Or to sleep—for goodness sake, Randar, quit being so damned morbid!

So now what do I do with a Troll baby?

"Come on, Cary, Pick up the phone man, pick up the phone. Come on brother man. Answer the God Damned..."

"Hello."

"Finally, fucker. Hey you're never gonna..."

"Got ya! This is Cary. I'm out right now so leave a message. I'll get back to you."

"Dude, you said you would be home for a few. I gotta tell you something important man. Real fuckin' important, bitch, so call me back. You will not believe what I found under a bridge today. Hurry up and call me Bro I need your advice on something major. Later. Oh and if you don't shit-can this message thing by the time I get to your place, I'm gonna bash it to smithereens with the first club or bat or big fuckin' stick I can get my hands on. This joke thing's getting' real old. REAL old! Later."

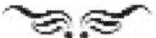

I grabbed up the bundled baby like a satchel, snatching a handful of cloth in my fist and turning, I headed up the embankment to the bridge. Eventually I made it to the gravel shoulder and picked up my grabber and left the bag of cans. I held her like that for the better part of the journey back to my house. I had to stop several times to rest and catch my breath. I'm no spring chicken and haven't been in any kind of shape in twenty years, so it takes me a while to tote a load like her across town on foot.

I finally set her down on my dining room table about an hour-and-a-half after I snatched her off that concrete shelf. I tried to peel off her dingy, dirty blankets and see if she was hurt in any way. She stank and she was filthy and she cried incessantly.

As I pulled at the layers of her swaddling clothes, I thought better of unwrapping her until I could get her upstairs and in a warm tub. So I threw out the garment pieces I had unwrapped and took her up the steps to the bathtub. I set her in it and went to find something clean to wrap her up in once I got her washed. The rest of her shit would have to go in the trash. All of it must be discarded, I decided. Maybe even burned. Whew!

"Randar, you better pick up this phone and talk to me Bro. This is getting trifling. We keep missing each other on this friggin' worthless phone system. What's your big secret news that you need to talk to me about, Brother Man? Did you finally get a girl to go out with you? Are you finally willing to admit that you're gay as a birthday tablecloth? What? Come on, bitch. You can tell me. Either you're coming out of the closet or you robbed a 7-11 and you need me to help you hide all the little coffee creamers and sugar packets from the MAN. Anyway, I'm calling you back for the umpteenth time today and if you want to get hold of me I'm going out to the pub for a ..."

"Cary don't hang up, don't hang up. Fuck, I had to run down the steps to catch the phone. I was upstairs in the bathroom. Give me second to catch my breath. Whew! Okay. Guess what the fuck happened to me today? Wait a minute...there. I had to pull up a chair. You still there?"

"Yeah, I'm still here. Just tell me. I don't feel like fuckin' the duck right now, dude."

"Yeah okay Bitch. So I'm walking around by the drawbridge, pickin' up empty cans, meditating and getting some exercise when I hear this baby crying off in the distance."

"Bitch, don't tell me you kidnapped a baby!"

"Well, not so much kidnapped, Bro. More like, I rescued a baby. And not JUST a baby..."

"The President's baby."

"Shut the fuck up dude, and let me finish."

"A Mafia mob boss's baby. Holy fuck dude..."

"Dude if you don't shut the fuck down and let me finish my story..."

"All right, all right, I'm sorry. It's just that you got me all fuckin' excited and..."

"A Fuckin' Troll Baby, Cary."

"A what?"

"Yep. A Troll baby. It's a girl and it's practically newborn and I found it under the draw bridge on the concrete pylon next to her two dead Troll parents. They had their sleeping Troll heads smashed in the draw while they slept and they left this Troll baby in some stank-ass blanket wrappings and a piece of torn sleeping bag. Dude, she's so ugly she's cute; know what I mean? Like a big watermelon-sized Shar Pei puppy with all those wrinkles and butterscotch colored skin."

"Dude, you're so full o' shit. I'm not falling for any more of your craziness. A Troll baby? Get the fuck out of here!"

"Cary, I'll swear it on your mother's grave. An honest-to-goodness Troll baby. I know it sounds like bullshit but you have to come and check her out. She's up in the tub now. I have to find something for her to wear when I give her a bath. She fuckin' reeks and she's hungry and cryin' and I need you to bring me some big toddler diapers and some whole milk and some mushrooms. And truffles. I'll need some baby food in jars too. And a couple of bottle rigs with nipples, big bitches. I'll give you the cash for it when you get here. Bring your girlfriend too, if you want. Babies love bitches. This kid needs to be cleaned up and fed like yesterday. Hurry up and get here. I have to head back up there before she screams herself unconscious. Hurry Bro. I ain't fuckin' the duck either, man. I need you. Later."

"All right man, I'll get all this shit for you and bring it to the crib but if you're lying to me about a Troll baby, you got a major ass whoopin' coming and I'm serious as a courtroom full of cancer patients. And you'll owe me double, so this better be legit. A fuckin' Troll baby huh? So this is a troll free call. Right? Heh-heheh. Wow! You don't see them every...fucking ever!"

"I know, Bro, right? Get here man. And don't make me say, 'Troll baby' again or I swear to God I'll punch you in the face."

"I'm on my way. A troll baby, huh?"

"Dude, what'd I just fuckin say?"

He came over with the grocery and baby goods and I had just finished bathing the baby in a bath of tepid water and mild dish soap. She was the color of butterscotch pudding and she had filth crusted in her folds and wrinkles. I had to change the bath water three times. She stopped crying as the warm water touched her leathery, pale brown skin and as she splashed the soap bubbles and water, she cooed and giggled softly. I noticed that she had no sex. There was only one hole for excrement and urine and she let loose with both when the warmth of the water covered her lower half. She shat and pissed simultaneously in my hand, and in my disgust, I dropped her in the tub and her body barely bumped the bottom of the big bath basin. She giggled and kicked and splashed in two inches of sudsy water slowly draining away along with a trail of feces and urine. The smell made me gag twice, vomit once, rinse and spit, and rub menthol vapor gel on my upper lip.

I let her splash away as I pushed all the fluvial detritus to the drain. The second bath was a bathing, scrubbing ordeal. The third bath was a playtime pastiche with a lick and a promise in the spots previously missed in baths one and two.

I put her in a miss-matched pillow case diaper folded in half and heavily powdered her with talcum. I wrapped her in a big beach towel for a blanket and took her downstairs. I handed her to my brother Cary and took the groceries out of the bags he had placed on the table. He held her away from him like she was made from pure shit and stood there stuttering at me in disbelief. I pulled the blender off the counter beside the sink and plugged it in. Then there was mushroom chopping and milk pouring and truffle stuffing and finally, Cary asks me, "So what do you feed a newborn Troll?"

"How in the federally funded loyal order of fuck do I know, Cary? I'm guessing here, Dude. You know, making it up as I go along? Let's see, Troll milk...maybe truffles and mushrooms and Whole Milk...Troll Milk. I'll start with that."

"Dude, are you seriously considering keeping this...this bundle of...this creature baby?"

"I don't know, Bro, she kind of grows on ya."

"Well fuck you Mister Understatement. Damn tootin' she's gonna grow on ya. You ain't gonna be able to feed this...this...later on. And what the fuck do they eat? Ain't it like, real live people? You know, the 'I'll grind your bones to make our bread' kind of shit? Maybe some road kill sampler platter appetizer before the 'people' main course? Come on Randar, get serious. You need to give her to the firemen or the cop shop, maybe drop her at some hospital ER. That's why they have those laws where they can't come back on you if you just turn her into one of those three drop-off points. It's free and clear. No appointment necessary, operators are standing by, this is a Troll Free Call. We'll pay the shipping and handling. Act now and we'll throw in this handy-dandy onion chopper do-hickey at no additional cost. Come on Bro, use your head."

"Yeah but..."

"But nothing! You gotta get rid of this. Randy, look at me dude. YOU HAVE GOT TO GET RID OF THE TROLL BABY THAT WILL GROW UP TO BE THE TWELVE FOOT TALL, HORMONAL GIRL TROLL WITH AN ATTITUDE, THEN THE GROWN WOMAN TROLL WITH WOMANLY NEEDS AND AN EVIL, HORMONAL, 'NOT-GETTING-ANY-TROLL-DICK' BITCH-IS-GROWN-AND-DANGEROUSLY-EMPOWERED ATTITUDE.Sorry Bro, but by then you'll be up to your ass in alligators and living in a borrowed tent next to the dog kennel in the back yard of the Poor House. No, fuck that! That's Bullshit and I won't have that for you. Give it to the authorities and be done."

"Yeah whatever, Bro. We'll see."

"WHATEVER! WE'LL SEE! ARE YOU ON THAT SHIT AGAIN? GIVE IT TO SCIENCE, YOU CRAZY FUCK!"

"We'll see, I said. Now drop it for a while. Shit."

"Oh I'll drop it. On its ugly fuckin' pug head."

"HEY! Give me that baby. Don't be evil, Mother Fucker. Give her back so I can feed her this soupy concoction of shitty shitake smoothie and don't you even think about dropping her."

"911...what's the nature of your emergency?"

"My brother has something that he kidnapped that will require the police and maybe a representative from social services. He's not equipped to take care of this baby he found and he lives at 5341 Applewood Drive. I think he might be on something, and I fear for the safety of this baby. Please hurry!"

"Please stay on the line sir and..."

"This is SEVEN ON YOUR SIDE breaking news desk. What can we help you with?"

"Bring a news team right now to 5341 Applewood Drive for the story of the century. There's a man barricaded in his home holding a baby...on mushrooms...kidnapping...police, fire and rescue in route. Hurry! 5341 Applewood Drive. Ambulances and fire and police...social services representatives. Explosive situation about to unfurl. I'm calling the three other television news outlets, so the first responding satellite feed truck to the scene will get the scoop. This is going to blow your viewing audience's mind. You really want to take this seriously, my friend. This will be Regional Daytime Emmy material."

That bastard I call a brother is the real creature in this shit storm story that is my life. Cary called the cops, the media, the social services people and the fire department to my home and they descended on me en masse and with swat-like precision and zeal. I never saw it coming. The monster had me arrested and the Troll baby taken away by a social service fucking ninja! This bitch disappeared instantly after taking the baby in her arms. The media never even got wind of her existence, that's how smooth this bitch was.

They had me beaten, thrown into cuffs, taken from my home, beaten again and tossed in a squad car, before I knew what the hell was going on. There were news people everywhere shoving microphones in my face asking me so many questions and bursting so many flashing lights in my eyes that I stumbled forward in a mute, dumbfounded, semi-shocked (have I mentioned, 'just been beaten'?) haze. They pulled me along at a rapid clip, holding tightly to each under arm, (also painful as hell I might add) whisking me past all the news parrots dressed in proper news plumage holding phallic microphones with bright channel numbers on them that they were obviously subconsciously reluctant to share.

I kept chanting the mantra, "Where's the baby?" over and over above the din of their cacophony of cackling questions. "Where's the baby, damn you people?" and still they swarmed and lunged at me with their foam-covered sound penises shoved at my face for comment. "Where's my baby?" And that's when one of the camera apes shot me dead on in the face, just as I looked into the lens, tears streaming down my cheeks, asking, "where's MY baby?"

I guess that changed everything. I went from crazed lunatic kidnapper to doting, loving father-type—a middle-aged man crying real tears of anguish and desperation over the usurpation and subsequent social services kidnapping and loss of his newly acquired baby of another species. I went from zero to hero in an instant. I was the lonely man with a bulging heart, ready to take on the slings and arrows of inter-species fatherhood at any cost. Damn the system that stole this man's baby. Listen to his heartfelt tale of wonder. Give him back his adopted newborn baby. I was flavor of the month on all the talk shows. I told my tale. News coverage and several days of investigations substantiated my claims. Necropsies were conducted of her biological parents. People wept. The footage of us being reunited after a series of court battles sparked a massive media frenzy and an outpouring of public sympathy and support. I named her Olivia Leanna. She likes Livie Lee.

Everyone from those baby supply super store chains to several disposable diaper companies and a plethora of pediatricians, child psychologists and scientists from all over the world would take an active role in her upbringing. Nutritionists would develop her nutrient rich, troll-specific, baby food. Costume designers from several Hollywood movie companies and New York fashion houses came and measured her and custom-made all of her clothing. She was later afforded scholarships and offers for future television appearances. My troll baby was going to be some kind of rock star.

"Uncle Cary...pick up. Uncle Cary..."

"Hey Livie, what's up Girlie-girl?"

"Dad says you have to go with us today on a secret journey so tell Auntie to dress you up all Sunday spiffy in your suit and tie, have her throw on a pretty floral dress and we'll pick you up by Limo in two hours."

"You're gonna fit in a Limo? Livie, honey you're twelve feet tall, for heaven's sake."

"I can fit if I step into the sun roof and stand up. Then I can ride it like a charioteer. It's either that or I have to walk to my own graduation and I...oh I told the secret journey surprise. Damn! Well anyway, then in two weeks we're taking me, by Limo again, to Yosemite so I can start my park ranger job. They've already built me a place to live from a converted helicopter hangar, and it looks so amazing! Ooh, Uncle Cary I'm so excited!"

"Honey, calm down, it's okay. We all knew of this surprise. Your graduation from college has all been planned out for weeks. We'll be ready when you come pick us up. We love you and we're really proud of you, Livie Lee."

"Love you both too, Uncle Cary. Aren't you glad you didn't drop me on my pug head now? Dad told me the story. I think it's hilarious how you two have been at each other's throats for over twenty five years and you love each other so much. Two old hard-heads, that's what you are!"

"Yeah...we're brothers."

Ken MacGregor
Disaster Blanket

My father taught me to always plan ahead. This has, for the most part, made my life much easier. I did well in school; I had a good job; I found a wonderful (and, it turns out, incredibly supportive) husband.

But, it was planning ahead that ultimately ruined everything.

Bill and I had our house—a fixer-upper we got for a song—our careers were both solid and we decided to have kids. Two: just enough to replace us when we're gone. I told him I didn't care, but secretly I wanted two girls. Still, I made the blanket yellow, just in case.

I started it when I was visiting Granny Bea. It was her 87th birthday, but she didn't want a party; just a few family members and the two friends she had left. Granny Bea had been an avid knitter, but her hands no longer worked right. I asked her if I could use her needles and some yellow yarn.

Everyone else had left, but we had a long drive, so Bill was napping. I had finished a few rows when Granny Bea asked what I was making.

"A baby blanket," I said. She beamed at me and said she had no idea and how wonderful.

"No, Granny. I'm not pregnant, just planning ahead." She frowned at me.

"Child," she said, "don't you know its bad luck?" I scoffed and went back to knitting.

"I don't think you understand, Jennifer; you never, ever make something for a baby you haven't conceived. Nothing good can come from it, child, and plenty bad."

"Granny, I know you are pretty old-school, but this is the twenty-first century. I just don't believe in superstitions. No offense, of course. You believe whatever you want, but once I get pregnant, I'm afraid I'll have too many other things to do, so I'm doing this now."

Granny Bea had very little to say after that. When we left, she gave me a dry kiss on the cheek, looked at me for a long moment and shook her head sadly.

In the car, Bill asked what was wrong, but I blew it off. Just Granny Bea being superstitious, I told him. Don't worry about it, I said. I would eat those words.

I finished the blanket months later; it was lovely and soft, bright and cozy. Almost immediately, I got pregnant.

Everything was textbook--oh, I had some nausea, but never morning sickness; I developed a strong aversion to the smell of cheddar cheese, which made me sad. Otherwise, I was healthy, happy and glowing. At the second ultrasound, the one where they determine gender (we both wanted to be surprised), we had our first inkling that something was wrong. The doctor made a small noise in her throat, unconsciously, I think. Bill and I looked at her. We couldn't see the screen.

"Oh," she said, smiling. "It's nothing. Just a slightly unusual phenomenon: during fetal growth, there is a tiny, vestigial tail; it's perfectly normal, and we all have it. However, by this stage it's usually gone, and your child still has one. It's rare, but hardly cause for alarm." In my mind's eye, Granny Bea is frowning at me and shaking her head.

"A tail?" Bill laughed. "Cool." I hit him gently. The doctor assured us that other than this tiny, unexpected-but-perfectly-harmless detail, the child appeared to be healthy: ten fingers and toes and everything coming along nicely.

My breasts and belly grew to truly alarming proportions and simple things like standing up from a chair had become Olympic level events. I watched a tiny, perfectly formed footprint glide from one side of me to the other, under my skin. I was filled with anticipation and love, yet I couldn't get that dinner scene from *Alien* out of my head. Eventually, the baby dropped. This is the term they use when the mother stops carrying high and the child is almost ready to come out. But, it's so appropriate; my whole middle went *thunk* down below. Well, not really, but it sure looked like it. This meant I was due any day now. I'd been dreaming of meeting my baby for a few weeks; sometimes it was a girl, sometimes a boy. I was finally going to know.

I think Bill was even more excited than I was.

Nine days later, my water broke; I was at the dry cleaners. They were very sweet about it, called me a cab and everything. I called Bill on the way, and he met me at the hospital mere minutes after I arrived. He was not quite panicking. It was cute.

I'm a little fuzzy on the details of labor. I know it was awful, but I think I blocked a lot of it out. I've done that a lot since then, too. The one thing I can still remember vividly is after the final push, the final moment of pressure and pain, despite the drugs, is that moment of silence when my child came out of me. I couldn't see, of course, but Bill could. His mouth was hanging open, his eyes wide.

"What is it?" I was starting to panic. "What's wrong with my baby? Why is it so quiet?" I tried to sit up, which was a mistake. Bill and a nurse took a shoulder each and eased me back down. They made soothing noises. I wasn't fooled.

"Bill," I looked at my husband. "What's wrong, honey? Why is everyone quiet? Why is the baby quiet?"

"Jenny, honey, it's okay. The baby's breathing. He's alive..."

"He? It's a boy?" Bill paused, too long.

"Yes," he hedged. "It's a boy. But..." He looked at the doctor, who was cleaning off my baby; I knew this because of where he was and the way he was moving, but he was between me and the child, so I couldn't see. The doctor turned his face, professionally blank, and brought a small bundle wrapped in a blanket to me. Bill moved a little away so I could take my son. He was tiny, so light. The blanket partly obscured his face so only one eye was visible and it was closed. Just this tiny part of my child's face filled my heart with pride and love. Gently, I moved the blanket off his face so I could see my son.

He was...wrong.

Bill was, I think, holding his breath as I removed the rest of the blanket. I think maybe I was, too. The lower half of my boy's face protruded, snout-like. His nose was two slits. I supported his head and looked at the rest. His arms seemed normal, but his hands were skeletal things, fingers too long, tapering to points. His legs bent backward at the knee, like a cat, or dog, or goat, or something. His ten toes grew together, connected by tough-looking skin, paw-like. I could see tiny white claws curving just below the surface. I could feel something odd on his back, so I turned him over. There was the tail, of course, almost as long as he was tall; I pretty much expected that at this point. The wings, though...those came as a shock.

Nobody spoke. I turned my baby boy back around and looked at his face; Inhuman, but not ugly . . . Sort of feline, really. He opened his tiny eyes and looked at me. I grinned at him and his green eyes sparkled.

"I want to call him Benjamin," I said to Bill. "It was his grandfather's name."

"Honey," Bill said carefully. "Are you okay?"

"Oh, Bill," I said, "I know he's different, but he's our son. How could we not love him?"

Benjamin only took a couple of years to show us how hard loving him could be. The media circus died down after a year or so, but once they left us alone, Ben started acting out. He was bigger than other kids his age, three-year-old-size at one. And strong. For a while, it was just tantrums and screaming. Every day. That's hard to take. But, that's parenting, right? You take the good with the bad. You develop a thick skin after a while.

Then, when Benjamin was almost two, he ate the cat.

Of course, that was unacceptable and he had to be punished. I hated to do it, but it was for good.

His third birthday party was a small affair; just the three of us. We put three small candles in a raw flank steak and tossed it to him. The heavy chain slithered across the floor as Benjamin moved to get his "cake". We didn't light the candles, of course. We were worried he'd get burned. He's just a child, you know? Bill and I sang "Happy Birthday", only a little off-key.

"I love you," I said. Benjamin looked up at me, bright green eyes reflecting the hall light. Blood from the steak dripped off his snout. He reached behind him and brought out an old, tattered yellow blanket. A blanket I had made. He held it to his cheek.

"Momma," he slurred. "I love you. Let me go." I cried, and told him I couldn't. I hated this, but two kids disappeared in our neighborhood. Their bones are at the bottom of the lake seven miles from here, but we can't keep this up. We're not monsters.

Well, Bill and I aren't.

Vessels by Niall Parkinson

Timothy Frasier
Daughter Mine

His nose flared from the coppery scent of fresh kill as he emerged from the forest. The snow was a brilliant red and sunken around the trap from the heat of the blood. Daniel Picket knelt down on the riverbank and examined the beaver's steaming carcass. The hide had been ripped to the point of being unsalvageable. He pried the trap open and tossed the grisly remains into the Catachut River. He didn't reset the trap. Sara would be giving birth any day now, and leaving her alone was risky.

A piercing scream in the distance startled Daniel and he spun around. He turned his ear to the direction he thought the sound had originated and tightened his grip on the broken axe handle in his calloused hands. It had sounded like a woman's scream. He'd just left Sara in the cabin, so he knew it wasn't her. Very likely a panther made the sound, and most likely that's what ruined the beaver pelt. A second scream make the hackles rise on the back of Daniel's neck.

"I hope it's my trap that has you screaming, you bastard!" His eyes squinted against the late afternoon sun as he headed west, downstream, smacking thorns and briers out of his way with the broken axe handle he normally used to dispatch animals caught in his traps. His rifle would have been handy just in case the cat got loose when he came upon it.

Daniel ignored the cold as he tromped through the six inches of snow in his worn out boots and threadbare trousers. The long, leather coat he wore was the only respectable piece of clothing he owned. His wide-brimmed hat covered shoulder length auburn hair and shaded brooding green eyes. A thick beard made him appear much older than his nineteen years. He was such a big man, standing nearly six and a half feet tall and of stout build, that many warned him about taking a small wife like Sara with her narrow hips, but love blinds most to common sense.

The cold began to penetrate Daniel's feet by way of his wet socks and crept up his legs as he tromped forward slowly. The trap where the scream came from was around the bend a short distance ahead. Moving shadows cast by the setting sun kept him on edge as his eyes darted back and forth from the wood line on his left to the river's edge on his right. An unusual stench, like a mix of pennies and sulfur, filled the air as he rounded the bend with his axe handle resting on his shoulder at the ready. Another beaver had been ripped apart, and like the first one, it appeared nothing had fed on it.

Daniel shook his head slowly and then scanned the wood line. Most predators killed for food, not for the hell of it. Something about this was not right.

"Where's the other tracks?" he said. The realization had struck Daniel in the face like a bucket of cold water. He looked closely around the trap and found only the beaver's tracks coming up from the water. He looked up. If it'd been a hawk or eagle, there'd be feathers.

The scream sounded again further downstream. Daniel threw caution to the wind and broke into a dead run until he came upon his next trap, still empty and un-sprung. He tripped it by smacking it on the side with his axe handle. "Thy rod and thy staff comfort me," he recited as he swallowed his fear and moved forward.

Another scream sounded inside the dense forest. Daniel hesitated, and then moved toward the sound. Ancient oaks, tall and straight, were interlaced with huge water maples with naked limbs stretching in all directions, giving countless hiding places for a panther seeking a perch for ambush. The forest felt surreal and foreboding, but he continued on undaunted, chasing screams amongst the shadows until the sun faded and was replaced by a low half-moon. Disoriented, he stumbled forward on legs numb from the cold, until the rush of water caught his ear and he followed it to the river bank.

"I must be losing my mind." He laughed when he came upon his first trap. Supper will be cold and Sara's temper hot, he mused as he reached the path to the cabin and broke into a run despite his exhaustion. When he reached the clearing and saw the black, hulking shape of the cabin, a sense of fear wound its way through his ribs and coiled in the pit of his stomach. Thin slivers of light escaped around the ill-fitting door and window shutters, creating eerie, rectangular outlines across the blackness which was the front of the cabin.

Daniel stepped upon the porch, kicked the sides of his boots against the post so as not to get a scolding from Sara, and then opened the door to an image from Hell. Sara was on the bed, lying on her side with knees drawn to her chest, and her gown wadded around her waist. There was blood. The bed looked like a stagnant, crimson river spilling over the mattress like a waterfall, pooling on the hardwood floor.

Daniel stood for a moment in disbelief before rushing to Sara's side. Tears poured down his face as he saw a tiny, blood covered leg protruding from her. It kicked feebly as he touched it, causing him to jerk his hand back.

"Pull it out of me, Daniel," Sara whispered. Her strength was spent along with her blood.

Daniel forced down the bile rising in the back of his throat and grasped the baby's leg.

"If the sun's shining tomorrow, I'm going to hang out those wet clothes," Sara said, in a child-like voice as she smiled up at Daniel. Her hair clung to her sweat-soaked face.

Daniel summoned his courage and pulled on the tiny leg until he felt the pop of its tendons. Blood flowed freely from Sara, pooling on the already saturated mattress, before finally soaking through. He swallowed hard and tried to push two fingers of his other hand inside her in order to find the baby's other leg.

Sara screamed and thrashed about, causing him to let go of the leg.

"What do I do?" he cried as he stood and paced back and forth. "What should I do, Sara?"

He knelt down and looked at the baby's leg. *It's got to come out or she'll die.* He pulled his skinning knife from its sheath and wiped it back and forth across the leg of his trousers to clean off the dried animal blood. *Should I cut her so the baby can get out...or cut the baby out of her?*

Daniel grasped the tiny leg in his huge hand and pulled it gently to the side as he inserted the tip of his knife into Sara. He yanked it back out when she yelped from the sting of the blade and tried to turn away from him. Her eyes rolled back in her head, exposing two slivers of white. Drool coated the side of her face. The small cut he made bled weakly.

Panic gripped him as he decided to sacrifice all to save his wife. He grabbed the baby's leg, roughly this time like it was nothing more than an animal in his trap, pulled the leg taut, and inserted the tip of the blade into its tiny thigh. He saw its toes wiggle and he pulled the blade out. *I'm going to lose them both!*

"I'm going after Jane," he said before kissing his wife long and hard. "Be strong for me," he pleaded as he rushed from the cabin and onto the porch. He looked toward the mule pen and did a quick mental calculation. The old animal was slow, and by the time he got her bridle on, he knew he wouldn't make it back in time.

Daniel turned and ran down the trail to Jane and Tom Duke's farm as fast as his legs would take him. His muscles screamed and his heart pounded in his ears. Twice he fell, but each time, he leapt to his feet and continued on.

Where were you, Daniel? Sara's voice whispered softly in his mind. Daniel threw up, barely slowing down. The guilt matched his pace perfectly as he ran for all he had. In the distance, dim light glowed from the window of Tom O'Brian's house.

Daniel pounded on the door and screamed for help.

"What's the matter?" Tom asked in his strong Irish brogue as he opened the door and began buttoning his shirt. "Is it Sara?"

Daniel nodded, unable to speak. He dropped to his knees and began to sob.

"Sara needs help, Momma," he called to his wife. "I'll hurry and hook up the wagon!"

"I'm going back," Daniel said between breaths, more in control of himself. "The baby's leg is sticking out!"

"The baby is coming breach. Hurry," Tom shouted to his wife as he started out to the barn. He turned to Daniel, "you help me get the wagon hooked up and ride with us. I'd catch you before you got halfway back."

The five minutes it took to leave the Duke farm seemed an eternity. Tom drove at breakneck speed with Daniel beside him and Jane in the back, bundled-up in a blanket with a scarf confining her long, red hair. The snow-covered countryside seemed foreign under the now risen half-moon.

"Don't know what I'll be able to do with the baby being breach," Jane yelled above the crunching sound of the horse's hooves. "I've had eight babies myself and I've helped deliver another three, but I ain't no midwife, Danny. All I can do is to try."

"I wasn't with her," Daniel said with his voice breaking. "I was out running the lines and got turned around. This is my doings." He slumped forward, appearing much older than his nineteen years.

The two mile trip back to Daniel and Sara's farm in the remote river bottom seemed to take only moments. The small, two-room cabin looked dead as they pulled up in front. Only the faintest hint of smoke drifted from the chimney.

"Dang it...I should've thrown wood on the fire before I left," Daniel stammered as he stumbled to the cabin door and shoved it open. He staggered forward into the cold room with Tom and Jane following, and then stopped. His body swayed back and forth like he was on the high seas.

Sara rested on her side facing them, the baby's head propped on her arm while it nursed. Like the keeper of a secret joke, a slight smile teased her lips, while her clouded, blue eyes were fixed on a lost moment in time. She looked content in her death.

The image was more than Daniel could take. He staggered outside and ran into the forest. His tortured legs screamed until the man, barely more than a boy, collapsed in a heap. He heard a scream in the distance as darkness took him.

Daniel watched the baby as she crawled off of the soft pelts and stood. The loose fitting gown she wore had belonged to Jane's daughter when she was two-years-old. Daniel's daughter was barely two-months-old.

"Thought of a name for her?" Tom asked. "She can't go through life without a name." He cut a chaw of tobacco and shoved it between his stained lips. He was a small, balding man of forty who dressed as poorly as Daniel, despite the fact he was one of the wealthiest men in North Carolina. Considered a shrewd businessman by many, only a few knew the truth, and that truth was that the real power in the Duke household wore an apron.

"I'll think of something," Daniel mumbled. He felt the hair on his scalp rise when the baby trained her unnaturally black eyes on him.

"Any of the clothes that are too small, just keep 'em for rags. Jane ain't having any more babies. Least with me she ain't," he laughed. "The garments that are too big will fit this one soon enough, it seems. Never seen a baby grow this fast."

The baby walked up to Tom and stared blankly. The black hair that nearly reached her shoulders accentuated her unusually pale skin.

"How's that bottle working out?" Tom asked, nervous, while cutting his eyes away from the infant. "Jane was afraid she wouldn't make milk when we were expecting our last. We ordered the thing all the way from Boston. We never needed it, though. She made enough milk to shame a cow."

"We haven't used it in a while," Daniel said while studying his child like one would a snake crawling through the weeds. "She likes more *solid* food."

"What would that be?"

Daniel pulled a piece of deer jerky from his pocket and held it out. The baby darted over and snatched it from his hand, causing both men to jump.

"Dang, she's fast!" Tom said. "And she has teeth?"

The baby's lips were pulled back as she devoured the jerky, exposing a set of viciously sharp teeth. The dried meat was gone in seconds and she looked up at Daniel blankly for more.

"I give you some more later," Daniel said, gruff. Then in a whisper, "Look at her hands, Tom. Look at them nails."

"Sweet Angel of Death," Tom said, tilting his head and leaning forward. "What's this mean?"

"It means I'm scared when I go to sleep at night." Daniel rubbed his bloodshot eyes. "After she was born, the cabin smelled strong of Sara's blood. It was soaked into that feather mattress she was so proud of. She was so happy when I traded for it, I couldn't stand to throw it out. I washed it and let it dry in the sun several times. But I could still smell it."

"Is that why you're stacking your pelts in here?"

"It covered the smell of her death with a different death," he looked at the bed in the corner of the room. "I came in yesterday and found feathers scattered across the floor, so I went over to the bed and found ..." He shut his eyes and set his jaw.

"What is it, Daniel?"

"She ate a big hole in the bloody part of the mattress," he said as he opened his eyes. "I took what was left outside and burned it."

"Don't mention any of this in town," Tom whispered. "They're a superstitious bunch."

"Remember that rat problem we had before she came along?" Daniel laughed like a man dancing in the shadow of madness. "We don't have a rat problem, now. Danged if she ain't better than a cat. Eats every one she catches, too."

Tom got up, walked to the door, and opened it. The girl's black eyes followed his every move.

"Tell me what's happening, Tom," Daniel pleaded.

"I wish I knew." Tom slowly turned and stared at Daniel. "I'll say a prayer for you and your daughter."

That night, Daniel shifted his weight, trying to get comfortable on his mattress of beaver pelts. He pulled the blanket up to his neck as the wind howled in the dark. His ears strained to hear her. There was a long moment of silence, and then the pitter patter of tiny feet across the floor. He pulled the cover over his head, just like when he was a child listening to things going bump in the night. Only now, he knew what the thing *was* that was going bump in the night.

The pitter patter came over to Daniel's bed and stopped. After an eternity of silence, he heard one of the floor boards creak inches from him. Every muscle in his body tensed as he imagined the feel of her teeth tearing into him, the pain of having his entrails pulled from his stomach and onto on the filthy floor.

"Go back to your bed," he croaked from under the cover with a dry mouth. His need to piss was extreme.

Silence...but he could sense her there, staring at him.

He began to sweat under the cover and felt a coward for hiding, but her teeth were so damn sharp. The blanket became taut as the girl climbed up on the bed. Daniel held back a scream as she moved up to his head. His heart pounded in his ears as he slipped his hand under the pillow and caressed the pistol he inherited from his great uncle.

He felt her leave the bed and then pitter patter cross the floor.

Silence.

The sound of the wind grew louder and the temperature dropped. He pulled the cover off of his head and realized she'd unlatched a window shutter and slipped out into the late-winter night. *Maybe she's gone back to Hell.* Guilt weighed on his heart. *She's the only thing of Sara I have left. And oh how she looks like her.* Daniel got up and went to the window. He started to shut it, but instead, went back to bed. His need to piss had subsided. A restless sleep took him as he listened for her return.

"I won't have any stock left by summer's end!" Daniel cried out as he glared at the remains of his last weaning-size pig. Once the girl had thinned out the wild game, she went for the easier pickings. Her appetite was insatiable. She was six months old and already as big as a twelve-year-old.

A familiar stench filled the air. It was the same stench that permeated the cabin and all his out-buildings. Daniel swallowed nervously, turned around, and found his daughter staring at him blankly. She wore the light-blue dress he'd placed on the porch for her earlier. Sara's favorite dress of the seven she owned, the front now stained crimson thanks to the girl's slaughter of the pig.

"Well, that's all the young pigs!" he yelled. "I guess you'll start on the sows next!"

The girl stood still, watching him.

Daniel turned and walked into the woods while caressing the pistol stowed in his belt. The surveyors from Carolina Timber should be here in a couple of months and he'd yet to mark off the area to be logged. The trail leading to the bluffs in the middle of his property was narrow and brier infested. Half way through, the briers thinned out and the ground sloped uphill. The trees were large and blocked out much of the morning sunlight.

An uneasy feeling came over him and he looked back to see the girl. "Get home!" he yelled.

She watched him.

Daniel started up into the bluffs, looking back over his shoulder nervously. When he reached the top, he couldn't help but smile as he thought of Sara. When they moved here two years earlier, he brought her here to see the view. She was so scared of heights, she had to sit down and scoot across to the edge to get a look.

Movement to the left caught his eye. The girl was there, kneeling on the uneven top and examining an odd pattern of stones. His stomach soured while looking at her. He turned back to the grand view before him. Nearly two thousand acres left to him by his great-uncle George Freemont.

"Before you came along, we planned on turning this into a real farm."

The girl stayed low and circled the stone pattern, oblivious to Daniel.

"Funny thing, what Sara looked forward to most from the lumber money was getting glass windows for the cabin," he said more to himself than his daughter. "She even wanted to build a room for you. We had no idea she'd be giving birth to a..."

She turned away from the stones, stepped to the bluff's edge, and squatted on her haunches. She stared intently at something on the ground two hundred feet below.

Daniel's attention focused on his daughter. She was filthy. Her hair was tangled and matted with rotten animal flesh. A fat tick dangled from her earlobe. All he had to do was take one quick step and kick. No one would ever know. His heartbeat quickened and his palms sweated as he measured the distance in his head. No one would know, but what if they did? Who would blame him? He licked his lips as he shifted his weight.

The girl lifted her dress slighted as she urinated, exposing the scar on her right thigh. The scar she received from his blade. Daniel's icy heart thawed slightly. Her life from the beginning had been filled with pain, he reflected as he relaxed his stance. Never once had he shown the girl any love. She finished urinating and dropped the dress. It fell into the stream of piss which was winding its way toward the edge of the bluff.

His heart was on the verge of bursting as the girl leapt over the edge.

"No!" he cried out. He rushed to the edge and looked down into the tree tops.

What had made her do such a thing? Had she somehow deciphered his thoughts and jumped to her death to save him the effort?

He climbed to the ground in reckless fashion and started around to the side from which she jumped. When he reached the other side, he found his daughter naked and devouring a large jackrabbit. A quick glance up revealed her blue dress hanging from the limbs of the tree she fell through.

"I'll put another dress out," he called, too afraid to go near her while she was feeding. "There's only four left, you best be taking care of them." He was amazed that she had room in her stomach for a jackrabbit after eating most of a weaned pig less than an hour earlier. He wondered uneasily what she would eat once the livestock was gone.

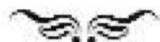

Ten months after Sara's death, Daniel pulled the wagon in front of the cabin. The girl, who looked every bit as old as Daniel, stood on the porch with her usual look of confusion. Her black dress was ripped to rags, exposing her muscular legs to mid-thigh, and most of her right breast. There was only one of Sara's dresses left untouched, and Daniel didn't know how he would clothe the girl once it was gone.

"I'll be back before nightfall, Sar—," he caught himself. She looked so much like her mother at first glimpse it was unnerving. When her eyes and mouth were closed during sleep, he would sometimes stare at her for minutes, quietly remembering the love he and Sara shared. But when those black, devil's eyes were open, an intense hatred brewed in his stomach.

"Stay close to the cabin," Daniel barked at the girl. He averted his eyes from her. The ancient mule harnessed to his wagon moved forward through the dry, multicolored leaves blanketing the trail. His trips to town were rare before Sara's death, and even more so now. He didn't feel like answering questions.

How would I answer their questions? I'm afraid to leave my farm because my ten month old daughter's eating all of my livestock! I'm afraid to bring her to town because she might rip you apart like that fox in my trap last week!

It took over three hours to reach town. He sold all of his pelts at the trading post, avoiding the small talk directed at him by the loafers sitting around the stove. Fur prices had dropped, causing Daniel to prioritize when he reached the general store. He had some change left after buying flour, salt, and other essentials, and courted the thought of buying a stick of candy for the girl. He decided against it and instead, purchased a bottle of whiskey.

On the way home, he stopped at Tom's and invited him over while flashing the bottle of whiskey at his only friend.

"I really shouldn't," Tom whispered as he stood next to the wagon. "I had a problem with it when I was young. Met Jane and been sober ever since. She's not much for nonsense."

"I'd like to go to sleep just one night without thinking about that abomination I sired," Daniel took in a deep breath and let it out slowly. "With a little whiskey inside me, I might possibly be persuaded to sell that pasture land you've been longin' for."

Tom smiled, "I don't think one drink will put me back on the path to Hell. Go on home and I'll be there shortly."

Daniel rode the rest of the way home, trying not to think of his daughter, but failing the effort. I can't move off and leave her. I can't take another wife and bring her here. Who could sleep with that horror just feet away from them? "I can." He answered himself.

She was nowhere to be seen as he unloaded the wagon, which he was thankful for.

Daniel placed the bottle on the table along with a couple of tin cups, and then seated himself facing the door. Soon, he heard Tom's wagon.

"Come in," Daniel yelled when he heard the porch planks creaking from Tom's weight.

Tom entered and took a chair facing him. "I ain't tasted the bite of good whiskey in a long time." He pulled a wad of tobacco from his pocket, cut off a chaw, and offered it to Daniel.

"Thanks, but I'll pass," he said while holding his hand up. "Tried it once and nearly threw my guts up."

Tom chuckled and shoved the chaw in his mouth.

"I'm not much of a drinker," Daniel confessed as he opened the bottle and poured it into the tin cups. "Here's to Sara. May her house in Heaven have glass in its windows," he declared while holding out his cup.

Tom touched cups with him and slowly raised the whiskey to his lips, kissing the rim like a long lost love. "That hit the spot," he said while slamming down the cup.

Daniel set his cup down, barely touched, and poured Tom another round.

"Been so long," Tom said as he stared into the clear liquid. "I forgot how much I loved her." He tossed it down and slammed his cup. "Give me another," he laughed.

An hour later, Tom sat across from his friend and cried. He cried because his wife didn't understand him. He cried because his children didn't listen to him as they should. Soon, his drunken sympathy turned from himself and latched on to Daniel.

"Oh, me lad," Tom said tearfully. "I'm so sorry for Sara. You had great plans for this place. You wanted children and all you got was a devil," The crassness of his words failed to register in his whiskey addled brain. "No disrespect, Danny boy. You love your little girl." He blew his nose and wiped his sleeve across his face while weaving back and forth.

"I blame myself," Daniel said as swirled the whiskey around in his cup. It was his second. "Tell no one this, but we gave in to temptations of the flesh before we married. It was my doings. I pushed and pushed until she gave in." He slung his cup across the room, causing Tom to jump. "Sara's blood is on my hands and my daughter is cursed by my sins."

"Daniel, me lad," Tom whispered while pouring another shot. "No one would know if you put a round ball through her. She's no more than an animal," his words slurred.

"I would not consider such a thing!" he said angrily and with a touch of guilt as he remembered that day on the bluff. "I meet my obligations, no matter what. I'm her daddy!"

Tom stared off into space for several moments. "Boy, things ain't the way you think they are." He then began to sob again for several moments before tossing his whiskey down his throat and then greedily emptying the remainder of the bottle in his cup. "I'll tell you the truth now, boy. You might hate me, but I got to clear me conscience."

"You're as honest a man as I've known." Daniel leaned forward and placed his hand on his friend's shoulder. "I'd take your word as gospel."

Tom's bloodshot eyes stared off in space for several moments.

"Jane comes from a cursed family." He looked Daniel in the eye while he took a sip of his whiskey. "In the old country, her Durbin ancestors were powerful people with powerful enemies. Legend has it that two hundred years ago, Kurt Durbin killed the son of a witch over a land deal. This witch then cursed Kurt's branch of the Durbin tribe with a banshee."

"What is a banshee?" Daniel asked as he leaned forward.

"A spirit of sorts," he said and then finished the whiskey and set the cup down. He shut his eyes for almost a minute. "All the women in Jane's family learn the black arts." He opened his bloodshot eyes and stared at Daniel. "It was the only way they could survive. They learn to push back the time of reckoning each time they're with child by using magic and blood sacrifice." He stood up on shaky legs and staggered to the open door and stared outside. "The last time, she discovered a spell to rid us of this thing forever."

"How did you get rid of it?" Daniel stared intently at Tom as the old man leaned against the doorframe and lowered his head. "Tell me, Tom. How did you rid yourselves of the curse?"

"By casting it onto your daughter," Tom said. His eyes were a blazing mix of anger and guilt.

Daniel didn't speak.

"Me wife cast it into your little baby, she did. And then she made it stay on your property with a holding spell!" Tom wiped his eyes with his sleeve. "I hate the evil bitch." He blew his nose, slung a wad of snot on the floor, and wiped his slimy fingers across his trousers.

"I don't believe in such things," Daniel said quietly.

"Just look at your daughter and tell me it's the natural order of things! What eats my soul is..." A sobbed racked his body. "Jane sacrificed our only daughter, Elizabeth as payment for the unholy transaction.

"You told me Elizabeth went back to Ireland!"

"Yes, we told everyone she'd gone back to the Old Country with my brother's poor wife because of the couple being infertile. The thing is, Danny Boy, I ain't got a brother. Jane took my six-year-old girl and butchered her like stock, without so much as a tear. Said it was the price for keeping our seven boys safe. She said Lizzy would never be able to do as much work as the boys, and we'd be out a dowry once she came of marriage age.

"This is hard for me to believe."

"You'd best believe it, Danny. My girl is dead and at peace. Your girl is another matter. Jane figures you'll have to kill her. You're the only one who can, you know, or she will eventually kill you. Either way, we'd swoop in and buy your land afterwards." Without a word of goodbye, he staggered out to his wagon and left.

Daniel's anger simmered slowly. Sara's death rested squarely on the shoulders of those he held dearest. The ceiling joist above him creaked and he looked up to find the girl, perched on her haunches. She slid to the floor and was out the door before he was able to speak. *How much of what Tom said does she understand?* He went outside and did his evening chores while he digested all that Tom told him.

The next morning, he went up into the bluffs to get a closer look at the stones the girl had been so fascinated with back in the summer. They were still there, forming a circle about three feet in diameter with a large, flat rock in the center. Something fluttering under the edge of the center stone prompting him to lift it and flip it on its side.

"Damn," Daniel exclaimed as he picked up a clipping of Sara's hair. He placed the hair clipping in his pocket and then tossed the stones off the bluff, listening with satisfaction as they made clacking sounds on impact. "What will this do to your witchery, Jane?"

A shrill scream echoed across the valley below. It was different than the screams he chased on the night Sarah died. This once carried an emotion that he couldn't identify.

"You bloody fool," Jane screamed. Her trembling fists were white. "You told him everything?"

"You know how whiskey does me." He rubbed his stinging cheek.

"And you knew better than to drink!" She paced back and forth. "Go fetch me a chicken! I have a spell to cast. Bring it to my spot in the corn." She went to her china hutch and removed an ancient book, its black leather cover cracked like the face of a weathered corpse. "The boy's apt to have loose lips," she mumbled. "What are you waiting for, you damn, drunken fool?"

Tom left the house and stumbled down the path to the chicken pen under the mid-day sun. Jane was angry, but she wouldn't stay that way. He slowed down before reaching the pen and marveled at the brilliant red covering the side of the chicken coup before it dawned on him that it was blood. Dead chickens and loose feathers covered the ground though the gate was still latched. He stood for a moment, not fully comprehending what had happened.

He walked the rest of the way to the pen slowly. Not a single chicken had escaped the slaughter. Most were ripped apart while a few had their heads bitten off. Fear seized Tom and his legs felt weak. He turned to go back to the house and saw a woman on the path in the distance. She was naked and moving toward him.

"Sara!" he called as she came near. But it couldn't be Sara. He helped bury her last year.

Indecision gripped him until a shrill scream escaped the woman.

Tom turned back to the pen and fumbled with the gate until it opened. He rushed to the coup, crawled inside, and dropped the sliding door which was there to keep out varmints at night. He gripped it tight and held his breath as he felt an effort being made to lift it.

"I know who you are," he cried. "It was my wife that did this...not me!"

Tom felt the pull against the door stop and pressed his ear against it. Silence. He lifted the door a few inches, placed his head on the floor in the chicken shit, and peeked outside. Dirty feet were right outside the door. Before Tom could let the door back down, two hands reached underneath, and ripped it off the coup.

The girl reached inside grabbed Tom, her nails tearing through his shirt and deep into his flesh. She dragged him out and lifted him to his feet. Her face was almost touching his.

Tom stared terrified into eyes that held no hint of mercy. Her mouth opened slightly, releasing a strand of slobber along with the horrible stench of her breath. With the speed of a rattler, she snapped her teeth into his face and shoved him down. He rolled on his side and put his hand to his stinging face only to find a ragged hole where his nose had been. Blood flowed freely down the back of his throat, strangling his screams.

The girl tore into him with her claws, ripping out his entrails and scattering them across the shit layered ground of the pen. She stood and circled him with her head tilted. A scent caught her attention and she darted off, Tom all but forgotten.

Tom gagged as he lay on his side, staring at the bloody intestines scattered in front of him. Something mixed in with gore caught his attention. It was his wad of tobacco! A moan escaped his throat as he painfully pulled himself within reach and grabbed his prize. He stuffed it into his mouth with a trembling a hand, and chomped down triumphantly as death embraced him.

Jane stood in the small clearing, hidden in a patch of sweet corn. She placed her book inside the circle, fashioned from field stone and paced impatiently.

"Drunken bastard," she mumbled to herself. If townspeople learn her secret, things will go to hell. And back to Hell is exactly where she needs to send this thing in Daniel's daughter.

A shrill scream in the distance startled her badly.

"Tom!" she whispered. She ran toward the house, detouring down the trail leading to the chicken pen. She slowed to a walk when the coup can into view. She stopped twenty yards from Tom, barely a breath left in her. "Damn fool," she muttered.

Jane thought of her boys, and ran back to the house. She entered through the backdoor and slid the locking bolt closed. The house was too silent. Her boys were constantly fighting or playing. The sound of furniture sliding across the floor or vases shattering into a thousand pieces was normally a constant. So much had been given to protect them. The life-blood of her only daughter had been shed to prevent what she now felt inevitable. The banshee had been cast into Daniel's daughter and trapped on his property. How can it be here?

"The damn stones!" she cried as she fetched Tom's rifle which rested next to the back door. Jane ran to the staircase and stopped as her mind tried to assimilate the horrible sight before her eyes. Blood streamed down the staircase from the hallway above. Chunks of flesh littered the polished steps. Halfway up, the head of her youngest son, eight-year-old William, rested precariously on the edge of a step with one eye open, the other closed.

"No!" she screamed. "Not my babies!" She went up the stairs with the rifle shouldered and her finger on the trigger.

Daniel's daughter met her at the top of the stairs, with Charles' head in her right hand and Zachery's in her left.

"Back to Hell with you!" Jane raised the rifle and fired. The girl staggered back at the same instant Jane tumbled backward down the stairs from the rifle's recoil, ending up in a heap at the bottom.

Jane stood on trembling legs. She grabbed the rifle and the accessory bag next to the door as she ran from the house. The faces of her boys flashed through her mind as she made her way through cornfield and to the only place she would be safe. She

---

ignored the burn of the razor-like cuts as she fought her way through the stalks, stopping often to listen for the girl. Maybe the rifle-shot killed her.

The clearing broke into view. Jane instantly leapt into the circle, falling to her knees while her heart pounded. Minutes passed and her breathing slowed. She stood up and spun slowly in a circle with the rifle in her hands. No one was there.

She looked down at the accessory bag and realized she'd not reloaded the rifle. With a practiced hand, she grabbed the powder horn from the bag and poured a measured charge of powder, then loaded the patch and round ball, tamping them down with the ramrod stored beneath the rifle's barrel.

Jane felt the heat of a stare and turned to find the naked, gore-covered girl behind her, standing at the very edge of the circle of stones. The two stared into each other's eyes, their faces less than two feet apart. The girl slashed at her, but the blow was deflected by an unseen force. Jane felt the dribble of warm piss running down her leg.

"Don't look like you can touch me," Jane said with mock courage. "Here's something for you...you bitch sow!" Jane took a step back, raised the rifle, and fired it into the girl's chest, knocking her backward into the tall cornstalks.

An idea came to Jane. She poured another charge of powder, but instead of a ball, she placed soil from inside the circle into a patch and rammed it into the rifle's barrel. She turned to find the girl behind her. The rifle roared as Jane fired pointblank into the girl's face, sending her shrieking back into the corn.

Jane smiled as she reloaded again the same as before. The dirt inside the circle was saturated with the blood of many animal sacrifices, and the more powerful sacrifice of her daughter, Elizabeth.

Jane saw movement out of the corner of her eye and turned to find Elizabeth standing in the circle with her. Her eyes were full of fire and accusations, the front of her white dress crimson from the cut of Jane's knife ten months earlier.

"No!" She screamed as she staggered back from her daughter, and outside the circle of stones.

Elizabeth's image vanished from sight like the dousing of candle flame. Daniel's daughter grabbed Jane by her red hair and threw her to the ground, out of reach of the rifle. Her clothing was ripped away and tossed to the side. Then the pain came. Jane felt the sting of teeth as the girl tore into her legs. A horrible scream nearly burst her eardrums and went on for several moments before Jane realized it came from her own throat. She thrashed about, serving only to increase the savagery of the attack. The murder of her sons was forgotten. She had room only for her own misery. The girl fed on her with an uncanny knowledge of what to eat, what to pull from Jane's open stomach which would not kill the woman outright.

Jane's eyes clouded as death finally came to her. The last image she saw before splashing into the depths of Hell was that of innocent Elizabeth, reaching to her from the corn.

Daniel stood on his porch trying to push himself into motion. What was the use? Sara was dead. His only friends had cursed him with a daughter torn from a nightmare. A nightmare he had endured for ten months. His time was nearly used up, she no doubt was saving him for last.

A scream from the path leading to Tom's house shook Daniel to his senses. He ran inside and latched the window shutters and grabbed his rifle. He walked back out on the porch, remembering what Tom had told him. He was the only one who could kill her.

Movement along the path sent chills through Daniel. A nude, bloody figure moved swiftly down the path toward the cabin. He looked down on the porch floor and saw the last dress, the one he'd placed outside for her that morning. "I don't reckon you'll need any more dresses after all." Daniel rushed in and bolted the door.

The door was rattled gently at first, then, more violently as the girl became angry. The shutters were tried next. She pounded against them relentlessly for over a minute, and then stopped.

"Leave this place!" Daniel shouted. There was only silence. He backed over to the bed and waited. Nearly an hour passed with not the slightest whisper. A sudden, heavy thud struck the door, causing him to jump. Seconds later, a second thud rattled the door. The third time she hit the door, it burst open, splintering the latch.

She stood before Daniel, wearing the dress he'd placed on the porch. She started toward him slowly, deliberately.

Daniel's hands shook as he raised the rifle and aimed at the center of her chest. He placed his trembling finger on the trigger and held it.

She stood in front of Daniel with the tip of the rifle barrel inches from her chest. She no longer seemed confused. Poised, with her back erect, she looked into Daniel's eyes.

Daniel lowered his rifle and then tossed it on the bed. His heart raced as welcomed death neared. His daughter moved close and wrapped her arms around his shoulders. He could feel her nails biting into his skin. Her mouth moved to his jugular, where, instead the sting of her teeth, he felt a soft kiss. He reached into his pocket and removed Sarah's hair clipping and held it next to her hair. The color matched perfectly.

Daniel was on the verge of screaming as she pulled her head from his neck. He looked into her eyes and was amazed to find the hint of blue. She was clean, her hair still wet from the creek.

In a cold, inhuman voice, the girl with no name whispered, "Daddy."

The flames seemed alive as they spread through the ground floor, hungrily consuming everything in its path. Up the bloodstained staircase it traveled to the second story. Soon, Tom's house was engulfed in an inferno. Daniel had placed the remains of Tom and Jane inside with their children earlier. What little of them that remained in the soil would soon be washed away by the storm that rumbled in the West.

The fire's glow would no doubt be seen from town. He prayed no one would follow for their own sake. Daniel placed his arm around his daughter and kissed her cheek.

The wilderness called. It was time for them to leave.

Daphne by Ashley Scarlet

M.C. O'Neill
Mommybook.com

Mommybook >> Main >> News >> Forums:

QueenBee (Moderator): "Hey, Mommybookers, we have a cool, new forum for you gals to post pics, vids and stories of your kids! This thread is geared toward toddlers and infants, so bust out those babies and don't be afraid to share! Ladies only!"

Within milliseconds, the moderator's inbox was assaulted with responses from all over the world. Mothers from every continent signed up mere moments after checking their inboxes. This forum was going to be a smash success. Queen Bee just knew it.

Bunnyfly89: "This is so cool! I've just come back from my vacation to New York City! We were in Manhattan, and the twins looked so adorable in their matching outfits. We even went to an art opening at P.S. 21! Hang on, and let me go get 'em."

TinaTexas90: "Heck yeah, I have tons of pics! Little Dylan just took his second poop ever! I've even got pics of the poo; I'm sure y'all are interested! I named him after Bob Dylan. I just love me some Bob Dylan."

PolishPrincess: "Hello, ladies!"

SwampScum91: "I have one of them poo-pics too! Little Connor done took his *third* shit, er, I mean, *poop*! He's gonna be a real slop-jockey!"

HotMummyUK: "Oh... This should be grand. Baby shite. Just what I've been chuffed to see all day, innit?"

RooMummaOz: "Oi, I've got pics of me lil' sprog's poo as well! Wee Sheila just ate her first Vegemite, and she already loves AC/DC! How the fack are you?"

HotMummyUK: "Foul... Vegemite."

The flood of baby pictures was relentless. Babies of all shapes, sizes and color came pouring in to the moderator's server like a torrent of infancy. Fat babies and long, skinny babies that resembled hot dogs entered the queue. There were pink babies and brown babies; babies with blue eyes, babies with dark eyes and even three specimens with ultra-rare lavender irises. Some of them were cute, and some... not so much.

Just like the digital deluge of children, pictures of baby turds were shown off and swapped. First shits and second shits were presented with motherly pride. There were big shits and little shits – each from every color of the rainbow. As with anything displayed on the World Wide Web, the judgments followed soon after the posts.

TinaTexas90: "See! This here is the poo I was talking about. Ain't it just amazing, y'all?"

HotMummyUK: "Erm... Dunno about that. If you look closely, his shite seems to have worms roiling within it. What have you been serving the wee lad? Mud pie, innit?"

TinaTexas90: "Are you trying to say I don't know what to feed my kid, you limey bitch? I take good care of my kids! At least I know who the daddy is, unlike you and your legion of chavs, or whatever the hell y'all call 'em over there."

HotMummyUK: "I most certainly am, you slattern."

QueenBee (Moderator): "All right, everyone. Let's calm down. There's no reason for me to bring out my pretty, pink banhammer, is there?"

TinaTexas90: "Hey! I just looked up 'slattern,' and it means, 'an untidy, slovenly woman.' That English whore just called me a slut!"

HotMummyUK: "Haw-Haw. I sure did... SLUT!"

TinaTexas90: "How'd you like to come down to good ol' Texas and say that to my face, Mommybook warrior? Remember, we kicked all y'all's asses in WWII! Let's see how you'd do in a rematch, skank. U.S.A.! U.S.A.!"

SiobhanOCowchip: "Aye, girl! Ye give that feckin' Royalist radge what-for! Up the IRA!"

HotMummyUK: "Good lord, now we have Fenians on the forum. Ahem... *TinaTwat*, as I was about to say, if you had cared to not drop out of primary school, you would have learned that our nations had been allies in that conflict. Oh, really, why must I explain history to the mentally addled? Don't cry just because you have mud in your teats."

QueenBee (Moderator): "All right, ladies. You've had fair warning. You girls are banned for the night. I refuse to have these catfights on my forum, and I won't allow Irish terrorists on it either. Say 'goodbye,' Siobhan."

SiobhanOCowchip: "Ah... Feck ye, then. Tiocfaidh ár lá!"

HotMummyUK: "Oh, whatever."

TinaTexas90: "Cheerio, bitch."

As the evening wore on, Queen Bee was shocked to see the immense numbers of subscribers grow by the minute. Mothers from even more nations flocked to the new Mommybook forum. America, Canada, Mexico, New Zealand, Russia and even a few women from Africa had joined. By the time the moderator's clock had struck midnight, her Alexa ranking was nestled within the firm, top one hundred.

QueenBee (Moderator): "Okay, we're really rocking now! So many thanks to all of the mommies from everywhere around the globe! I just can't believe what a great turnout Mommybook.com has had in only its first night! I admit, we've had a few bumps in the road, but I think we have all those trolls solidly weeded out. So, come on, girls, share those pics and flicks!"

HoosierMomma21: "Well, as you can probably guess, I'm from Indiana, and I've just given birth to a precious baby girl. Little Jayden was only six pounds, seven ounces at birth."

QueenBee (Moderator): "Welcome, HoosierMomma! Congrats!"

BroadofCanada: "Hey, everyone! I just had a lil' hoser of my own only a month ago, eh? I think the daddy is the lead singer of Dayglo Abortions, but I'm not sure, eh? Maybe Skinny Puppy. Oh, I also had sex with Gordon Lightfoot a while back. At least the birth was at no cost to me because of our totally awesome free healthcare, eh? Winnipeg Jets fuckin' rule!"

QueenBee (Moderator): "Um... Congrats?"

HoosierMomma21: "I heard Gordon Lightfoot was dead."

BroadofCanada: "Naw, you're thinkin' of Anne Murray, eh? Gordy just got cloned."

HoosierMomma21: "Oh. My bad."

PolishPrincess: "Canadian chicks are all hot! Every one of them!"

HoosierMomma21: "Troll! I freakin' knew it! You're really a dude! Pervert! Psycho-stalker! Give him the banhammer, Queen Bee!"

SwampScum91: "Hell yeah, sister! Get that toad-sticker outta here!"

RooMummaOz: "Oi, that sheila's a joey! HA! HA!"

BroadofCanada: "Ya! Go back to Germany, ya fuckin' Polack!"

QueenBee (Moderator): "Don't worry, girls. *Polish 'Princess'* is totally banned. Remember, folks - ladies only."

HeidiVon666: "Greetings from California. In moments, I shall post images of my daughter for all of you to marvel at. Perhaps some of you may know who I am?"

QueenBee (Moderator): "Eh, okay. We can't wait for you to bring on the marvel. Welcome to the forum, Heidi. Are you a celebrity or something? We'd always welcome celebrity on this forum."

RooMummaOz: "Oi! You're that world-famous fashion designer Heidi von Lindsenmann, ain't 'cha? I've got loads of your shoes—they're the best! I even have a couple of pairs from your Premium Collection. Can't wait to see your wee sheila!"

BroadofCanada: "Not me. All's I need when I go out is a Winnipeg jersey, blue jeans and my moose-kickers—and a case of Molson, don'cha know?"

HeidiVon666: "Oh, how 'charming.' I'll be sure to keep the doughnuts warm."

TuiEnZed: "Feh, typical Aussie elitist, you, *RooMumma*."

RooMummaOz: "Harden the fack up, you Kiwi slag! It's not my fault you're just jealous. Go have a suck or a fackin' cry about it. And it ain't my fault you can't afford a solid V-8 Falcon, either, Tui."

QueenBee (Moderator): "Aw... Not this shit again. Let's behave, girls. Look, we all know very well that the nations of Australia and New Zealand are currently at war, but this is a happy place, so let's keep the peace, okay?"

RooMummaOz: "Fair enough, Queen Bee, even though Tui's a sheep-shagger."

TuiEnZed: "Yeah... Too right, Queen Bee, even though *RooMumma* shags koala bears."

SwampScum91: "Well, I ain't sure about the rest of y'all, but I gotta agree with *BroadofCanada*. Ain't much one for high fashion or any of that gup—mostly just wife-beaters and Daisy Dukes for good ol' *SwampScum*. Well, except on Sunday—for church, you know."

HeidiVon666: "Enough of your whinging, fools. Yes, I am Heidi von Lindsenmann. Now that we have that fact established, allow me to post pics of my child. Her name is Minerva, and one day soon, you will all bow down to her."

With every pair of eyes glued to their screens, the image of the little "girl" sent freezing chills down the collective spines of the spectators. Rendered in high-resolution, there was no doubt to anyone viewing her that this child was not human, nor was this photo a product of digital manipulation. Primordial fear of awesome beauty and pure evil invaded the minds of the worldwide onlookers as emotions of dread and wonder entranced them all. No matter their experience and telluric exposure, or their lack of it, they all knew by natural instinct that the baby they were seeing had not been conceived within the belly of a woman; it had been forged in the bowels of Hell.

AztecaMamacita: "Aye! Giantana Santa Maria! Diabla! Diabla!

Demonia! In nomine Patri, et Fili, Espiritu Sancte!"

HeidiVon666: "Your foul Virgin will not save you, *Mamacita.* Her time is over. Prepare for the Day of *my* girl, *conia*! LOL!"

BroadofCanada: "That thing is from the pits of Hades!"

HoosierMomma21: "Dear God! This kid is the Antichrist! Look at her eyes! They... *glow*. That isn't P-shop. This is for real!"

HeidiVon666: "She has her Father's eyes, you corn-husking dolt. And your point?"

BroadofCanada: "Sweet Jesus! Who's the daddy, ya goof? James Roy Daley?"

RooMummaOz: "Oi, look! That sheila has horns on her head and

a barbed tail! What the fack is up with this kid?"

TuiEnZed: "Although I hate *RooMumma's* guts, she's right! I just saw an exposé about Heidi von Lindsenmann on New Zealand's very own *The Tommy Westwood Show*, and I know for a fact that she's in the Illuminati! It's the truth! Fackin' devil-worshiper! Illuminati scumbag!"

HeidiVon666: "Haw! The Illuminati can eat the peanuts out of my shit. You need to do better than that, you meat pie addict."

MamiWata: "Mokele M'bembe!"

SwampScum91: "Get thee behind me, Satan!"

Little Minerva von Lindsenmann's image was an exposition of disgust and hellish shock. What appeared to be a banal photograph of a fashionable, young blonde mother holding her child was besmirched by the subtle details of a baby with scarlet skin, citrine, pulsating eyes and a pointed, pink tail whipping from under the blanket swaddling her. The most uncomfortable features were the tiny ram's horn buds erupting from her forehead and swirling around on either side of her beautiful, red face.

Where, thousands of years ago, a humble Virgin had held her baby boy in a filthy rag, on this night, an opulent fop held her infant daughter in a cloth dripping of unholy silk and luxury. It was an exorbitant, bastard mockery of empyreal birth and life.

Bunnyfly89: "Hey, even though your baby is the devil's daughter and stuff, I have to admit, her blanket is just divine! Is it Gucci? I almost bought little Cameron and Connie ones quite like it in New York City. You *must* tell me the designer."

HeidiVon666: "Thank you, Bunny! No, I designed it myself. It's made of silk from finely-filleted human skin and pure, fourteen-carat gold. Hey, you're pretty cool. I just might let you live tonight."

Bunnyfly89: "Um... Thanks?"

HeidiVon666: "Don't mention it. Don't fuck with me, either."

Bunnyfly89: "Yeah, we're cool. We're cool, Ms. Von."

HeidiVon666: "Yes, we had better be."

HoosierMomma21: "Oh, your veiled threats are nothing against the power of Jesus Christ! What could you possibly do to harm us over an Internet forum? Show us more pictures of your Satanic baby?"

SwampScum91: "Amen, sister! You tell that monster's mother where she can stick it. Praise the Lord!"

HeidiVon666: "So funny of you to ask, *HoosierFrightwig*. Allow me to demonstrate..."

A low grumble boiled from down in the bowels of the elitist dandy. It growled with the strength of a million damned souls, channeled into her lithe fingers as she tapped out the heinous incantations on her golden keyboard. Languages known long before the rise of Rome and forgotten by most men burned across the screens of all those on that ill-fated forum. They challenged Heidi von Lindsenmann for Hell and that was exactly what she gave them. To pack in this deadly prayer to her evil gods, the young mother of the Antichrist ended it in mundane Latin.

HeidiVon666: "In nomine Dei nostri Satanas Luciferi excelsi... Weitiko! Weitiko! Weitiko!"

At first, profuse sweating and the horrid vibes of raw doom trailed through the bodies of the mommies populating the website. A terrible transference of sinister energy coiled up their arms and infiltrated their eyes and senses. Soon, feelings of vomitus and retch overcame their collective guts. Not long after that, their orifices began to weep blood.

RooMummaOz: "Oi, not feelin' so good, am I?"

AztecaMamacita: "Aye! Demonia!"

SwampScum91: "Why, I feel like I done ate the bad bean! I'm gonna ralph."

BroadofCanada: "My nose is gushing! Help me!"

TuiEnZed: "Oh, shite, I really need to get to hospital, yeah? Me phone ain't working."

QueenBee (Moderator): "Please, girls, this is just mass hysteria! Keep calm! I'm not feeling well either, but don't let her get to you. I'm trying to ban her, but the server isn't responding. It must be some kind of virus."

HoosierMomma21: "Good Lord, do something, Bee! I'm bleeding to death! I can't feel my arms!"

Gleaning the protests of panic across her screen, Heidi laughed. So many pleas of misery were posted by those jealous mothers. They knew deep down inside that they could never bear such beauty, grace and poise as that of her little Minerva from their inferior wombs. How dare they deign to insult and mock the sweet child of Satan? Power is born inherent, she knew this very well, and none of these curs had been blessed into it. After ten minutes of their dying blithering, only one member remained active and online.

HeidiVon666: "Hello, Bunny. And how are you doing tonight?"

Bunnyfly89: "Uh... hey, Ms. Von. Really stoked you didn't kill me and stuff. Eh... So, when is your autumn line-up going to be released?"

HeidiVon666: "September Twenty-first. In New York. Lots of maxi-dresses this year."

Bunnyfly89: "Oh... Nice."

Edward Ahern
The Foundling

Michael vomited again. Silas trapped most of the spray in a cotton diaper. The other parents in the waiting room ignored the upchucking, focused on their own problem infants.

A short woman with Aztec features came over and took the soiled diaper, giving Silas a clean one. Silas stared at her scrubs and name tag. Apparently the waiting room was frequently defiled.

Michael started to cry. Even reddened and tear swollen, his face looked gaunt. Silas gently rocked his son in his arms, brushing the top of his head with kisses. Michael was all he had left of Beatrice.

At home Silas sometimes cried along with Michael when Michael cried because he was hungry. Silas, because he was no longer a husband—and unless Michael could be treated, would soon not be a father. His name was called.

"Silas Mortenson?" Come with me please."

The examination room held only two chairs, a high chair with feeding tray and a plastic sheeted crib. Cleansing agents were lined up on a side shelf.

"Mr. Mortenson, I gather that Michael still isn't able to keep solid food down?"

"Or most liquids--all he can keep down is diluted fruit juices. Not enough to keep him alive."

"When did this problem start?"

"Three weeks ago."

"Did anything change in his diet at that time?"

"He'd been receiving breast milk from my wife." Silas coughed roughly. "Until the day before she died."

"I'm so sorry for your loss, Mr. Mortenson. And you've tried the various milk formulations on the market? Soy milk for example?"

"Yes, of course!" Silas snapped, then regretted his outburst and spoke more gently.

"Michael can't tolerate any sort of milk, nor solid food. He's starving. He bolts down everything I put near his mouth, but pukes it all back out almost as fast."

Michael had resumed crying. Silas' voice was a gentle sing song. "There, there, my baby boy, my baby son." He'd prepared a nursing bottle of vitamin laced fruit juice and nudged the nipple into Michael's mouth.

Michael sucked violently, then spit the nipple out. Silas' voice was sad. "He knows it's not what he needs."

The nurse's name tag read Helen Quinlan. She looked somehow frightened.

"Mr. Mortenson, the results of Michael's blood and DNA testing were atypical. While you're here, we should try one of our liquid formulations —protein, calcium, and so forth. You'll need to remain here for two hours after Michael's feeding to see if he regurgitates the formula or retains it. Would that be acceptable?"

"Of course, anything," he said

Helen left and returned ten minutes later with a nipple bottle containing thick, rose colored slurry.

"Please try this and see if it helps. Don't be surprised at its warmth. It's pre-heated to body temperature."

Michael took the nipple with suspicion, and almost spit it out when the unfamiliar taste hit him. Then he devoured it, leaving only an empty plastic liner inside the bottle. Silas, used to Michael's violent spewing, didn't put him over his shoulder for burping, but held him to his chest against a diaper, waiting for the upheaval. But Michael gave a normal soggy burp and went to sleep.

"He hasn't upchucked!"

She waved a cautionary hand. Silas noticed that she was trim but nicely rounded. "The next two hours will tell us the story. If he regurgitates, we haven't found the answer. If he holds the food down, we'll have an idea of what to do next."

Michael's breathing was easy and slow. Silas felt a burst of relief and joy at being able to hold his son without anxiety, but eventually laid him down in the bassinet. *Maybe Bea...just maybe,* he thought, and as his tension continued to ease, he fell asleep in the chair.

"Mr. Mortenson?"

Silas started and lurched toward the bassinet, but Michael was still sleeping. "Yes, sorry, Ms. Quinlan. I fell asleep. He didn't get sick!"

"Call me Helen, please. And no, he seems to have held it down." Her voice was calm, but worry lines still crisscrossed her forehead. "I'll prepare a kit with enough formula for the weekend. If Michael's able to hold his food we'll follow up on Monday. If he resumes vomiting, bring him back in immediately."

The ride home and the evening feeding were blessedly normal. Silas grinned when Michael pooped, his first real defecation in days. Silas whispered to him through the feeding and well past the time he fell asleep, nursery rhymes, and how they'd go hunting when Michael was grown, and resonant sounding babble,

Silas realized his own hunger, and that he'd been losing appetite and weight along with his son. He thought about a beer, then gave himself a mental dope slap. He needed to be sharp if anything happened. He prepared a sandwich and brought it back into the bedroom to eat. Michael's crib was next to Beatrice's side of the bed, and Silas had no heart to move him over. Her belongings lay undisturbed from the day she'd been ambulanced to the hospital.

By Monday, Michael's coloring had gone to pink, and his arms and legs had lost their old man flabbiness and reflated toward baby chubby. If he hadn't been carrying Michael, Silas would have skipped into the clinic's waiting room.

When Helen Quinlan led him into the examination room, there was a white frocked man waiting. "Mr. Mortinson, I'm Dr. Victor Strigoni."

"Aren't you the owner of this clinic?"

"I am. Michael's case is quite unusual, and I'm going to handle it personally. Thank you Helen, that'll be all." Helen Quinlan looked as though she wanted to say something to Silas, but simply shook his hand and turned around to leave. She seemed tense.

"Mr. Mortenson, Michael's blood and genetic test results, and his positive reaction to our formula confirm an inability to process normal foods and liquids. The formula he has been taking for the past two and a half days is specially selected so that Michael can digest it. This is a chronic condition, one which he'll have to be accommodated for the rest of his life."

"I don't understand what you're saying. Michael's going to need an artificial diet? Is it available in stores? How much does it cost?"

"Ah, no, this formulation is only available here at the clinic. It's expensive, but we can make it available at one dollar per feeding if you allow us to see Michael on a regular basis so we can follow his progress. He's quite an interesting case."

Silas scrutinized Victor Strigoni. He was not thin, but sinewy, as if his body fat index approached zero. "Dr. Strigoni, you mean that Michael can have a normal life?"

"We'll have to verify that his recent lack of nutriment hasn't damaged any of his functions, but, yes. In all but diet, he should pass as normal."

They arranged for weekly provisions and clinic visits, and Silas walked out. Helen Quinlan was standing outside the front door when he exited.

"Mr. Mortenson!" she hissed.

"Ah. Helen. How are you?"

"Never mind; Get the formula examined!"

"Pardon me?"

"Have the food tested. You won't believe me until you do. Use a lab in another city, and make sure they do complete genetic testing. Don't tell them it's food. Call me when you have the results. Here's my cell phone number."

"But . . . what?"

"I can't be seen with you. Just have it tested." And Helen Quinlan darted back into the building.

Michael recovered steadily for two weeks before Silas decided to have the food checked. After all, he thought, I've got no idea what they've giving my son. Bea would have had it tested two weeks ago...

Testing services like he needed didn't advertise on Facebook. It took Silas two days of research before finding an out-of-state facility. The uninsured cost was almost $5,000, but Silas finally justified it to himself. He described the slurry as being of an unknown origin and composition.

He received an irate phone call four days after the parcel was received.

"Mr. Mortenson, we're not in the habit of practical jokes, even if they're paid for."

"I beg your pardon! The sample was sent to you in good faith, but obviously the results are abnormal. What have you found?"

The lab analyst's voice slowed and lowered. "Mr. Mortenson, the complete results will be sent to you, but in brief the sample is of human origin."

"What do you mean?"

"Human. Bone calcium, blood and sera, muscle tissue, organ materials. Human. We're discussing reporting this to the police."

Silas' mental wheels slipped, then got traction. "That's not necessary. The material came from an authorized medical facility and I'm just verifying its composition for my own benefit. Involving your clinic in a police investigation and press coverage is surely not desirable."

The voice on the phone paused and hardened. "Please do not send us any samples in future. We accepted your sample for testing in good faith, and will provide the results. But we want nothing further to do with you."

Silas felt vaguely guilty, although he'd done nothing wrong. "Of course, if that's how you feel. Just send me the results and the matter is closed."

He hung up the phone and stood next to it for several minutes, thoughts swirling. Jesus, Bea, I've been feeding our son cannibal food. And he's digesting it! Like he relished your breast milk, but wants nothing from a cow or a plant. Quinlan's phone number...here it is.

"Hello, Helen? What the hell is this formula you've been giving me?!"

Quinlan's words were strained. "You can't ever tell Strigoni that I told you to test it! We can't talk about this on the phone. Can you meet me later this evening? Saint Stephens' church on Boyle Street?"

"Silas sputtered, then said, "All right. 7 p.m.? If Michael starts crying, they'll kick us out, you know."

Helen Quinlan was seated in a pew next to the confessionals. Silas set Michael's bassinet between them on the pew and turned toward her.

"What the hell is going on, Helen?"

"I'm going to leave here in ten minutes, so listen closely. Strigoni has been looking for a child like yours for a long time. He's not going to let go of Michael. And you may want to let him have it. You know what he's been feeding Michael?"

"Now I do! How the hell can he feed that to an infant?"

"Because it's the only thing that'll keep Michael alive. And I think it gets worse."

"How?"

"Strigoni says that Michael's going to develop physical and mental oddities that will make him a danger to others—and maybe to you as well."

"That's impossible!"

"Like only being able to absorb human flesh? You needed to know, that's all. I just wanted you to know before Strigoni tied you up too badly. I'm leaving."

"Helen, wait. I've got questions..."

"And all the answers suck. I'm still leaving.

"But, wait, if you hate this so much, why are you working there?"

"Because I can't get a job anywhere else. And Strigoni knows it. You're going to find out that he's already intimately familiar with Michael's problem."

He sat in the pew for several minutes after Helen left, Michael still sleeping. *Bea, he's yours as well. What do I do?* But neither Beatrice nor the resident God provided an answer.

Silas agonized, but saw no way to turn down what gave Michael life. Michael and Silas settled into an almost self-contained universe for several more weeks. The rituals of bathing, feeding and clothing Michael filled the spiritual hole in Silas, like the priests Silas remembered from childhood, treating cloths and vestments and chalice with reverence.

And then Michael began to teethe. His first milk teeth were incisors, and he began snapping at Silas's fingers if they came too close to his mouth. *My son, my boy is a carnivore, a sport. And may be dangerous?*

Silas mentioned the pointy teeth to Dr. Strigoni, whose lips moved upward without really smiling.

"We need to talk, Mr. Mortenson. Michael has special needs that soon will be beyond your ability to handle. When that time comes, we would like to place him in a facility that can accommodate his needs without risk of injury to others."

Silas reddened. "I may be unemployed right now, but he's my son—mine—and he lives with *me*. I know what you're feeding him Strigoni, so we don't have to pretend. I had the formula tested. You're making a cannibal out of my son!"

Strigoni walked over, locked the door to his office and returned to his desk, all in silence. "Mr. Mortenson, I'll deny everything I'm about to tell you. You put both Michael and yourself in danger if you reveal this to anyone else.

"Michael, as you've gathered from testing the food, is a genetic cannibal. That is to say that he can only digest human tissue and fluids. Not his fault, not yours. Once in every few million births a child like Michael is born. Most die of starvation or malnutrition before they're even as old as Michael. Almost all of the survivors die when those around them realize what's been done to keep them alive. A very, very few survive to adulthood and are able to fend for themselves.

"These rare biological sports are the source of the werewolf and vampire legends—fanged, blood and flesh eating, feral carnivores.

"Michael's a baby, for Christ's sake! He'll grow up, except for his diet, just like other kids."

Strigoni lost his temper. "You still can't conceive of how bad it will be. Until he's matured and conditioned, Michael will rip apart his little classmates and devour their entrails. After puberty, Michael will prefer cunnilingus while his girl is having her menses. He has to be trained like a dangerous circus animal, Mr. Mortenson, while under restraints. We can provide that here. You can't."

Silas looked down at Michael, still sleeping. And in the silence noticed something. Strigoni had begun sweating while yelling at him. He smelled like Michael did before a bath—a rotten flower smell.

"You're one of them aren't you? Where's your fangs?"

"What're you talking about?!"

"I should have guessed. Who else would spend the money and time to get the food and set up this facility?"

Strigoni stared at him. "It wouldn't make any difference to your situation if I were, or if I'd had dental work done to grind down the incisors. We can provide Michael with nourishment and habitat until he's adult enough to fend for himself. You can't. Sometime soon you'll need to turn him over to our care, for Michael's own good."

"I'll go public, you bastard. Once people accept what Michael is, he'll be treated well."

"He'll be treated like a side show freak, and put down the first time he maims or kills someone."

Michael had awakened at the shouting and started crying. Silas picked him up and glared over Michael's shoulder at Strigoni.

"Look, Mr. Martinson—Silas—deep down you know that I'm right. That Michael needs our help. Take Michael home with your usual supply of formula and think it over. We'll talk again in a few days. I encourage you to keep our conversation secret, as any attempt to go public would end very badly for you and Michael."

Silas moved with the measured, strained pace of a pallbearer out of the office and into his car. He fed Michael with a peculiar mix of fear and great love. *This is our body, this is our blood, Michael. Eat and live.* After putting Michael to bed he sat down, not to think, but to somehow get a sense of what must be done.

Bea, I can't give him up...I can't. Even the most vicious guard dog obeys his master. And that's what Strigoni wants to become, forcing me out.

Two mornings later he called Strigoni's private number. "Dr. Strigoni. I know it's early, but Michael has been rejecting the formula."

"That's impossible."

"Maybe, but I just finished cleaning up the puke. Could you stop by and just look in on him? I don't want to wait another few hours, in case it's serious."

"All right, all right, where are you?"

Silas let Strigoni in thirty five minutes later. Strigoni hadn't taken the time to shave. "Where's Michael?"

"Through there. Go ahead; I'll bring in some more formula."

Strigoni took two quick steps toward the bedroom. At the first step, Silas pulled his shotgun from behind a curtain and fired. Strigoni leaped impossibly quickly to one side, and only a few of the buckshot pellets caught him in the ribs. Silas fired again, this time blasting Strigoni full in the chest. Strigoni dropped to the floor, coughing blood and spittle onto the carpet. Silas fired a third time into his back.

Michael had started crying at the explosive noises. Silas laid down the shotgun and loped in to pick him out of the crib. "There, there, my little boy, my little prince. Daddy's got to go and prepare your dinners." *Don't worry, Bea. I used steel shot, so no danger of lead poisoning.*

Carrick McCleary
Paternity

Jude made his way downstairs to greet his daughter, who grew within her a miracle...

Long hours of a working single father left Jude's fourteen-year-old Kyrie largely alone. But she was a good girl: studious, thoughtful, and considerate. As she'd been for three days now, Kyrie was locked in the basement, restrained to her bed. But her new restraints were gentle and allowed her some freedom. That comforted him whenever he had to be away.

It was only a week ago that Jude got home and found Kyrie in front of the television, crying over the phone during one of Maury's "baby daddy" episodes. The host and his audience mocked her ruthlessly, calling her a liar and a slut, while others shouted censored epithets. It sounded like someone sending a message in Morse code.

Jude tore the phone from her hands, disconnected the call (after shouting some of his own censored epithets), and turned off the idiot box. He pulled Kyrie close and asked her what was wrong, though the answer was already clear enough to be undeniable. Kyrie drew a shuddering breath and wiped her tears. Both her hands massaged her belly, one over the other. She closed her eyes, took another deep breath, then opened her eyes and looked at her father. Finally, Kyrie told him she was pregnant...and that she was still a virgin.

Despite her pleading and swearing that it was a miracle, her disbelieving father ordered Kyrie to terminate her pregnancy. He also wanted to know what little bastard, which little *punk* was the father, but Kyrie held tight to her story. There was no boy; she'd had a dream that Angels came to her. They sat on each side of her bed, caressing her face, playing with her hair. A bright glow appeared at the foot of her bed and the Angels held her still when she became afraid and began to struggle. Her blankets were moved; her nightgown was pulled up and her panties down. Her body, naked and exposed, was slowly filled with the bright soft light. It entered her and she told her father that she felt it suffuse her whole body from her head to her fingertips. She closed her eyes as the Angels continued to touch her everywhere, even those places that she had never touched herself. The warmth of the light within her growing warmer, the hands and fingers of the

Angels dancing across her skin and slipping inside her, and she told her father how unbelievably amazing it felt. She wanted to explain how the tingling she felt down there, especially when the Angels made it more intense with their hands over her breasts and teased her nipples, and how her body tensed and surged when their fingers slipped inside and out of her and the unworldly scent that she—

"Enough, Kyrie! I don't want to hear any of that!" Her father had let go of her and inched backward. Kyrie's cheeks were flushed; her legs rubbed together slowly, her hands together between her thighs as if in a different kind of prayer. "Maybe somebody drugged you! Maybe it was just a very strange dream. I really don't know. But one thing I do know is that it wasn't real!"

Tears in her eyes altered their appearance from sky blue to sapphire, bright and shimmering. "But it's all true! It has to be. All I remember...after, was waking up. And when I woke up, I did believe it was a dream. But then I saw my underwear on the floor. And I was still really warm inside and there was still tingling down there. And the feathers!" She grabbed her father's hand and rushed into her bedroom. She opened the top drawer of her nightstand and withdrew a handful of multiple-sized, waxy, white feathers. She put them in Jude's hands. He felt them, milling them with his fingers. They were soft and surprisingly pliable for their size. He remembered when she'd had him get thread for her comforter because it had torn somehow. Jude took the comforter from the bed and examined it closely. He tried to ignore the scent of Kyrie's sheets when finally he found what he was searching for: the repair she'd made to her comforter had torn more and come unraveled. The feathers he took from it may not have matched exactly, but they were close enough for a plausible explanation. *Definitely more plausible than an orgy of God and a couple of Angelic child-molesters inseminating her with the Second Coming*, Jude thought. He shook the disturbing image out of his head.

But a serious question remained that would help his fourteen-year-old child to admit the truth, "Kyrie? When did you have your dream?"

"It was a miracle, dad. Not a dream." She had gathered up the feathers and was putting them back in her nightstand. She closed the drawer and looked at her father. "Two days ago."

Jude winced. "Two days?! Your mother didn't even begin to show until her second trimester!" Jude grabbed his daughter's shoulders and looked closely into her eyes. "Kyrie, you need to tell me the truth, now. No more games. It's impossible to show after two days. You look like you should be at least two months along, maybe more."

They argued, going around and around, for hours; Kyrie pleading her case and swearing over and over that it was an honest-to-God miracle, her father trying to stay calm while he explained and interpreted each aspect of her dream to be something from her subconscious trying to deal with what she refused to admit to herself. Somehow she had blocked out what really happened months before. It was completely understandable...and it was the only thing that made any sense. Jude had been so focused on his work that someone could have easily broken in and assaulted her with the door wide open while he was in the very next room. It was his fault; he knew that she would never lie to him about something like this, and if she was seeing someone, Jude would know. His daughter would have told him long before she and a boy would even become serious in any way.

Kyrie was a good girl. And ultimately, she complied with her father's order. The pregnancy would be terminated.

Jude called Planned Parenthood, and an appointment was made. Jude was told that after a short meeting with Kyrie alone, and an even shorter one with the two of them together, the termination would be completed in a completely anonymous procedure.

The following morning, Jude put his arm around Kyrie and hugged her, then led her outside to the car. He squeezed her hand, promised her that everything would be all right, and opened the car door. As they drove, Kyrie stared straight ahead, her hands clasped in her lap; even the rise and fall of her chest barely noticeable. Every now and then, Jude would steal a glance at his daughter, who sat strong, upright, and pointedly emotionless. Jude took her hand and gave it a reassuring squeeze then brushed her hair back with his fingers. He touched her face gently, though she neither returned nor rejected his intimacies. Kyrie always accepted her father's love as a matter of course.

As they passed Evergreen Street, a maroon Honda appeared over the crest of road ahead. It was speeding and swerving in and out of their lane. As it sped closer, Jude could just make out the driver through the windshield. It was a frightened woman, who was shouting something and waving one of her arms for them to move out of the way. The Honda veered into Jude's lane, and the trees lining the shoulder allowed him no room to get out of the way. When the Honda was close enough for Jude to read the vanity plate (hairdressers do it with STYLE!), Kyrie gripped the dashboard. The Honda ahead slid sideways, back into its lane, and flashed past. Jude slowed and looked into the rearview mirror at the Honda until they reached the hill and disappeared over the other side.

Jude looked at his daughter. "Wow! Are you okay, Ree-ree?" Kyrie looked at her father and smiled weakly, and her dull stare offered nothing more. They continued on to the clinic.

When they arrived, Jude filled out the paperwork as a nurse took Kyrie into a room and closed the door. When the door opened sometime later, the nurse took him aside.

"She's a remarkable young lady, but she believes her pregnancy to be a possible miracle."

"She told you?" Jude leaned forward and rubbed the stubble on his face.

The nurse raised her hand. "I understand that it's complete fantasy, but I wonder...is Kyrie devoutly religious?" Jude shook his head, and the nurse continued, "I didn't think so. Her story offers details that would never be accepted in most faiths; most of it seems tantamount to rape. The only reason I'm saying this is because this may very well be an instance of rape that she doesn't, or can't, deal with at the moment. She is approximately four or five months along, just short of the limitation for the procedure in this state."

"So there's no problem? We can get this done and put it all behind us?" The idea of his daughter being four or five months pregnant left many more questions in his mind, and Jude didn't want to accept that he was ignorant the whole time. Or maybe he just chose to be.

The nurse smiled comfortingly. "Everything will be fine. I just wanted you to know that it might be a good idea to set up a counseling appointment if Kyrie shows any sign of lasting depression or begins to act strangely and noticeably unlike her normal self. A termination can be a stressful and difficult thing to accept, and Kyrie might need help dealing with her decision in the future."

Jude nodded, the words her decision echoed harshly, accusingly. It was a burden that she seemed to be accepting upon her own shoulders alone. They went back into the room together, Jude holding his daughter's hand, and sat while the doctor, William Grayson, explained the procedure.

After she undressed and slipped on her gown, Jude met Kyrie in the operating room at her request and held her hand through the entire procedure. After the fetus was partially delivered, the doctor injected or cut something (Jude couldn't tell exactly what) before drawing the rest of it out. Kyrie caught a glimpse as the doctor carried the fetus behind her and placed it on a metal tray. Jude looked over at it. It was a boy...or would've been. A nurse picked up the tray and carried it from the room and the doctor followed, his brow furrowed.

Kyrie wept quietly and Jude put his arm around her, kissing her forehead. "It's all right, Ree-ree. Everything will be all right." The doctor returned quickly and injected Kyrie with a mild sedative. After Kyrie fell asleep, the doctor directed Jude to a nearby office.

"I thought I should speak to you over a few matters of importance." Doctor Grayson moved a chart aside and put his elbows on the desk, fingers intertwined. "First, I want you to know that your daughter was intact."

Jude sat forward in his chair. "I don't understand what you mean by 'intact'...is she all right?"

Grayson nodded. "Of course; I meant that her hymen was intact."

"If that's true, then how..."

Dr. Grayson interrupted. "How did she become with child? It's uncommon but not unheard of. Pregnancy happens when the sperm gets inside the vaginal opening and travels up to fertilize an egg. Direct contact through genital rubbing, partial penetration with ejaculation, and pretty much anything that ends up with sperm entering into the vagina can lead to pregnancy. There was even a recent case where a woman was impregnated when a couple had intercourse in a hot tub and she got in a bit after the couple had left. And she left her bikini on." Dr. Grayson shrugged. "So it can happen under many circumstances."

"Thank you. I don't think that will help me sleep at night, but it means Kyrie might not even know how she got pregnant. No wonder she concocted that story." Jude shook the doctor's hand. "I'd like to be in the room with her when she wakes up, so if there's nothing else..."

"Well, there is one other thing," Dr. Grayson took a pair of glasses from his pocket and put them on. They gave him a more clinical appearance which also gave him more personal distance from Jude. "It seems after the, well, remains were taken to be disposed of, the fetus began to move. I don't understand how it happened, but I must have missed the spinal cord. I sincerely apologize, but I had to make quite a severe cut before the fetus finally expired. I am only telling you this because the nurse your daughter spoke with now seems to believe it may be something more than what it was: a simple mistake." Dr. Grayson paused for a moment, and then added, "The nurse seems to be of the belief that it... that it is divine in nature. Now, I don't subscribe to that nonsense, but I have to admit that I'm a bit taken aback by today's circumstances."

This was revelation (the word itself caused Jude to roll his eyes) he could have gone a lifetime without knowing. He stood up. "Okay, fine, it's over now, so please keep that woman away from Kyrie. She doesn't need to know any of this." The doctor agreed and Jude left the room.

When Kyrie awakened, her father sat with her until she was ready to leave. She dressed alone and met him in the lobby. He hugged her tightly and drove her home. She was quieter than usual, and Jude had agreed to let Kyrie stay home from school until she was ready to return. But the following night, when Jude returned home from work he noticed his daughter's belly actually seemed bigger than it ever was. Jude attributed it to inflammation from the procedure, but the next morning showed him to be wrong.

Kyrie's belly continued to grow more swollen, as Kyrie herself began to unravel. She had terminated her pregnancy yet here it was again, still, now moving and kicking within her. She told her father than God wouldn't allow His child to be killed again, and that both Jude and Kyrie herself would suffer for their sin after His birth. Kyrie decided that to protect both her and her father, she had to make sure that the baby would not ever come to term. She took a butcher knife from the kitchen and stabbed herself belly multiple times before her father could wrestle it away from her. They both watched as the wounds healed before their eyes, leaving not a single scar behind. It was a miracle, and that meant the *child* was a miracle! Kyrie snatched the knife back from Jude and slashed her wrist deeply before he could get it back, and Jude could see the muscles and tendons flexing as she bled. Unlike the wounds on her belly, her wrist did not stop bleeding or heal. Jude took the knife from Kyrie and left the room. He returned with a needle and thread, rubbing alcohol, and bandages. Kyrie thrashed and screamed for her father to let her die, but eventually she stopped struggling and Jude was able to clean, wash, sew, and dress her wound.

"Look, Ree-ree. The baby won't allow you to harm it, but you can harm yourself. Now we know that this truly was a miracle. And I think the baby, through you, saved us from that car yesterday. I was wrong, Honey, and I'm so sorry for not believing you." Jude touched Kyrie's belly. "You need to keep this child safe from now on, okay? He needs you, and we all need Him."

Kyrie looked away. "I don't want it inside me. I want it gone. I didn't ask for this, and I never had a choice." She smiled. "As soon as I'm able, I am going to get rid of this...thing. Even if I have to kill myself to do it."

For her own protection, and especially to protect the miracle child, Jude bound his daughter to the bed with rope, twine, and bungee cord from the garage. As Kyrie's skin was scraped raw bleeding from her struggles, Jude promised himself to replace it with more gentle bindings. He didn't want Kyrie to suffer; he only wanted to make sure she brought her little miracle into the world. It was no longer her choice.

He purchased Kyrie's new restraints from an Adult store. Though he was not lost on the irony, Jude knew that it was by far the best place to find cuffs, shackles, and such that would allow for restraint and security without causing serious injuries. When he took them home, he found a dog in his yard, scrounging through their trash cans. When he tried to scare it away, the dog growled and began to approach. Jude sprinted toward the front door and the dog gave chase, its garbage dinner forgotten. When Jude opened the door and rushed inside, he turned to close the door and found the dog halfway in, growling and snapping, lunging. Jude shouted for his daughter, "Kyrie, are you all right?" The room filled with a high pitched squeal, and the dog's growls faded to a whistle-whine as it frantically tried to pull its head out of the doorway, no longer pursuing Jude. The sound grew louder and higher, and the dog struggled harder, thrashing and digging backward. Jude pulled the door open just enough and the dog escaped so fast it looked like it vanished. He gathered himself for a moment before heading down to the basement. Kyrie was still tightly bound; her belly was noticeably shifting and squirming from within. Kyrie looked at her father and gestured at her belly with a nod of her head.

"He did it." Kyrie wiggled her hips, causing her belly to wobble. The child inside of her shifted and lay momentarily still. Her voice became a haunted whisper. "He can make things happen."

When Jude started to exchange Kyrie's old bonds with the new ones, Kyrie didn't struggle or fight him. "I believe you, Sweetheart. He saved us from the car the other day, and he just saved me from that dog. See? We're doing the right thing, Ree-ree."

"If you say so." Kyrie had messed herself while he was away, so after he'd stripped and cleaned both Kyrie and the bed-sheets, Jude brought a bucket from the garage. Now that she had more comfort and room to move, that unfortunate incident wouldn't happen again. When Kyrie asked for something to eat and drink, Jude was elated that his daughter was finally grasping the enormity of their situation. After returning with a sandwich and some milk (that she refused to drink), he carried his mini-fridge from the den to the basement, stocking it with food and beverages. "Maybe you'll be hungry later. And if you promise not to hurt yourself or the baby, I would love to take the restraints away." Jude sat beside her on the bed and leaned over her. "You are going to give birth to a miracle, Ree-ree. And you are a miracle...you know that, don't you? It's time for us to pull together as a family and look forward to His birth." Jude caressed her belly and the child pressed back, touching his hand. "It's going to be very soon, I think."

Kyrie shook her head, and Jude's heart tumbled. "As soon as I am able, I'm going to kill it. And if I can't kill it, I'm going to kill the baby and myself." She glared at her father. "And I'm willing to kill us all to make sure."

Jude sighed as he checked her restraints, kissed his hand and touched Kyrie's forehead with it, and locked the basement door before heading upstairs.

Jude checked on Kyrie in the morning before work and discovered rats scurrying around the basement. He noticed that they approached Kyrie and her unborn child, momentarily pausing at a safe distance before hurrying off into the shadowy depths of the basement, as if the baby made a protective barrier around mother and child to keep them both safe from harm. As he looked upon his daughter who lay sleeping, one of the rats bit him on the ankle. "Ow! Dammit!" Jude grunted through his teeth, reaching down to smack the rat away. But the rat was prepared and bit down as Jude's hand swept by. It clung to the meat of Jude's palm, and another much larger rat approached from between some boxes against the far wall. It was huge; it approached bravely if not warily as Jude waved his hand wildly to get the rat latched to his hand to let go. But it held fast, and the large rat was only a foot away. To Jude, it looked the size of a small dog, and it made an odd chittering noise as it drew near. Out of desperation, Jude swept his hand down, smacking the large rat with the small one. The small rat dislodged its teeth, tumbled over the large rat and went sliding against the wall. The large rat was only momentarily stunned; it hissed, shook its head, and continued its measured approach.

The rat in the corner was already coming back as well. And in the other corner, by the door, yet another rat was peeking around the doorframe. "Oh, God!" Jude stepped back as the large rat lunged. Its clamping jaws caught his pant leg; the large rat dug its claws into Jude's flesh and began to chew. Jude kicked his leg back and forth, against Kyrie's bedpost. The large rat would not let go, while the smaller rat jumped for Jude's hand, barely missing, and rearing back on its haunches to try again.

The large rat smashed against her bedpost and jarred Kyrie awake. She saw the large rat on her father's leg; the other rat jumped and found the webbing between her father's forefinger and thumb, and chomped down securely, as yet another rat stealthily approached him from behind. Kyrie sat up in bed and put her hands out; her belly squirmed for a moment then lay still. The large rat released its jaws from Jude's leg and lumbered toward the basement doorway; the smaller rat let go of Jude's hand and plopped to the floor before scurrying back into the shadows. The rat that approached from behind froze in place; Jude wheeled around and stomped it dead. The other rats hissed in unison and came forward, but only for a moment before returning to their hiding places.

"Thank you, Ree-ree," Jude exclaimed as he sat down at her bedside, "and thank you, little miracle-man!" Jude considered putting down rat traps before work, but he'd seen that, even while Kyrie slept, they could not get near her. Only Jude was vulnerable.

He asked Kyrie if she would like to be released, but instead of answering his question, she repeated once more that she would kill them all to end the baby's chance at birth. "I don't understand. He's been performing miracles! He's saved us, and he's saved me more than once. It's not a coincidence, either; right?"

Kyrie shifted and lay on her side, her head propped by her arm. "Miracles; Yes, okay. But there's something else happening! Attacking rats and a dog, a car out-of-control? Something else is at work here, too. Can't you see that?"

Jude finally left the room with his daughter bound and the beady eyes of the rats watching him from the darkness. Once work was finally over, Jude found that he'd missed the train due to a car crash that happened before his very own eyes. One of the cars had veered toward him, while to other crossed two lanes to hit the first on the driver-side. Both drivers were killed. After he waited for the police and gave his statement, he hurried to the station only to find the South Shore had already departed. So Jude waited impatiently, wanting to get home and thank the unborn child for yet another life-saving intervention. The earlier accident proved absolutely that there was much more involved than a miracle baby...something else was just as determined to stop it, and stop Jude in the process.

When he finally pulled into the driveway, his heart was racing. He turned off the car and opened the car door slowly. He cautiously scanned the night for anything coming to harm him before stepping out. He got out and closed the door quietly. The latch clicking into place echoed loudly in the night air. Jude tried to take a deep breath, but it hurt painfully; his heart was galloping. He sneaked to the house and crept inside, closing the door behind him and locking it securely. He must have been gripping his keys too tightly in his left hand because it was tingling up to his forearm. He put down the keys and looked at his hand, the indentations were lighter than he expected, but the paleness of his hand showed his grip had been too tight.

Now, as Jude crept down the stairs to the basement, he thought about the rats. The pounding in his chest began to worsen. He unlocked the door and pushed it open, and leaned against the doorway. His heart raced unevenly, his heartbeat rushed and roared in his ears. He peered in and saw his beautiful daughter. She was sitting up, looking back at him as if she'd been waiting.

Something dark and furry squirmed in her hands.

Jude clutched his chest, and his legs grew unsteady. "What do you have there, Ree-ree? Is that a rat?"

Kyrie showed him the rat, and smiled as she bit into it. There were scattered rat carcasses littered all around the bed, chewed and almost unrecognizable. The large rat from the morning sat perched on the bedpost beside her shoulder. "It is a miracle, father. I understand now." She took another bite. "I understand everything."

She chewed thoughtfully as Jude collapsed to his knees. Jude said, "Kyrie, you shouldn't be doing this! Your baby is special. It's going to be born and change the whole world!"

"Oh, I know, father. He's *very* special, like I told you in the beginning." She looked at Jude, her piercing eyes stripping the truth until it was laid bare before him. "But you didn't believe me."

Kyrie picked her teeth with a fingernail, examined it, and flicked something away. She smiled at the large rat and the large rat looked back at her. Kyrie stroked its fur and outstretched her free hand toward her father. Jude's heart began to sputter and his breath caught in his throat. "Please..."

"No, Daddy. I agree with you: I was chosen. I alone was given a gift to bring to the world. Now, just like the first time, I was right about this baby. Only this time," she closed her outstretched hand, crushing Jude's heart from within his chest, and added, "he has a different father."

Dave Eccles
Grandma Knows Best

Tamara sat opposite her grandmother in the day room of the Chiltern House Retirement Home, silently sipping her cup of tea while trying her best not to make the fine bone china cup clatter in its matching saucer. She knew that Grandma Nancy hated noise of any kind, which is probably why she chose to live out her days at the home in the first place. Other residents were in attendance, but apart from the odd tell-tale rasp of flatulence, they each remained seated and unmoving; general fatigue and senile dementia being the main reasons for their silence.

Peering over the rim of her teacup at the wall clock behind her grandmother, Tamara made a mental note of the time and tried just by force of will to make the minute hand revolve more quickly. It felt like more of a chore than a pleasure to visit, and although Tamara only stayed for an hour every weekend, waiting for that hour to be up was torture; she felt like a child longing for the home bell that signaled the end of a school day. She tried to dismiss her guilt and reminded herself that she needed to get home soon anyway. It was nearly time for her to take her medication.

As much as she loved her grandmother, Tamara couldn't forgive or forget the cutting remarks she would continually make about her four year-old son, Daniel; utterings that dripped with pure venom yet were delivered in such a casual, off-hand manner. Everyone who had ever met Daniel considered him to be a typical blond-haired, blue-eyed angel, which made it so hard for Tamara to understand why it was that her grandmother exhibited such animosity toward him.

"Don't think for a second that I don't see you eying up the wall clock, Tamara!" spat her grandmother. Startled by her grandma's sudden outburst, Tamara spilled her tea, the cup rattling noisily in the saucer. "Really, girl, you're such a bag of nerves!" Nancy tutted and shook her head, her jowls wobbling as she did so. "Then again, it's only to be expected, I suppose."

Grandma, you can be such a bitch sometimes...

"I don't know how you can stand to be around such an ugly baby every second of the day." Nancy drove that remark home with a withering stare over the top of her horn-rimmed spectacles then broke eye contact, pushed her glasses to the bridge of her nose with one finger and brought her teacup to her puckered lips for a generous, noisy slurp of tea.

Apologizing for her clumsiness while at the same time trying to dismiss this latest slating of her son, Tamara set her cup and saucer down on the occasional table that separated them, her nervous smile giving away nothing about her true feelings toward her grandmother at that particular moment.

"By the way, Grandma, I brought Daniel with me." She smiled again weakly before adding, "He's on the grounds somewhere, exploring in the bushes. I thought it best to leave him playing outside, and the gates are locked—so there's no danger of him getting into any kind of trouble."

Grandma Nancy leaned forward in her armchair, a barely audible grunt being the only thing that signaled her discomfort at the pain in her arthritic joints.

"Listen, child, and listen well." She paused to organize her thoughts, but also for effect. "I know he's your child, and a mother's supposed to love her child no matter what. But the fact of the matter is there's something wrong with that boy. I see it as plain as the nose on my face, and I know that someday, others will too. I want you to open up your eyes to the truth, girl, and maybe you'll see it yourself. There's ugliness in that child. Ugliness so deep that not even he knows it's there."

"Enough, Grandma," Tamara snapped, and, feeling embarrassed by the volume in her own voice, looked around to see if she had woken any of the other residents with her outburst. Not one of them stirred; they all continued to enjoy their afternoon nap. Tamara lowered her voice to a heated whisper. "I've had all I'm willing to take of your snide remarks about Daniel, Grandma." Visibly shaking, she continued, afraid that if she stopped talking now she may never again have the courage to speak her mind and stand up to the nasty, spiteful old battle-axe seated in front of her. "He's just a normal four year-old child, Grandma, nothing more! I don't want to hear any more of your nastiness. If you can't say something nice about your own great-grandson, don't bother to say anything!"

Her mouth felt as dry as the hottest desert imaginable, and though there was nothing she would have liked more than to be able to pick up her cup and saucer and quench her thirst, the adrenaline coursing through her bloodstream caused Tamara to shake so much that she couldn't trust herself to handle the fine bone china without dropping it.

Grandma Nancy just quietly sipped her tea, took a small bite of her chocolate chip muffin and said nothing.

The rapid breathing and hurried footsteps of a child's sandals slapping the floor announced Daniel's arrival. He skidded to a halt in the doorway, chest heaving. "Mommy, can you help me? I've tried to put it back together, but it doesn't work anymore."

"Of course I'll help you, sweetie. What is it?" Tamara turned toward her son, her eyes wide in abject terror. An uncontrollable, unearthly scream escaped her lips and she recoiled in her armchair, throwing herself backward as Daniel deposited the sticky, dripping remains of what had once been a young blackbird, its breast plucked bare and its ribcage folded up over its head. The bird's entrails hung from the gaping wound caused by the child's crimson-stained fingers; the same fingers that he used to caress his mother's soft cheeks during the moments when she really needed to feel loved and appreciated; the same fingers that had held the hand of his baby sister only a few months ago, before the fatal "accident" with the pan of hot oil in the family kitchen that tragically cut short her young life and promoted Daniel to the rank of "only child".

Tamara had shouldered all of the blame for the terrible loss of her daughter, and she had cursed and cried herself to sleep for weeks, regretting the decision she made to leave the two tots together while she answered a telephone call in the lounge. The grief had very nearly consumed her, but with the love and care of her family, a carefully monitored dosage of the appropriate medication, and lengthy counseling sessions, she had begun to claw her way back from the edge of the abyss and had slowly begun to rebuild her shattered life.

Until now.

"What's wrong, mommy? Why are you crying?" Daniel reached out to his mother, his tiny hands caked in the rapidly congealing blood of the avian he had rent asunder. The evidence of his inherent bloodthirstiness was also apparent on his T-shirt and his shorts. He wiped his bloody mitts on his stomach and proceeded to lick his fingers. Tamara retched.

She saw it now, the thing her grandmother had warned her about: The ugliness that had hidden itself deep within her son. Daniel's eyes were no longer blue; they were blacker than black, if that was at all possible. No light reflected from those terrible orbs; they looked even darker when contrasted with his straw-colored locks.

Tamara knew in that moment that little Nicole's "accident" had been anything but that, and that Daniel's burns had not been from trying to help his sister. The whole room seemed to contract and fold in on itself, and Tamara felt her vision blurring and consciousness slipping away.

The barest hint of a smile played upon Daniel's peachy, angelic countenance.

Grandma Nancy snorted contemptuously as Tamara slumped in a dead faint. "You should've listened to me, child. Didn't you know that Grandma *always* knows best?"

Tom Johnstone
Meconium

Week One

They never told me its face would look so old. The health visitor said that would change, but its black, beady eyes are still staring at me out of a wizened face, wrinkled like the rest of its baggy skin, as if it's spent too long in the bath. Well, I suppose it has—about nine months in the womb, give or take a couple of weeks.

Joe says I should call it he, not it. But he's already gone back to work, so *he* doesn't have to spend all day with its constant feeding, then it's puking it up as runny milky porridge or shitting it out as an awful green tar. He's right of course, I suppose. It *is* human. But there's something weird about the baby: it just looks so alien, with its over-sized, bald old man's head and berry-black eyes. It looked strange enough when it was just a silvery, flickering blob on the ultrasound scan. It reminded me of that creepy, grainy black and white film of the Roswell alien autopsy. I hoped I wouldn't feel like this when it actually came out. But now I feel worse if anything. Joe doesn't see it. "Don't you love him?" he asks. Of course, I do. I think. Maybe I'm just not the maternal type he hoped I'd be.

Of course, I know it's a boy: I can just about see its wrinkled little winkle, underneath the rotting twist of umbilical cord with the plastic clip still attached. And if I forget it's a he, it's quite happy to remind me by pissing up in my face whenever I change it.

And whenever Daddy gets home from work, he's too tired to take his precious son off my hands. He eats and falls asleep, almost as soon as he walks through the door, it seems, looking like a baby ought to look himself, so peaceful and vulnerable.

Week Two

"When does that blackened thing fall off?" I ask the health visitor.

"Well, it varies. Every child is different."

Then she says: "How's Baby pooing?"

I love the way she calls him "Baby", assuming I haven't given him a name. As a matter of fact, I haven't. I'm so tired I can't think of one, and Joe hasn't bothered to give his opinion. So maybe "Baby" will just have to do. But I've started calling "Baby" him instead of it, after the looks she started giving me. I felt like saying: *I'm not the maternal type, get over it.* Joe was the one so desperate to have a kid: maybe *he* should do more.

He hasn't got much to say for himself now, with the health visitor here. Hardly surprising really: he wouldn't know what baby shit looked like if I served it up for his dinner. Come to think of it, maybe that's not such a bad idea. I could pretend it's mustard. He probably wouldn't even know the difference.

"How's Baby pooing?" she asks again.

"Sorry. Drifted off. Well, he's stopped doing that icky green stuff."

She says what it's called: Mekon-something.

"Mekon-what?" I ask. He certainly looks like the Mekon.

"Meconium."

Well, it's certainly murky.

"Right," I say. "Anyway, it's still quite sticky, but smells sort of nutty, and mustard-colored."

"Good!" she coos. She must really love baby shit or something. "Good Baby! Let's have a look at the little man, shall we? Oh..."

She breaks off, taken aback, slightly alarmed even.

"What?" Joe frowns, stroking his beard. "There's something wrong with him?"

It speaks! Well, God forbid there should be anything wrong with his precious son.

"Oh, no!" she replies. "No, it's just he looks so mature, so grown-up, in his face, I mean. Those eyes! He's a deep one, I can tell..."

Here we go. All together now...

"...And I can see, he looks *so* like his Dad already!"

She simpers, and Joe smiles back bashfully. If you ask me, it's the other way round. He's starting to look more like a big version of "Baby". Not his body, which is hardened from working on the road maintenance crew, but his face seems as pink and soft as, well, as a baby's bottom. For all I know his dick's as small and shriveled as the "little man's" little man too by now: I haven't seen it for months and probably won't again for years. Maybe it's getting exercise elsewhere. I watch the health visitor with her baby shit eating grin. Did I catch her eyeing him up?

Before I know it, he's showing her out, while I'm left holding "Baby".

After she's gone, I realize I forgot to tell her. Or maybe I didn't want to, because I knew it would sound so stupid. The baby shit is mustard-colored, just like it's supposed to be, just the way she likes it.

But I still keep finding the other stuff, the murk-whatever it is, all over the place: on the bath, in the kitchen sink, even in the bed.

And "Baby" doesn't even sleep in our bed. No fear! He's staying in the crib, the cot, the Moses basket, whatever. He's not coming anywhere near the bed, my one sanctuary.

At first I thought it was Joe washing after work, and not cleaning up after himself. He didn't even notice it. But then he never does notice when he leaves a mess, the filthy pig.

Week Three

Joe's at work today. Just me and Jimmy. Yes, he's got a name now. We finally agreed on one.

Jimmy keeps looking at me, as if to say: *just you and me here, on our own.*

That health visitor may have been soft in the head, but she did have a point. His face does look almost adult. He's got quite a bit of hair too, thick and black like Joe's, not the bald baby head you'd expect. Still, at least that's some evidence the baby's Joe's. I did wonder for a while if he might be, well...

Not that I cheated on Joe, but the dates didn't seem to tally with the last time we had sex. Seems like such a long time ago. But when he was born he seemed so weird, so freakish. Everyone said that's what newborns look like. But the point is, now he looks even weirder. Jesus! I think he's even got tiny black hairs under his nose and chin. A bearded baby? And the look in those eyes...

I'll say one thing for him: he doesn't cry, just lies there staring.

But the look in those eyes...

I don't like it.

I sit down to take the weight off my feet, and get away from those black, shining berry eyes. I rest my hands on the arm rest.

Then I lift them up again in disgust at the cold, clammy stickiness I feel there.

Try to lift them up.

Dark green tarry threads pull them back down again. My backside's stuck down on the chair too, and my feet glued to the floor.

I look over to the cot, where Jimmy lies helpless, unable to move, still staring at me through the bars, with that strangely knowing look, as if to say: *now you're helpless too!* There's something different about his face. But babies are constantly growing, constantly changing. Sounds like something the health visitor would say.

"So like his Dad...!"

And he is, he's looking more like him by the minute.

Then I remember the dream I had last night, one of the ones I crammed into fitful snatches of sleep between night feeds and changes. I was lying trapped in wet, green tarmac that was spurting thickly from Jimmy's backside, while Joe was driving a vast machine with a great metal roller toward my helpless body. As it began to pulp and splinter my bones, my screams awoke me.

In the dream, the muscular driver of the machine had a tiny, grinning, bald baby head, while the tar-shitting baby lying nearby on the road had Jimmy's bearded face, out-sized and screaming in an adult voice at what was about to happen to me.

As I awoke, they blended into Jimmy's cries for a feed.

But he's not crying now. It's as if he knows something I don't.

Rubbish. He's just a baby, isn't he?

As Jimmy again turns his cool gaze onto me from the cot, I try to struggle again, but the tar has set, pinning me to the armchair. I try to scream, but my lips are tarred together.

Still, I mustn't panic. After all, what can a baby do to me, lying there in his cot? He's as trapped as I am. I just have to sit tight until Joe gets back. Sit tight is all I can do, though I'm starting to need to pee. By the time he gets back, I'll be sitting in my own shit, like a baby whose parents haven't bothered to change him.

Then I see what's happened to Jimmy's head.

It's not Jimmy's head any more. He doesn't just look like his Dad. It really is Joe's massive head on Jimmy's tiny shoulders, staring in horror at me through the bars of the cot, Joe's adult brain making the puny body wriggle uselessly in its wooden jail.

And when I hear the key turn in the front door lock and think of the tiny, bald, grinning baby head that must now sit on top of Joe's broad shoulders, and what its cold, alien brain can make his hard, muscular frame do to us, I start to scream through my glued-together lips.

Suzy Saylor
Lucy

She looked down at her arms. Pale and scarred, they told a story of a younger version of her. She used to cover them up, but finally gave up and decided that owning her past was infinitely better than pretending it never happened—especially since it still visited her in her dreams. She tapped her foot nervously and waited for the doctor. God, how she hated doctor's offices. She hated the stupid paper gowns that always tore around her too-ample hips, how the nurses and doctors were always judging her. Memories of her mother dragging her from one doctor to another never seemed to stop flooding her brain during every visit. Living with a parent with a mental illness was rough enough, but in addition to her own traumatic past, it made for a great recipe for a Nuthouse Special. She had been served that before, thanks to Mommy Dearest. St. Augustine's, St. Mary's, and St. Bernadette's all knew her by first name. Six weeks in each will do that, especially when you visit them more than once.

"Why do they make you wait?" she asked. "This is just cruel. I swear, they just do it for dramatic effect." Her husband was tapping his fingers on the counter across the exam room.

"These things don't just instantly give results. You know how it goes, Lil." She knew he was nervous, too. He tried hiding it, but it came through in his voice. She sighed, tapped her foot some more. He tapped his fingers, and a terse silence filled the tiny exam room again. The door opened and she jumped.

The doctor spoke without looking up from his tasseled loafers. "Well, there are still options available to you. There's surrogacy, there's adoption, and then there's always another round of in-vitro. If you do decide to do another round, I would suggest it be your last. Your body has been through hell and back with these procedures, and none of them have taken. Not to mention the financial aspect of it—it's got to be wearing you thin. I haven't met the couple that it doesn't weigh heavy on, and most have done fewer rounds than you. I'm sorry Lily. I wish this was better news for you." Lily just looked down at her paper-covered lap, trying to hold back the tears that always came. The silence seemed unbearable. The doctor left the room without saying a word, and Adam walked across the room to his wife. Five times they had been through this, not counting the three miscarriages prior to these procedures. She wrapped her arms around him and sobbed softly into his chest before pulling away and wiping her eyes.

"I think we should stick to the old fashioned way," Adam said with a mischievous smile as she tried without success to hop gracefully off the table.

"Seriously? *GET OUT*," she said, and pointed to the door.

As he closed the door behind him, she let herself cry. Why wouldn't her body just work like every other female on the planet? Had everything she done to herself made her so terrible that the cosmos saw fit to torture her like this? All she wanted was a child to love and care for...to show the beauty that she herself had finally discovered in this world after living in darkness for so many years.

Fuck it, she said to herself, and tore off the paper gown. She walked out of the room, past her husband, and out the front door. Adam gave her some space and caught up with her at the car. They rode home in silence with the exception of the radio.

That night, after skipping lunch and dinner, she took a pill to calm her nerves and went to bed. Before she knew it, the TV was getting blurry and waving at odd angles as she tried to focus on the screen. She finally gave in and fell asleep.

She kept hearing the voices from the TV in her dreams, narrating a bizarre reality. She kept wondering why cartoons sounded like *Law and Order*. Somewhere in the mess of colliding realities, she heard Adam's voice and smiled with the thought of him, as she tried to understand what he was saying.

"No, of course she has no idea. Why would I ever let anything jeopardize this?" She heard him whisper, but couldn't find where his voice was coming from. "It's the right time, finally. Yeah, this was the last procedure. Yes, I'm sure. They said her body couldn't handle another one. Stop worrying...no, you know she has to be the one...I'm sure it's her...She wants it so bad, she would never give this up. She trusts me more than anyone, she'll do whatever I say...Yeah, anything...it'll definitely be a night to remember..." and then his voice drifted off into the ether as she sunk into sleep completely.

She kept dreaming of something that she could never see—she knew it was there, but she couldn't see its face. Its voice was like the sound of twisting metal and screams of the tortured all at once, yet it entranced her. She wanted so badly to just look upon it, but every time she turned toward it, all she would see were horribly broken bodies, bent in impossible ways, twitching and rising up from a blood-soaked ground. The bodies didn't bother her; all she wanted was to touch the face of that voice. She loved it—she longed for it—why couldn't she see it? She gave chase to the voice, stepping over, even on, the endless field of mutilated corpses in grotesque positions. The ground squelched underfoot from the oversaturation of blood and fluids. She could smell iron in the air, like too many pennies held in your hand, from all the blood. It mixed with the stench of death and made her wretch. She was running now, dodging the undead in her way. She couldn't make out what the voice was saying, like it was whispering and screaming all at once.

She begged the voice to stop, to let her see them. But it never even hesitated. Every nerve ending was on fire, as if she had rolled around in a pile of hot coals. She came to a sudden stop at the edge of a massive crevasse. She could hear tortured screams and could feel a great heat upon her face as she looked down. The walls squirmed and twisted before her, oozing a viscous fluid from every crack. She tried to breathe in, but there was no air at all. She scratched at her throat, panicking for the first time. As her terror peaked, something grabbed her face like hot razorblades and whispered in her ear, "Would you die for me?" And without a thought, she exhaled, "Yes." She felt herself falling into the chasm, and could feel the heat becoming more and more intense. All she could do was smile.

Lily awoke in a puddle of sweat, all tangled up in her sheets. She never had a dream feel so real. She tried to remember what had her so worked up, but all she could recall was smiling at something she knew should have terrified her. She hopped in the shower, trying to shake the unsettled feeling she woke up with. She was still trying to recall the bizarre dreams she knew she had, but they seemed to turn into vapor the second she tried to catch hold of them in her mind. She assumed it was all just nerves because of the bad news the day before, but she made a mental note to call her shrink anyway.

As a young girl, she had always felt different, felt alone. It didn't help that her birthday was Christmas day, so she could never have birthday parties, like "normal" kids. If she got presents, she was lucky. She had always been told she wasn't worth the money. Her mother exploited her insecurities to anyone who would listen, casting her as the demon child. As an adult, Lily knew that she had underlying issues from the mess that was her childhood, so she found a doctor a thousand miles away from her mother, sought her own treatment, and started a new life. She knew that because of her history of anorexia, it could be difficult getting pregnant. But no one ever said it could mean she couldn't carry a child. When she miscarried, she should have gone to her therapist—but she only trusted one person. Adam.

After the third miscarriage, in vitro fertilization was the next logical step, so they went all in. Five times they went through the process, and as of yesterday, five times it failed. Lily could feel herself getting angrier and angrier as she shampooed her hair. "FUCK THIS!" she yelled out loud. She rinsed off the last of the soap and stepped out of the shower.

As she dressed, bits and pieces of conversations came back to her from her dreams. She remembered Adam talking to someone last night, something about the time was right, and jeopardizing something, and she remembered someone asking her if she'd die for them. She shivered, attempting to shake the bizarre feeling she got when she thought of that and tried to go about her daily routine.

She heard Adam eventually come in and got up to go greet him. "You look so down! Why don't we do something, to cheer you up?" His tone seemed almost pushy. "Let's go out, get sloshed. Can you remember the last time we actually drank?" Lily looked at him. This wasn't the usual Adam, but a little voice in her heard whispered, "why the hell not?"

"Ok. Where did you have in mind?"

"I heard about this...club in West Latham," Adam said as Lily walked into the bedroom. "I thought we could check it out." Lily just rolled her eyes and headed to her closet. She didn't notice Adam had been texting on his phone the whole time. She could use a good night of drunken idiocy to kick this crappy mood she was in, so she grabbed her sluttiest dress, her highest stilettos, and prepared for a good time.

She felt her heart race...the heat on her skin was intense. She gasped for air. Skin on skin. Sweat was pouring off them; she could feel it running down her body. Every sense heightened, she gave herself over to the fervor. It felt...familiar. The world slipped away. Adam yanked her hands up over her head with one hand, and pulled her into him. He put his lips to her ear and whispered, "We can give you everything you ever wanted." She looked into his eyes, "Yes," she exhaled. There was an intensity from him she

Ugly Babies

had never felt before. She felt like a piece of her was shaking loose, a part of her that she hadn't unleashed for many years.

"I'm Apollo." He shouted over the music in the club earlier, but somehow he still managed to sound like he was purring. Now she felt him envelop her. Body like a Greek god, and a...well, that was God-like as well. Brown hair, cropped short, perfect smile and eyes as blue as the Caribbean Sea. She couldn't tell if this was real or a dream, but she didn't much care. Adam spun her around into Apollo's hands, and she grabbed him like a hunter snatching its kill. The pressure of Adam's body against hers as she pressed against Apollo brought out the beast within her. She couldn't think of anything but RED. It was as if something inside awakened and utterly consumed her. She played the slut card once before in her life. It left her feeling primal, carnal, and hungry for more. It controlled her, instead of the other way around. She felt forced to reign herself in, to grow up. No man wanted a whore for a wife. At least that's what she had thought. Eventually she felt herself drift off to sleep amongst her gods, fulfilled in every sense of the word.

She dreamed of being pregnant. Her belly grew rapidly before her eyes. She could feel it moving and kicking. She knew it was different than any other child, but she couldn't tell why. She felt as if this child wasn't even hers, like it was simply using her until it could get out. The taste of blood and ash mixed in her mouth and she craved meat. She could feel her heart pounding faster and faster and all she wanted to do was strike a match and watch the world burn.

She awoke frightened and confused. She was lying in the middle of a barn, naked, save for a blanket. She tried to remember the night, but it was all snippets in red. Red dress. Red shoes. Red lights in the club. Red as she touched Apollo's chest. Red as she touched Adam at the same time. Red as she felt her thighs begin to quiver all over again and her face flush. She shook her head to clear her thoughts. She wrapped the blanket around herself and stood up to go find Adam, only to turn around and run into him.

"JESUS! You scared the shit out of me, Adam!" She leaned into him and whispered, "What happened last night?" She tried to keep her voice even, but her nerves got the best of her. He looked down at her with something resembling excitement. He didn't even seem like the same person she knew. She had never seen him like that before.

"Sweetie, I just wanted to give you everything that would make you...happy." Adam said. But it didn't even sound like him.

"I don't—I don't even remember..." she protested. But as the words were coming out of her mouth, she felt the intensity creeping back from the night before. "Trust me." Adam breathed into her ear. She closed her eyes, and everything went red again. She could recall the taste of salt on his skin, the need, and the want for more. She didn't even notice Adam was no longer there.

A pain in her stomach hit her so hard she fell to her knees. She opened her eyes, confused. She was alone again. She gathered herself up and slowly wandered out of the barn. She knew she needed help. She stumbled up some stone steps that led to a massive house. The pain was so great, she never saw the many eyes that watched her every move with a hungry anticipation from their hiding spots.

She banged on the door, and it swung open slowly. As she walked in, she momentarily marveled at the beauty of the place, but something seemed...*wrong*. About it all. Things twisted in ways that didn't look quite natural, shadows appeared where the sunlight should be. Where the hell was she? A sudden stab of pain grabbed her and she collapsed in the middle of the great entranceway, gripping her stomach. She could swear it felt bigger, harder. Before she knew it, hands were upon her, from all directions, carrying her. She was in so much agony that she couldn't even resist. They laid her down on a massive four-post bed and as suddenly as they came, everyone was gone. Not so much as a peep as to why they had just dropped her there. She grabbed at her stomach, which was now the size of a small beach ball. What was happening to her? *Am I still dreaming?* she thought. There was so much pain that she knew she had to be awake. She closed her eyes against the pain and could faintly hear a whisper. She suddenly remembered chasing that voice and without thought, she yelled out.

"I just want to see your face!"

Adam finally came into the room. Lily was pale; hair plastered to her face, her whole body glistened from the sweat. Her face contorted with pain.

"Adam! Help me please! I need a hospital! *Please!*" she screamed as he entered the room.

"Everything you need is right here," Adam said in an eerie tone. "Don't worry. We're all here to take care of you."

"What the FUCK do you mean by that?" she panted at him.

"I told you I wanted you to have everything, didn't I?" he asked. "Well, now I—well, we—have given you what you most wanted. See, we're kind of a package deal, he and I. We had to have the combination of all of us to make it happen. Man, God, and the

Whore. Always knew you had still had that slut inside you," he said smugly. "There's nothing wrong, Lil. This is what you've always wanted. A child so special, you have no idea what it'll bring to this world." The tone of his voice was anxious and scary all at once. "So just relax, and let it happen," Apollo cooed in Lily's ear. She didn't even know he was there until that moment. "But how am I—and how is this—*who the hell are you*?" Lily screamed in time with her contractions.

"Like I said, package deal. Man, God, together. We are one in the same, really," Adam said as Apollo came to his side. The room burst into activity and Lily's mind raced in a thousand different directions.

"But...but how? We just—" she stammered, out of breath.

"It works a little differently for the Gods, my dear," Apollo answered. "They demand immediate results." Lily went to respond, but all that came out was a guttural scream as her body took over and did what it was made to do. She tried to regain control of it, but her stomach contracted and her body pushed without her even trying. She cried out in agony as she felt her insides rip and tear away. She put her hands down between her legs and all she could feel was warm, wet tissue between her fingers. She held them up and they were covered in blood and a membranous film that was BLACK and fetid, like rotten flesh. Then a smell hit her she wished she didn't recall, the smell of iron and death. She looked around the room, panic-stricken and horrified. Around her she saw writhing shapes she couldn't identify, faces that were contorted in terrifying ways, bodies that bent and split apart. She looked for Adam, but what she found was Adam and Apollo's bodies melding into one.

"You're bringing us the Slayer of Gods! He has been waiting thousands of years for you! Lilith Pandora Belial—you were chosen from birth for this," their voices now chanted in unison as their bodies twisted and melted together. They laughed a strange sort of noise, like the grinding of rocks and glass together. She tried to cover ears, but the searing pain in her abdomen had her clutching the bed sheets instead. She could feel her flesh splitting apart and bones snapping like twigs as she screamed. There was nothing around her but pain. Then a sensation like an explosion came from somewhere inside her body and she truly thought she had been torn open from the inside out. She looked down at her waist, and she couldn't understand what she was seeing—it was like looking at raw hamburger meat. She thought for a moment that she must be delirious, but as she blinked and tried to clear her vision, she saw it for all that it was—a mass of bleeding flesh wriggling about. She didn't even see a head, but this—thing—was somehow moving and making a sound that turned her brain inside out. There were cries coming from all around her; praises and creatures falling in worship of the wiggling pile of meat. She watched it squirm as the four arms of Adam/Apollo carefully cradled it, fluid oozing from orifices that opened up as it moved. It stretched and grew before her eyes. Flesh elongated out of its middle, cracking and bubbling as it stretched upwards, bulging pockets pushed to the surface, black and bulbous. Teeth, a jaw, what looked like a skull formed in bony patches, poking out of the swirling goo. Something resembling a claw reached out toward her, and as it grew closer, she watched muscle form, then fatty tissue and blood, and then skin appeared just as it reached her hand. She jerked away from it, trying to back herself up—but couldn't move. She couldn't feel her legs at all. She heard a scream that sounded familiar, and then realized it was her own.

She saw the pulpy mass squirm out of the arms of a creature she once loved (or lusted) and land with an audible plop at the end of the bed. She watched as bone grew from cartilage, shredding ligament and sinew in its path, blood leached out over the surface of its newly stretched muscles. She vomited uncontrollably all over herself.

The creature shrieked as it stood up, raw red skin forming over its gory figure. It was scarred and emaciated and looked as if it had been beaten without mercy. Now the size of an adult, it turned to face Lily with dead, black eyes, and spoke with the voice from her dreams, that catastrophic noise that drew her in like a moth to a flame.

"You gave me these scars, Mother. Every time you ran that blade across your skin, every time you starved your body because of the hate in your heart, it came to me. Every time your mother pummeled your pathetic carcass, your hate for her made me possible. It grew within you and waited. Waited for me. Here I am, Mother. Here's the face you so longed to see. Look what you have given me, Mother. Is this what you want your child to look like? Scarred, withered, worthless? To be as hideous on the outside as you were inside? Is this the beauty you wanted me to see?!" it screamed at her. Then it smiled and outstretched a hand. "Or will you take them from me, Mother? Will you make your child perfect?" The arm was bleeding and covered in pus from slices made all over it. There were stitch marks, but no stitches—just open wounds. Lily looked at the hand waiting before her. It was her child. How could she not?

She took hold of the extended hand and the world snapped into focus around her. She felt pain as she had never felt it before. All over her body, her scars split open. Her hair began to fall out with bloody chunks of scalp, her skin shrunk back, her ribs protruded. Her annihilated pelvis exposed its broken edges. Her body convulsed and flailed in agony, and she begged for death to just take her. The pain was relentless.

"Don't you wish you could have given back *your* scars to that wench you suckled from?" chided a voice like satin with a razor's edge. Lily pushed herself up onto her elbows and she couldn't believe what she saw—a stunning beauty, hair as blonde as corn silk, eyes as blue as a tropical ocean, body of a Grecian Goddess. "But then again, your dear daughter is a bit more important than you'll ever be." She leaned into Lily's face. "There was no more room inside me to hold all of your putrid ugliness along with what I plan to do to the world, so I figured you could have it back. It served you so well in the past. I mean, when you're evil incarnate, how much more do you really need?" She chuckled and pushed Lily's forehead back, forcing her backward into the bed, landing with a splat in a puddle of her own blood and piss. "I hope you don't think you were picked at random—just look at your name! Seriously, your mother was a God damn freak! Let's see; Lilith, first wife of Adam, who left him to sleep with the *'Man'* himself. I call him *Daddy*." She placed a hand on the mutilated being that was Adam and Apollo, who now had become a beast with two faces and arms and legs that flailed in fragmented sections: "Pandora, the woman who let loose all the evils of Heaven and Hell in the world; and then Belial, the lawless and lustful. You were just born to bring destruction to this world, and that you did. Aren't you just so proud?" she mocked in sweetest tone of hatred Lily had ever heard. "It's just beautiful irony that you share a birthday with the *'savior'* of this worthless world, don't you think?" Lily looked at her "daughter", but as she blinked, the beauty she had seen moments before was now a writhing mass of maggots and dead flesh, pus and fluids oozing from head to toe, fibrous tissues stretched thin over bony protrusions that jutted out at unnatural angles from its body. There were no eyes, or even a face—just massive jaws with row upon row of jagged teeth between which vomit and bile poured through. Lily tried to scream but something squeezed her throat shut. She looked up and saw one of the twisted face of one of the crawling things that had been on the floor. They were all over her...she could feel them pulling and digging their nails into her skin. "Wait one moment, my friends," Lily heard her "daughter" say. She glanced back at her and she was once again the beauty Lily has seen earlier. "What will be my name, Mother? You must name me before I go into the world."

"Lucy," Lily said. Lucy smiled.

"Clever mother. Enjoy my friends," Lucy said as she turned away. The creatures swarmed Lily, tearing her apart like ravenous dogs. The fusion of Adam and Apollo looked at Lucy.

"Daddy's little girl," they said. Their gravelly voice hung in the air as they grabbed Lucy with their awkward limbs, touching and grabbing, fondling and kissing like lovers. Then all three slithered out of the embrace and dove into the feeding frenzy. As they joined in and tore a ragged piece of flesh from the pile, Lucy wiped her mouth and walked out of the room.

She strode down the hallway, stopping in front of a large antique mirror to admire herself from head to toe.

"Damn, I'm good looking," she said to herself, a flash of black glinting in her gemstone eyes.

Caroline Kepnes
The Stars Said Trudy

Parents loved their children. But parents did not have to like their children. Elsa's parents probably weren't calling their friends to complain that their daughter still played with dolls and had no friends. But they were thinking that stuff. And it was harder to think stuff if you never got to say it out loud. They loved her. But love was nothing without like. Without like, love was just obligatory, nipples for kittens, coffee without cream. Elsa's mother was always making coffee and complaining about forgetting to buy cream. Elsa's mom would be in a bad mood for the rest of her life, it seemed. She was always lighting cigarettes off the gas stove and leaving half-full cups of forgotten coffee all over the house. One time, Elsa tried the coffee even though she knew kids aren't supposed to drink coffee. Her mother caught her.

"Elsa, you know better."

"I only had a little."

"It doesn't matter. Do you want to stunt your growth and ruin your life and be addicted to coffee?"

Elsa didn't want any of those things and the coffee tasted bad anyway so it was no big deal, leaving those cups alone.

Elsa's father was always griping about those cups—staining the counters, perched on counters, all the waste—and the only thing he griped more about was the way his wife forgot to shut off the burners on the stove. He said that one day she would kill them all because she didn't turn off those burners. He didn't say this like it was bad, more like a matter of fact. Elsa's parents were named Marley and Brett and they were really good looking with lots of friends. All their friends had kids but their kids didn't like Elsa. Their friends didn't come around as much and though they didn't say it, Elsa knew that they had a lot more fun before she was born, before she was talking and weird.

They tried to do nice things. Last night, they surprised her with a doll. But it was an ugly doll with yellow hair and knee socks and a gingham dress. Elsa tried, "If you have the receipt, maybe me and Mom can return this doll after school. I wanted Ariel from *The Little Mermaid*."

Her dad dropped his paper. "A doll is a doll is a doll."

Her mother snapped, "Elsa, at some point we all have to grow up. Would you want everyone at school to know that you still play with dolls?"

This doll wasn't a gift. This doll was meant to get her off dolls. It wasn't heroin; it was methadone. They hoped that she would take this doll and all the others and throw them in the basement. The burner went tick-tick and Elsa's mom flicked ashes in the sink, "Stop pouting."

"Sorry."

"You wanted a doll, you got a doll. So you may as well try and love it."

"I'm sorry, Mom."

And Elsa was sorry. She knew about her mom's sadness. She knew about the miscarriage that happened before Elsa even existed. She found out about it when she was snooping in the basement and saw her mother hunched over a pink blanket with the name TRUDY on it, pink and puffy.

She opened her mouth: "Surprise!"

Her mom screamed and dropped the blanket. Her face looked crazy and her hair was messy. Maybe it was just the lighting in the basement. Elsa ran.

Later that night, her parents visited her, together, which was weird.

"I'm sorry I ruined the surprise," said Elsa. "I want a baby sister."

Her dad rubbed his forehead. Her mother said there wasn't a baby on the way.

"Who's Trudy?"

Her parents looked at each other. She knew she shouldn't have asked. She wanted to take it back.

Her mom started pacing. Her dad rubbed the sides of his head where there were tiny grey hairs. Sometimes she wanted to tell them they could be sad if they wanted. She didn't care.

"Elsa," her dad said. "Your mom had a miscarriage before you were born."

Elsa repeated the word, "Miscarriage."

"Don't say that," her mom said. "It's a bad word."

Miscarriage meant that you were bad at carrying the baby. It meant that they made Trudy together, but that Elsa's mom messed up carrying her all the way into the world. It meant that they had all this stuff for someone who didn't exist and kept it in the basement as if she was gonna come back for it. Which she wasn't, because she was dead, so why did they keep all that stuff?

"Because we love her, Elsa," her mom snipped. Then her mom looked in the mirror and pulled at her eyebrows and sipped her cold coffee. "We'll always love Trudy. Our first baby."

"Why didn't you name me Trudy?"

Elsa's mom started to cry. They left and the next morning Elsa brought her mother's forgotten coffee mug downstairs and put it in the dishwasher.

Elsa ransacked the basement and found more presents for Trudy. Butter soft blankets, bunny dolls and sweaters. All the gifts were embroidered and every time Trudy's name announced itself in puffy, feminine pale letters, Elsa's heart sank. She hid Trudy's presents under her bed. One day, she looked and all Trudy's things were gone. She never went looking for them again.

Elsa's mother was driving jerky, braking hard for no reason, speeding up and slowing down. She let a cigarette with a match and dropped the match and dropped the match and they had to pull over even though Elsa swore that she saw it land in an old cup of coffee. Later she lit a cigarette on the wrong end and they had to pull over again. Maybe her mom was upset about taking Elsa out of school in the middle of a school day. She even gave her an iced coffee as soon as they got in the car.

"You said kids can't drink this."

"Iced coffee is different. Drink it. It's good for you."

She said they were going to Elsa's doctor but Elsa looked out the window and saw run down houses with junky cars and busted washing machines in the front yard.

"Is this a new way to Dr. Kelly?"

"We're going to a new doctor."

"Why?"

"Did you finish your iced coffee?"

"Almost."

"Finish all of it, Elsa."

Elsa stared at her mom's puffy face in the rearview mirror.

"Don't stare, Elsa."

"I'm sorry."

It was scary being the car when her mom was crying because it felt like they might die. Finally they arrived at the new doctor's office, even though the office didn't look like an office because the front deck was covered with cob webby dream catchers. And her dad was there, which was weird. He hugged her mom and told her it was okay. Elsa worried. Her mom was crying. Her dad was whispering and trying to get his mom to go back in the car but his mom shook him off and wiped her eyes.

"Elsa, did you finish your drink?"

"Do I have cancer?" said Elsa.

A woman in a black robe came outside and waved. "Do you have the doll?"

Elsa's mom popped the trunk. She got out the crappy doll. Elsa was scared. Her dad was in his car with his dead down. Her mom was staring at the doll and Elsa's heart was pounding but that could have been coffee or cancer.

"No, honey," her mother said. "Now come on."

That was the last thing Elsa remembered.

A few weeks later, Elsa's parents decided to home school her. She was sickly; the iced coffee from that day stunted her growth. Her skin was stiffening. She was like the Dr. Seuss poem that goes *oh heck it's up to my neck* because the gluey-skin feeling was worming its way up her legs. Her feet didn't feel like feet when she squeezed them, they felt ceramic, like the time in art class when they poured hot goop into trays and baked them and then out had come ornaments. The ornaments were mangy and Sienna Grady laughed that all parents are so stupid cuz they hang this crap up as if kids don't know how ugly it is. Elsa thought of her own parents, throwing the ornaments away. Her mother hated junk. Her father said everyone couldn't be an artist.

There was a going away party for Elsa at the end of the day but she didn't want any the cake. She was hungry less every day. Kids laughed and the teacher told them to stop laughing but then the teacher offered her a plate, "Just a small piece, Elsa. It's good manners."

She took the plate but she couldn't eat the cake. She didn't have a belly anymore. She watched the kids and none of them were talking about how much they were going to miss her. Nobody seemed sad that she was going. They all seemed happy to have cake and she felt good, like at least now she would be remembered for making birthday cake magically appear on a Wednesday when it wasn't someone's birthday. Not one kid seemed upset about her going and she figured she was really bad at being a kid. She'd been quieter all the time lately. It had been getting harder and harder to talk and she had fewer things to say every day. Someone popped a balloon and she startled and looked down at her vanilla cake with white frosting and pink flowers and the kids really did look super happy and maybe the cake would make her feel better and she dipped her finger into the frosting but when she put it on her lip it just sat there and she couldn't move her tongue to get it to go in. She shook her head and it fell on the plate.

"You're weird," said Adam Halstead. That was the last thing any kid said to her except for when the teacher made them all say goodbye at the same time.

She rode the bus for the last time. The bus driver gave her a hug, "Don't be a stranger, Elsa."

Elsa said she would visit but deep down she knew she wouldn't. You can't visit a bus driver. That would be weird.

Elsa's parents fought harder all the time. They threw glasses and platters. Elsa knew there wouldn't be a party for a long time because the trays for crackers were all in the trash now. There were coffee stains on all the walls because now her father threw forgotten cups when he found them instead of putting them in the dishwasher. Her mother drank out of Styrofoam cups but he threw those too.

They didn't make her do school work. It was like they weren't even trying to teach her anymore. And now that she didn't eat food there was nothing to look forward to, really. She asked her mom to go get a new doll and her mom told her to play with the doll she had. She slammed her door. She missed school.

One day, while they were yelling she took scissors and cut her hair until she looked like a boy and then she cut more and now she looked like a sick toddler. She cut more. She knew why she was cutting. She thought if she cut her hair and looked crazy enough that her parents would stop yelling at each other and start yelling at her and then they would fall back in love and go shopping for new glasses and platters. When she felt the hair it felt like fake hair from a doll head. Her arms were so sore from working the scissors she thought she might die and she sat on the bed with her feet on the ground and listened to them yelling, the way they talked into and over each other it was like the words were all coming from one bad place, not from two different people:

You're a monster no you're the monster oh fuck you that's a brave one Marley real fucking brave and original takes one to know one asshole I believe there were two people there that day I believe there were two people who agreed to do this No I agreed to go I did not agree to do it you cunt you cunt you drugged her before I could make up my own mind Oh fuck you Brett just fuck you

In the morning her parents were very quiet when they saw her head. They didn't yell. They didn't seem to be on the same side like she had hoped. Her mother left the kitchen to check the laundry. Her father ate Cheerios.

"I'm sorry," she said.

"Me too," he said.

Nobody yelled for a day or so. But then the yelling started again.

It was obvious that her hair wasn't growing back and she probably had coffee kid's disease that you can't fix. That must be why they got her a TV set for her bedroom. She always begged for one but they had always said no. Maybe dying wouldn't be as bad now. And she did think she was dying. She was moving less every day. That doctor they went to, the dream catcher doctor, whatever she did to try and fix Elsa hadn't worked. She must be so upset. You try to help someone and you give them drugs and then they get worse. How awful. Elsa didn't want to be a doctor when she grew up. But she knew she wasn't going to grow up and that's probably why she didn't have to do school work anymore. If you're dying from caffeine kids disease, it's okay to sit around and watch TV.

Sometimes her dad sat with her. He laughed at stuff even though he didn't think it was funny but because she was laughing. Then her mom would call him away to do something. Sometimes he carried Elsa outside. She liked to go outside. She basically couldn't walk anymore and talking was too hard so it was nice when her dad took her out. She liked thinking he could read her mind. She missed walking in the woods. She missed running. Her dad put her on her bed.

"Thank you for my gifts," she said.

"Gifts?"

"My doll and my TV."

Her words came like burps now, burps she had to work for. She breathed.

"Don't thank me."

"Is she mad at me?"

"Mom?"

"The doctor. Because I drank the coffee. Mom said I could but I know I shouldn't have."

Her dad's teeth chattered and he kissed her forehead. "Sweet dreams."

But she didn't need to sleep anymore. She was sorry about so much. She was sorry she had been a weird kid. She was sorry she had acted like such a jerk about the doll they got her. She knew what a brat she had been that day.

She had it all wrong before and she wanted to tell her dad that she knew that love was much harder without like and that her parents were better than she thought. She hadn't even tried to love that doll. Sure, she loved her new TV but it was easy to love a big TV. A good girl would have found a way to love a cheap doll. Love was only real if you were beating out your bad feelings, your judgments, your bratty wants and picky obsessions. Simple love, for a TV or a kid with a lot of friends, well that wasn't as good. That was just getting what you want. Brave love meant loving what you got. She knew that now, but her dad was asleep next to her mom in the other room and the farthest she could walk was the dresser.

She didn't know exactly when the new girl showed up because she didn't know the days of the week anymore. She only knew what was. And the facts were as follows:

A girl in a gingham dress, close in age.

She smiles a lot.

She wears knee socks.

She kisses Elsa in the morning.

She kisses Elsa at night.

In the day it is sunny and the girl is away.

Elsa sits on the dresser all day.

Her mom turns on the TV in the morning.

Her dad turns off the TV at night.

Sometimes the girl brings Elsa to bed.

Sometimes Elsa spends all night on the dresser.

In bed they lie by side with their eyes open and look up at the ceiling.

On the ceiling there are puffy pink plastic sticker stars that glow in the dark.

The stars spell Trudy.

The girl does not snore.

Trudy has lots of friends.

Trudy goes to school.

A calendar goes up.

The Little Mermaid is on top and the month of June is on the bottom.

Trudy makes a red x on a day every day.

After there are eight red x-es, Elsa's mom brings a suitcase into the room. *The Little Mermaid* is on the suitcase too. She cuts the tag off with scissors.

"Pack smart," she says. She kisses Trudy. She leaves.

Trudy smiles. She picks up Elsa. She looks in her plastic eyes: "I am taking you to Disney World."

Elsa's face is in a smile. It is always in a smile.

It is dark. Trudy is in the bed. So is Elsa. There is screaming. Mom opens the door. "Elsa, you gotta get up. We're gonna leave now."

"Elsa?"

"I mean, Trudy. Damn it."

"Who's Elsa?"

"Someone, no one. Honey, just get dressed."

Mom leaves. Trudy packs. Dad opens the door.

"Trudy, you have to get in the car now."

"Who's Elsa?"

"Who told you about Elsa?"

"Who is she?"

"Trudy, get in the car."

"Who is she?"

Dad grabs the suitcase and Trudy follows him.

The front door opens and they are gone. The front door opens and Dad is back. There is screaming:

You told her I told her nothing She just told me you told her She doesn't know what she's saying Oh yes she does Oh fuck off Well this is a nice start to a fun family vacation Then maybe I should stay here You know what, sweetheart, that's what you're gonna do Peter what the hell do you mean Just what I said honey just what I said you and your misery and sick cold heart are gonna stay right here Good Get the hell out Oh that's what I'm doing baby you just do me a favor and wait a minute before you light that butt Oh fuck you Love you too

The door closes. Mom is crying but then throwing things. The stove goes *tick tick tick* and then the noise like a firecracker inside of your body coming out your ears out your eyes and then nothing.

Elsa was not a doll anymore. She was a girl again. She had to pee and she peed in her pants because she couldn't remember how you hold it in. The stench was bad, overwhelming the stale coffee and cigarettes of her mom's car. Her dad said it was okay. But he always said things were okay. He put down a *Little Mermaid* on the seat. Elsa had skin again and eyes and a mouth and a pulse and she shrieked and pounded on the window of the car when she saw their house in flames. She was the only one in the backseat and her dad was in the front seat at the wheel. His knuckles stayed white. They didn't change.

Trudy was a doll again, same gingham dress and knee socks same cheap hair. Elsa would have asked her questions but she couldn't remember how to talk. She couldn't ask what happened. All she knew was they had been driving for a long time. It had been light and dark and light and dark. She pooped once and they pulled over and he carried her into a bathroom in a roadside diner that smelled like burnt coffee and cigarettes and she thought of her mother and realized that her mother was dead and she thought she might cry but she didn't. Her dad wiped her bum like she was a baby and put her in a brand new *Little Mermaid* bathing suit. She peed again in the bathing suit in the car and she used the Trudy doll to soak up the mess. It was the first time her dad laughed a little and his knuckles were almost pink, they were changing, finally.

They crossed into Ohio and Elsa leaned forward. It had been more darks and lights. It had to have been several days. She had practiced talking and she felt like she could get some words out. "Dad," she said.

He pulled over. He turned off the car. He turned and looked at her. He had new grey hairs on the side of his head. He looked dirty.

"What is it, honey?"

"I'm not mad at you."

He shook his head. "Elsa, Elsa it just happened so fast."

"No, it didn't," she said.

He was wrong. It happened over years and years. It started when Mom lost Trudy and it happened when she tried to fix her bad mood by making Elsa and then it happened when Elsa turned out to be less like the Trudy that Mom dreamt up. There was nothing fast about any of it and her dad showed up at the weird place that last day, the day she drank the iced coffee and left school. He hadn't shown up with a police car. He had shown up alone.

"Elsa, I don't know what you mean. You must be tired and I bet you have questions but sometimes it's best to just take a deep breath and sleep on it."

"You wanted Trudy, too," she said.

He was wearing one of his button-down shirts. The shirt looked stupid when you looked around at where they were, cornfields all around, he was dressed up for no reason. Elsa had never been on a road like this one, high grasses never ending. The road was so straight ahead and straight back and didn't turn even a tiny bit as far as the eye could see either way. It was a world without choices and she liked it. She pointed at the grass. "Is that corn?"

"Yes."

"Can we get out?"

"You can do whatever you want, honey," he said. And he hit the unlock button.

Elsa grabbed Trudy and stepped out of the car. She could hear the grass and the corn swish-swish. She carried her doll like a baby and she made way into the cornfield. Her dad didn't follow her and she wasn't scared. She knew it would get dark, but she also knew that in places like this the stars fill the sky with light. She would see a big farmhouse soon and the people inside who take care of the corn would be kind. They would like a little girl with strange short hair and a smelly doll. She loved them already even though she didn't know them and they didn't have neat restaurants nearby or big TVs or trips to Disney World or glow in the dark stars. She loved them the way mamas love their babies when their babies are still in their bellies, when they're not pretty or ugly, when they're just blobs on the inside to be carried all the way home. She stopped and closed her eyes and kids coffee disease was reversible. She knew it because in this new quiet place, she would swear that she could actually hear her hair growing.

Little Girl by Ashley Scarlet

Angela Meadon
Tiger, Tiger

TYGER tyger, burning bright,
In the forests of the night,
What immortal hand or eye
Could frame thy fearful symmetry?

In what distant deeps or skies
Burnt the fire of thine eyes?
On what wings dare he aspire?
What the hand dare seize the fire?

And what shoulder and what art
Could twist the sinews of thy heart?
And when thy heart began to beat,
What dread hand and what dread feet?

What the hammer? what the chain?
In what furnace was thy brain?
What the anvil? What dread grasp
Dare its deadly terrors clasp?

When the stars threw down their spears,
And water'd heaven with their tears,
Did He smile His work to see?
Did He who made the lamb make thee?

Tyger, tyger, burning bright
In the forests of the night,
What immortal hand or eye
Dare frame thy fearful symmetry?

-William Blake

Genna held the sleeping baby to her chest and pressed her eyes shut. She could love him as long as she didn't look at him. She could ignore the shocked faces of the horrified nurses. She could love him.

Holding him against her, she could almost believe that he looked like the other babies in the maternity ward. But then she would hear someone gasp, and the image would come tearing back into her mind. How could this happen to her?

Why, after three years of trying to conceive, had she been given a baby like this? She opened her eyes and peeked out at his misshapen features: Only his tiny face was visible, the rest of him swaddled in a pastel-blue receiving blanket. Her throat constricted as she looked at the angry red wounds where his eyes should have been. She repressed the urge to cry out when she saw, again, his tightly stretched lips.

There was a gentle knock on the door, and Genna looked up to see Doctor Livani, her obstetrician, whose face did not disguise her concern.

"How is he?" Dr. Livani said.

"He's sleeping." Genna wanted to leave it at that, but opening her mouth had released the flood gates and a huge sob heaved in her chest. Tears streamed down her cheeks. "What am I going to do? Where is Tom?"

"We will have a specialist here in the morning," Dr. Livani said, "Someone who has experience with cases like this. He's already flying in from Johannesburg. Until he gets here, we will do our best to keep the baby comfortable."

Genna was disheartened that the doctor ignored her question about Tom. He'd left as soon as the baby was born. No explanation, no promise to return. He'd just disappeared.

"Thank you, doctor." Genna wiped the tears from her cheeks and tried to smile at the woman who had helped her give birth to this creature. "Should I nurse him?"

"Breast milk would be best for him, but I don't think he will be able to latch on. We will bring in a pump if you would like to express, or we could feed him formula."

The doctor examined Genna and left, promising to send a nurse with the pump. Genna put the baby in the bassinet next to her bed and watched his tiny chest rising and falling in the bundle of blankets.

She had dreamed about inspecting her baby's tiny body from the day she'd found out she was pregnant. She had longed to count his fingers and toes, to run her hands along his smooth skin and sing him lullabies while he nursed at her breast.

But that would never be.

His skin was hard, and instead of bending to his shape, it tore whenever he moved. Raw wounds marked his body in angry red lines like stripes on a tiger. The risk of him catching a deadly infection was so high that she could not run her fingers over her own child's body.

Where the hell was Tom?

He would know what to do—or at least be able to console her while she looked down at their broken baby. *What god would allow a child to be born like this?* Genna shook her head to try and clear the anguish from racing mind.

A nurse brushed the curtain aside and deposited a large box on the nightstand. It had wires and plastic tubes coming out of it and suggestive cups attached to it.

"The pump," the nurse said. She shot a terrified look at the sleeping infant, crossed herself, and fled the room.

Anger swelled in Genna's chest. *What is wrong with people? He's only a baby.* She threw her pillow across the room and it thumped against the wall outside.

A high-pitched wail tore through the room, and it took Genna a moment to realize that it was coming from the baby...her baby.

He sounds like he is in terrible pain, she thought to herself. Of course he was in pain. Every movement tore his skin open. She picked him up and held him to her again, gently rocking and singing to him. But he didn't calm down; his cries only became more frantic and insistent.

He's hungry, Genna thought. The pump lay on the table beside her bed, like something out of a dairy farm, and Genna decided then that she wouldn't be able to express. She stood, clutching the wailing infant to herself, battling to control the rebellion in her knees and fighting back the wave of nausea. She hobbled out into the corridor and down to the nurses' station.

The maternity ward was dark, most of the mothers and their new babies were sleeping soundly. Only Genna and her baby moved. She found a nurse at the duty station. The woman held a book of crossword puzzles in front of herself like a shield.

"Do you need something?"

"My baby is hungry, but I can't feed him. The doctor said you could give him formula through a tube?"

Panic flashed behind the woman's eyes and she stumbled away from the desk. "Yes, I will get someone to help you." She walked a little too quickly toward the kitchen.

Genna fumed. If she had gone to a proper private hospital in the city they wouldn't have to deal with the superstitious country-nurses. They'd also have had a specialist see their baby immediately. Maybe Tom wouldn't have left. *Where the fuck is Tom?*

Genna screamed a wordless wail that contrasted and amplified the baby's squalls. She noted with some satisfaction that other babies in the dark ward started an answering chorus. She waited

---

in the hall, listening to the women calm their babies, for a long time. Nobody appeared with milk for her baby though.

She stalked to the kitchen and threw open the door. Inside she saw the three on duty nurses, huddled together on the floor and praying in hushed voices.

Would people always react like this to her baby? Would they always fear him? He did look terrifying, Genna had to admit. But he was only a baby. These women, these *nurses* couldn't even bring themselves to feed him. *Should I?*

She wandered back to her room in a daze, the infant in her arms still mewling with hunger, but the strength was leaving his body now. How long would it take for the specialist to arrive? Would he know what to do?

She closed the door and sank, crying, into her bed. She pressed the tiny body to her chest and closed her eyes. She remembered the first time she'd felt him move within her. The jabs and pokes and rumbles as he turned and stretched in her womb. *Had each of those movements hurt him? Torn at his skin?*

She had felt such joy at the thought of bringing a baby into the world, but now that he was here she felt only pain. Her pain couldn't compare to his. She pressed his face into her chest and held it there until he stopped crying.

She placed his tiny body in the bassinet and watched him. His chest no longer rising and falling; His suffering was finally over.

She had loved him.

"Have you fed the baby yet?" Doctor Livani's voice penetrated the fog of grief that held Genna in its unforgiving grip.

"No, I couldn't," she pulled the blanket up around her shoulders. The doctor would soon realize that the baby was dead, they would blame her, Genna knew. She shivered and held her breath for the accusations that were sure to come.

"He's looking...better."

"I don't know what...what did you say?"

"His skin seems to be healing. Look at his lips."

Why would a doctor lie to me? Genna knew the baby was dead, she'd smothered him herself. She'd watched his body turn cold and blue before succumbing to the grief.

"Look at him Genna!" The doctor put her warm hand on Genna's shoulder and rolled her over to face the bassinet.

Morning sunlight filtered in through the lace curtain on the window. In the gentle glow the baby did actually look like his skin was healing. The wounds were pinker, the skin itself looked more elastic.

Maybe it's because he's dead, Genna thought. Maybe the muscles relaxed or something.

Doctor Livani reached her hand out toward the baby, her long fingers hovered just above his skin. *She's going to touch him and know I killed him!*

"Don't, don't touch him!"

The doctor looked at her for a moment, the look in her eyes going from puzzled to understanding. "Of course," her lips parted in a warm smile. "He's your baby, why don't you hold him so that I can check him?"

Genna's heart trip-hammered in her chest as she watched the doctor slide her hands under the bundle in the basinet. As she did, the baby stirred in his blanket. His mouth opened as he yawned a greeting to the day.

"His improvement is remarkable." The doctor handed the baby to Genna. "Look at how his eyelids have grown closed. He might not lose his vision! This is a miracle!"

Genna was too stunned to speak. A few hours ago she had smothered this infant, now he lay in her arms nuzzling at her breast.

"You should try and feed him, his lips look like they have healed enough to latch now."

"But, this isn't right, last night he...I..."

"New born babies are remarkably resilient, we'll still ask Doctor Pohl to look at him, but he seems to be recovering."

The doctor walked out of the ward and drew the door shut behind her.

What happened? Genna asked herself over and over again as she fed the baby. She'd killed him, she was sure of that. She'd felt him stop fighting her. She'd watched him lie, dead in the basinet. Was she imagining it? Had she dreamed it?

I must have dreamed it.

When the baby finished feeding, Genna laid him on her bed and slowly removed his blanket. His arms and legs were like the antennae of a stick insect protruding from his body. She couldn't deny the improvement though.

But there was something strange about his fingers. The bones seemed fused together, curved in a rigid, claw-like grasp.

By the time Dr. Pohl arrived, every nurse in the ward had come to inspect the baby. They were alarmed, and relieved, by his progress.

"You say this baby had a severe case of Harlequin Ichthyosis?" Dr. Pohl asked as he pushed his glasses up the bridge of his wide nose and peered at the marks on the baby's body.

"I've never seen anything like it," Dr. Livani replied. "This is what he looked like at birth." She held up a smartphone and showed him pictures she had taken.

"Remarkable. Yet now he has a mild case."

The two doctors spent the better part of an hour inspecting every part of the baby's body and eventually they decided on a course of treatment.

Genna watched this in silence. She couldn't shake the feeling that they would discover what she had done to the baby. There might be a bruise or a scar that would reveal her deeds. Had she even done anything to him?

I must have dreamed it. Babies don't die and then come back to life. This is the real world, not a horror story. She chided herself.

The doctors were so positive about the baby's progress that, when they left, Genna decided that it was time to give him a name. She and Tom had agreed to call him Bryce, but with Tom having abandoned them she couldn't honor his wishes. She decided to call him William, after her father.

Genna felt herself relaxing. The nightmare about him dying faded from her mind and was replaced with his soft skin and milky breath. By the time she fell asleep with William in the crook of her arm, she knew that she would love her baby more than anything.

Genna awoke to a sharp, pricking sensation in her left breast accompanied by something hot and wet running down her ribs. William was still snuggled up against her.

His diaper must have leaked. Genna rubbed her eyes to clear the sleep from them. Her hand was covered in fluid and it left a sticky mark on her cheek.

"Ah!" Genna cried softly as she felt a sharp pain in her breast. The room was dark, the sun had already set and little light filtered in below the door. That must have been why the pool of liquid spreading across her gown looked so much like blood.

Genna flicked the light switch and this time her scream was so loud that William started crying. She threw the baby onto the bed, drops of blood splashed across the white linen and soaked into it.

His wailing grew louder, but Genna ignored him as she pulled the ties open behind her and dropped the blood-soaked gown to the floor.

"What the hell?"

Genna lifted her arm and looked in the mirror above the washbasin. There, in the crease below her milk-swollen breast was an oval wound. *Are those tooth-marks?*

Genna pulled a wad of paper towel from the dispenser and pressed it against the seeping bite. She crossed to the bed where William lay screaming, waving his arms in protest at the way she'd treated him. His mouth was ringed with blood, the sanguine fluid covered his chin and stained his clothes. Within that mouth Genna saw dozens of needlepoint teeth.

"Oh, Jesus, help me," she whispered. She reached out and gently slid her finger into William's mouth and pressed the tip to one of the teeth. His jaws clamped down and she felt the tiny points piercing her flesh.

"Let go, you little bastard!" She used her free hand to pry his mouth open and wrenched her finger out. He started wailing in protest. Genna could do nothing more than stare at him, dumbfounded.

I must be dreaming again. This can't be happening. Day-old babies don't grow cats' teeth.

William's cries grew louder and Genna's breathing quickened. He sounded like a kitten, she realized; his cries filled the room like a mewling cat. Even his hands, scrabbling frantically at the air, looked like the claws of a tiger.

Genna pulled her robe back on. She picked William up, holding him so that his mouth was turned away from her, and rocked him until he stopped crying.

Should I call the nurses?

The baby wasn't hurt, and her wound had stopped bleeding. They would probably think she had hurt the baby. *What will they think of his teeth?*

Genna took the baby into the small washroom and filled the basin with warm water. She bathed him carefully, keeping clear of his teeth. Once he was clean she put him in the basinet and took care of her own wound.

This is not right. This can't be right. She winced as she wiped the dried blood from the wound. Something evil had brought William back from the dead. That something was still inside him.

Genna knew that there was only one thing she could do. Before the doctors saw him and thought he was a curious medical oddity that they must study. Before his...whatever was wrong with him became worse.

Genna walked back into the room and lifted the pillow from her bed. She leaned over the sleeping form of her tiger-striped baby. It was the only thing she could do. The only way to undo the damage she had already done. She had to send her baby back to wherever he had come from. Back to whoever had made him the way he was.

Tears streamed down her cheeks as she bent over him and pressed the pillow onto his face. He only struggled a little. When he stopped moving she dropped the pillow onto the floor and wailed wordlessly until she thought the pain would break her in half.

She picked William up, his body limp in her arms. His little head lolled on his shoulders and his mouth fell open to reveal the soft pink gums inside. There were no teeth.

She spun and held him up so that the light shone straight into his mouth. The teeth were gone. Had they ever been there?

What have I done?

Genna slammed the door open with her shoulder and ran toward the duty station. "Help me! My baby isn't breathing! Help!"

"You did the right thing," Doctor Livani said. She gently brushed a strand of hair away from Genna's eyes and smiled at her. There was no irony in her smile. "It takes a while for new born babies to work out how to breathe properly. William is lucky you were so alert."

Genna looked at the baby, drinking happily from the bottle she held in one hand, while the doctor inspected him.

"And would you look at him? It's almost as if he'd never had anything wrong with him. I can hardly see a scar on him. Even his eyes are completely healed. This really is remarkable."

It's not remarkable, it's evil. Genna knew that nobody would believe her if she tried to explain why the baby had healed so well. *I can't tell them I killed my own baby twice. They'd lock me up!*

"We're just fortunate, I guess." The words sounded hollow to her and Genna knew the doctor would hear it to.

"You've been through an awful time these past three days, would you like a sedative?"

Genna shook her head. What would the baby do to her if she was knocked out?

"We'll take care of William," the doctor pressed the issue. "You need some good rest. We'll bring him back soon. Don't worry."

If the baby wouldn't be in the room she would be grateful to get some good sleep. "Please make sure they wake me?" She hoped her fear came through as maternal concern.

"Of course, you'll be amazed by how good you feel after a good sleep."

Genna accepted the small blue pill when the nurse brought it to her a few minutes later. She swallowed it with a sip of water and settled into the spongy embrace of the hospital bed.

Genna slipped in and out of a deep sleep all through the night. She shuffled groggily to the toilet in the darkness and when she returned the nurse was tucking William into his basinet.

"He's all right dear," the old woman said. "You'll be going home tomorrow." She patted Genna on the arm and left the room.

William was sound asleep, his perfect skin showed no signs of the hardships he had endured and Genna allowed herself a moment of optimism before she fell asleep again.

Genna awoke again to the pre-dawn light shading her curtains. A weight pressed down on her chest and she blinked the murk from her eyes. A sudden tearing sound turned Genna's blood to tar in her veins; her heart ached with the effort of pumping it.

Why couldn't she lift her arms? What was happening...?

"Aah!" Genna moaned as sharp teeth dug into the flesh at the base of her neck. Her voice strangled by fear and her parched throat.

Am I still sleeping? Is this a nightmare?

More needles pricked into her arm, breast and stomach while the creature on her chest strained at the mouthful of flesh it held in its teeth. A sickening wet squelch filled her ears as Genna watched dark liquid arch up and splatter against the ceiling. Warm drops fell down and struck her face. The smell of her own blood filled her nostrils like the tangy scent of autumn leaves.

Hot blood poured out of her neck, seeping into the sheet beneath her and tainting the air.

The teeth sank in again, deeper this time. Hot breath chilled her skin as the baby breathed on the wet flesh of her neck. His tongue snaked between his teeth as he bored into her neck.

Dark spots spun on the edges of her vision as Genna strained to look down at the baby on her chest. She could just make out his feline form as he crouched, feeding on her. His skin once again bore the stripes he'd been born with, tiny claws protruded from the ends of his fingers.

But it was the angry red eyes that bore Genna away from the pain and fear. Darkness swallowed her as she stared into those eyes with one thought in her mind.

I tried to love him.

Dusty Davis
The Thirteenth Child

A full moon watched over the little cabin in the woods where Alda Mae Watson sat in her rocking chair knitting a sweater for her unborn child. The crackling of the fireplace soothed her as an animal howled somewhere in the night outside. She clenched up as her abdomen was racked with pain. With a hand on her belly, she took deep breaths until the pain subsided. Alda Mae knew what to expect. This was her thirteenth child.

Alda Mae bit her lower lip as she pondered her family legacy which said that the thirteenth child of a witch would be cursed by the Devil himself. Alda Mae and her husband both knew the sayings of her family but they both had wanted a lot of children. They had planned to stop at twelve and were shocked nine months ago to find out that she was with child again.

The fire crackled as a fierce gust of wind slammed into the cabin door, startling her and causing her to drop her needle. She picked it up off her lap and stuck her finger with the point. Blood started to spill from the hole in her finger, ran down her hand and dripped to the floor with a splat. As she rocked herself up to her feet the cabin door swung open allowing a cold wind to enter that sent a chill racing through her body.

Ezekiel Watson rushed through the doorway followed by the town midwife, Hazel Douglas. Alda Mae reached for her husband as another labor pain shot from her belly around to her back and doubling her over. Outside, the wind howled along with her as another gust forced its way in, extinguishing the inferno in the fireplace and cast the cabin into darkness.

Alda Mae fell to her knees from the pain as she heard Ezekiel and the children rush to her side. The pitter pat of the smaller children's feet sounded like rats scurrying across the cabin floor.

"Don't let them get my baby!" She screamed in fear as she fell to the floor and wrapped her hands around her stomach to protect her unborn child from the imagined rats. Ezekiel rolled her over onto her back.

"Alda Mae, nobody is going to take our baby," he told her as he looked over his shoulder at Hazel, who stared blankly at the witch on the floor. "What do you need us to do?" he asked, getting her attention again.

"We are going to need blankets," the midwife said as she crouched in front of her. Alda Mae could see the look of fear in her eyes as the sound of rushing feet filled the cabin again, as the children scrambled to do as they were told.

Jacob, the eldest boy, reappeared out of the darkness a moment later and handed Ezekiel a thick quilt, which he put under Alda Mae's head.

"Here—lay down on this," he said, and guided her head down with his big, thick hands.

Light returned to the cabin as the children got the fire started again. Ezekiel wished that it would go back out, because now he could see the pain that was etched on his wife's face. Her lips were curled back in a snarl, and wet tears streamed down her cheeks. Her hands were at her head gripping fistfuls of her thick, black hair.

"I see the head!" one of the children exclaimed, giving Ezekiel an excuse to leave Alda Mae's side. A baby's head was squeezing its way from her loins, tearing her open. Blood was oozing from her, soaking the cabin floor.

Hazel Douglas tried to get a grasp on the head, but it was too slippery from the blood. Wrapping her hands in a blanket, she grabbed it and started to ease it out but immediately stopped.

"The cord is wrapped around its neck. I need something to cut it, quick."

"Get this Devil out of me!" Alda Mae screamed in pain. Ezekiel shot to his feet and ran to their little kitchen area. He returned a moment later with a large knife and handed it to the midwife. She took it and with a look of fear in her eyes, gently cut the cord from the baby's neck. The baby shrieked as its head came out, followed quickly by its torso.

The cabin was pervaded with the pungent aroma of blood as the baby's legs slid out, shining with the crimson substance. Ezekiel let out a sigh of relief when he saw that the child looked to be normal.

"Let me see him," Alda Mae said with outstretched arms. The midwife put the crying baby into her hands and saw the smile that lit up her face. She held the baby boy up close to her and coddled him as her tears of pain became ones of joy.

Everyone gathered around Alda Mae to get a peek at the new baby. Alda Mae smiled down at the boy in her arms as an inhuman growl escaped from his mouth. The baby stretched its tiny arms and they turned into the wings of a bat. Convulsing, the baby's head grew outward in length. Alda Mae looked on as it took the shape of a horse. She felt something against her thighs where the baby was pushing off her lap, flapping its wings. Looking down, she saw that a tail had sprouted from its spine, and his once tiny feet had grown three times their original size and were now cloven hooves digging into her thighs, trying to escape from his mother's grasp.

The creature growled and screamed as it started to take flight. Everyone screamed along with it, running and hiding behind whatever they could find. Alda Mae looked on calmly, understanding what was happening to her son. It was not cursed by the Devil...it was his offspring. She released the creature and let out a shriek of laughter as it dipped and flew.

The monstrous thing landed on the floor with a thud, flapping its wings so hard that it threatened to blow out the fire. With a growl, the entity grew to over four feet tall and its skin turned a dark green color. Hard scales jutted from his back and ran down his spine. Once the transformation was complete, the creature scanned the room with eyes that burned as red as the fires of Hell.

Hazel Douglas was cowering behind the rocking chair when the thing saw her. With amazing quickness, it was upon her. She screamed in terror as the creature grabbed her with its sharp clawed hands and ripped at her house dress. The material melted away like butter in a fire as the devilish creature pushed her to the floor. It straddled her and shot out a forked tongue, which caught her on her cheek and seared her flesh. The creature then mounted the midwife, trying to get inside her. She screamed as she felt the tip of his fully erect cock against her thighs and kicked and squirmed to get away.

Ezekiel grabbed a fire poker and rushed to the midwife's aid. He swung at the creature with all his strength and hit it in the head. The beast rolled off Hazel onto the floor and shot back to its feet.

"Don't hurt my baby!" Alda Mae screamed at Ezekiel from across the room as she was trying to sit up.

"This thing isn't our baby!" he screamed back, staring at the creature and waiting to see what it was going to do next.

Alda Mae stood up on shaky legs and came at Ezekiel, causing him to turn away from the creature. She grabbed him around the waist, distracting him as the creature attacked. The thing wrapped its clawed hands around Ezekiel's head, and with one movement, ripped it from his shoulders. The creature flew toward the ceiling, cradling the head in its arms and raining blood upon everything below. Ezekiel's body stood motionless for a moment before crumpling to the floor in a heap.

Ugly Babies

The thing shrieked and bit into Ezekiel's head with razor sharp fangs before flying up the chimney and out into the surrounding woods. Everyone's gaze moved from the decapitated body to the chimney and back again. Some of the younger children cried while the others simply looked on in shock. Hazel clutched her torn gown to her bosom and gently rocked back and forth with her arms draped over her knees. Tears fell from her face to the blood soaked floor.

Alda Mae sat back down in her rocking chair and looked at the carnage in the small cabin. A shriek of laughter tore from her lips as she turned her attention to the chimney and hoped her son would come home soon.

Triplica by Ryan Rice

Matt Kurtz
Teddy

"Sissy," Rachel said, barreling toward the dark attic doorway.

An opened padlock lay on the carpet beside the entrance. She raced past it then up the creaky stairs, taking three at a time.

Reaching the landing, she stumbled into the large, shadowy space, finding the four-year-old under the room's single light source—a 60 watt bulb, half-covered by a metal dome, attached to a cord that stretched up into the black void above the rafters. The lighting appeared straight out of a police interrogation scene from an old noir film. Only instead of a two-bit hood sweating it out under the strong light, a cute little girl was sitting on the floor, Indian style, with her back to Rachel. A ring of padlock keys sat on the ground a few feet away.

Catching her breath, Rachel stepped forward, the floorboards squeaking under the slight weight of each step. "You're in big trouble, missy."

Sissy ignored her. She sat motionless, stiff as a board, gazing at the teddy bear that lay on the dusty ground just outside the light's perimeter. The little girl's pale complexion and blonde hair were bleached white from the harsh glow. As if snapping from a trance, she suddenly spun and locked eyes with her new babysitter. "I'm tellin' Daddy that you scared Teddy."

Rachel's glance shifted from the girl to the teddy bear lying in the shadows. Instead of scolding the child, possibly upsetting the girl enough that she'd tattle the incident to her father, Rachel tried a softer approach. She crouched beside the girl. "I'm sure your daddy is gonna already be upset with me if he knew we were up here. This isn't a play area. It can be very dangerous."

"Don't be silly. Teddy's here. He won't let anything bad happen to me."

Rachel looked back at the bear lying on the floor's thin layer of undisturbed dust. The stuffed animal's plush back kissed the wall of darkness that stretched deep into the murky attic. "Well, here's an idea. How 'bout we bring Teddy downstairs with us? So you two don't have to play up here anymore?"

Sissy shook her head. "Don't be silly. Teddy always stays here. He likes the dark."

Rachel glanced around the shadowy attic—at the ghostly outlines of sheet-draped furniture and stacks of boxes just beyond the safety of the bright light. A cold chill raced up her spine and exploded along her scalp, eliciting a hearty shiver.

She slid closer to the child and gently grabbed her hand. "C'mon, kiddo. Let's get back downstairs, okay? Please?"

Twenty minutes earlier, Rachel had been on the phone, comparing notes for an upcoming Trigonometry test. She looked up and found Sissy gone, her Crayons and coloring books still spread across the plush carpet in front of the glowing television screen.

Quickly hanging up the phone, she tossed aside her spiral notebook, sprung to her feet, and scanned the large living room, finding no sign of the girl. Her gut twisted at the notion that the child could be *anywhere* within the large house.

"Sissy?"

Only the faint voices on the television responded.

Rachel snatched the remote and shut it off: "Sissy?!"

Nothing.

She stood frozen. If this were a game of hide and seek, should she just ignore it and wait for Sissy to return after growing tired of waiting?

No. Because what if it weren't a game, what if she wandered off and, God forbid, had gotten hurt?

It might put a real crimp in her (fledgling) babysitting career if Mr. Murlock returned early from his business engagement and found Rachel clueless as to his daughter's whereabouts. So the other option was to play along and search the house—which also seemed unwise since Murlock had given her strict instructions to remain on the lower floor of the three-story home at all times. The upper levels were off limits. He was so adamant about the demand that, at Sissy's bedtime, the little girl was to fall asleep on the living room couch rather than being brought to her room on the second floor. Only Murlock was to put the child to bed upon his return home.

Rachel really didn't want to have to disobey such a simple request, but if it meant doing so to find the missing girl, then so be it. Murlock seemed no-nonsense from their first meeting—one set up after she answered an online ad for a sitter—but he still seemed like a sensible man. She hoped he'd understand that she wasn't being insubordinate, but that his daughter had left Rachel no choice.

Rachel exited the room, walking past the hallway table lined with pictures of Murlock, Sissy, and Murlock's wife, Amanda.

Upon her job interview, Rachel was a little weary of meeting at Murlock's home, especially when informed that Mrs. Murlock wouldn't be attending. What if he was some rich pervert that didn't actually have a wife and child and was only trying to get young girls alone at this house?

But her apprehension became short-lived when Sissy answered the front door. And more so when Murlock informed her that he was a widower, his wife having passed away from a tragic accident three years prior. Rachel saw a hint of sadness that still lingered in his eyes whenever he mentioned Amanda's name. Whatever happened to her, *his* wounds had yet to heal.

Mr. Murlock and Sissy seemed like good people. She was really hoping the job could become something lucrative, maybe a weekly gig if she continued to earn Murlock's trust. And if so, she'd put whatever money she earned toward her freshman year of college, with the hopes of becoming the first in her family to get a degree.

Of course, Rachel had to find Sissy first. And the longer she went without doing so, the better the chances of the child informing her father how little his new sitter really sat for him.

She quickly brushed aside the guilt over any invasion of privacy and checked every cabinet, room, and closet on the first floor before pausing in the lobby. She stared up the long flight of hardwood stairs to the second story's dark landing.

"Sissy!"

A floorboard creaked somewhere above.

"Sissy, this isn't funny! Get down here, right now!"

Soft footsteps padded across the ceiling.

Rachel sighed. She *had* to go upstairs in order to get the girl. What would look worse? Being a babysitter incapable of watching a four-year-old? Or one that's willing to break a rule for the welfare of a child?

Rachel slowly ascended the steps.

The second floor was murky. She felt for a light switch and found it on the far wall.

The hall lit up, revealing a long stretch with three doors to each side. She went to the closest one, reached for its brass knob, and paused.

What if there was some sort of individual alarm on it? If she tripped it, Murlock would surely know she'd been trespassing.

Ugly Babies

But, technically, she'd *already* accomplished such violation just by climbing the stairs.

She twisted the knob. The door creaked open, the hall light spilling into the room--a guest bedroom. Rachel quickly checked under the bed and in the near empty closet then moved to the other rooms; another guest room, a small office, a bathroom . . . And Sissy's room. All void of one impish little girl (that was going to be in big time trouble once found).

The final room at the end of the hall was a nursery. The walls painted blue. Except for the thin layer of dust coating everything, the crib and other furniture still appeared new. Never used. Rachel found it odd since Murlock only had a daughter. The room looked like it was somehow frozen in time...and rightfully so, with the calendar on the wall that hadn't been changed in over three years.

Returning to the hall, she heard a little girl's giggle echoing from the third floor.

Then the jingle of keys floated, and the creak of a door.

"Sissy, Get down here this instant!"

Rachel didn't wait for a response. She bolted ahead, whipping around the corner and up the next flight of stairs. She stopped on the landing and stared down a corridor of black. Finding the closest light switch, she flipped it and a pair of wall mounted lamps erased the darkness, revealing a heavy wooden door at the end of the hall.

With a sprung padlock on the ground beside it, the door was wide open...inviting her in. A set of stairs inside led upwards and dissolved into shadows. It was the attic, a place where little children are certain to get hurt if left unattended.

Heart already drumming in her chest, Rachel sprinted down the hallway toward the opening, terrified the child might be up there, injured and bleeding.

"I don't want to go downstairs," Sissy said. "I wanna stay here and play with Teddy."

Rachel scanned the darkness beyond the overhead light and squeezed the little girl's hand tight. "Fine, you can play with Teddy. But downstairs," she told the child. "Or if you want, we can color in you coloring books together. Just you and I--would you like that?"

Sissy shrugged. Not interested. The child stayed put, only staring into the gloom ahead.

"Hey, Sissy," Rachel said, trying to get the girl's attention. She squeezed her little hand again. "Sissy..."

The child ignored her sitter.

Rachel rolled her eyes. Didn't take long for the brat to emerge, huh? Rachel stepped in front of the girl and knelt, forcing Sissy to look at her. Putting her back to the darkness, something in Rachel's gut squirmed, demanding she check over her shoulder. She saw nothing except the teddy bear on the floor. She returned her attention to the girl, hoping to convince her to leave so they could get the hell out of the spooky place.

"Then...how about...hmmmm...how about some ice cream?" Rachel said.

Sissy's eyes lit up; "With chocolate syrup and sprinkles?"

Rachel didn't know exactly what was in the stocked pantry, but she felt confident they'd have all the staples of a typical sundae. "Sure, whatever you want."

Sissy squealed in excitement, sprung up, and ran for the stairs.

So that's what it took to get the kid to move . . . fattening frozen ice cream and high-fructose corn syrup?

Rachel leaned over and snatched the key ring off the floor. She'd have Sissy show her where she got it and return them before any ice cream was removed from the freezer. Now what she was going to tell Mr. Murlock about going upstairs was still completely up in the air. She'd be foolish to try to act like it never happened because, not only was a four-year old incapable of keeping a secret, but her and Sissy's footprints were all over the attic floor. It was obvious that they were the first ones to disturb the coating of dust in quite some time.

"If I'm gonna get ice cream," Sissy said, twirling with joy on the landing. "Then Teddy wants to eat too."

Her back to the girl, Rachel stooped to pick up the bear. "I know, sweetheart. So what's Teddy's favorite flavor?"

"Oh, he doesn't like ice cream."

"Sure he does." Rachel said. She held the bear to her ear and nodded. "Okay, Teddy. He just told me he wants whatever you're having."

Sissy looked confused as Rachel walked toward her.

"That's not Teddy, silly," she said, nodding at the stuffed animal. "That's BoBo." She pointed at the darkness above, somewhere within the rafters. "*That's* Teddy. Up there."

A guttural growl sounded from overhead.

Rachel stopped dead in her tracks, under the lamp. Her eyes clicked upwards and immediately winced from the bulb's white hot brilliance that blinded her from whatever Sissy was pointing at.

Something dripped onto her.

Hot. Stringy. Clear.

Rachel had only a moment to register that it was saliva running down the front of her shirt before a deafening roar was unleashed and an elongated hand shot down. Spindly, quadruple-jointed fingers throttled her, completely engulfing her neck like a constrictor. Clawing at the deformed hand, Rachel's bulging eyes locked with Sissy.

The little girl stood frozen. Not in fear. But admiration.

A split second later, Rachel was viciously yanked upwards, disappearing into the shadowy rafters. One of her shoes flew loose and landed on the attic floor with a loud clunk.

Sissy squinted and tried to see what exactly was taking place in the gloom above. But only the wet sounds of flesh tearing and bones snapping could be heard.

Sissy waited for a long moment.

Then something was tossed out of the dark, sliding across the wooden floor with a metallic jingle, and stopping at Sissy's tiny socked feet.

She stooped and picked up the ring with the padlock keys. Sissy looked up into the darkness once more, still unable to see much of anything.

"Bye-bye, Teddy." She playfully waved then turned and carefully descended the stairs.

Padlocking the attic door, she placed the key ring back in its secret place within her parents' room. She hoped Daddy wouldn't get mad at her again for feeding her younger—but much, *much* larger—brother, Teddy.

After all, losing another sitter might lead to the discovery of the family's dark little secret, one that originated when a monstrous baby boy tore his way out of his mother's belly over three years ago.

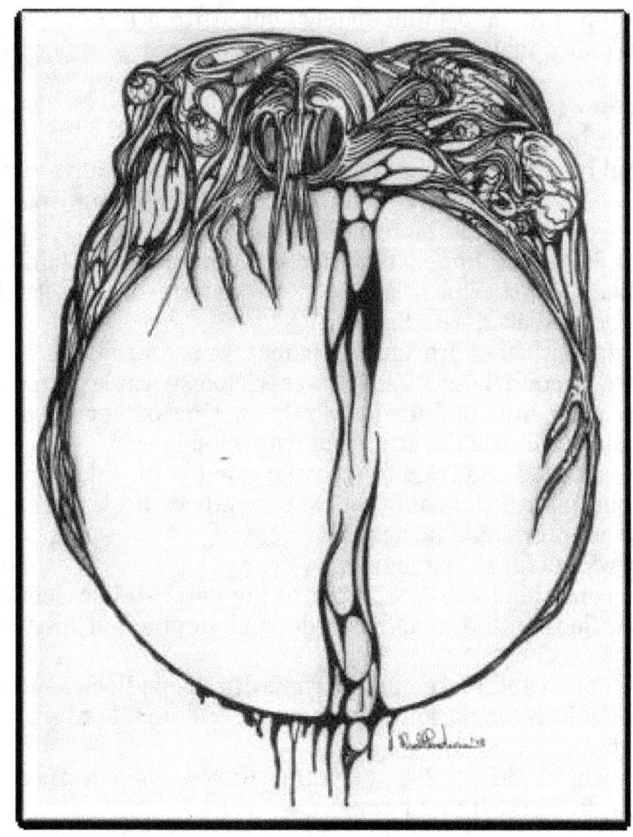

Cancer by Niall Parkinson

Dan Dillard
Henrietta's Skirt

Henrietta, or "Hen" to her friends, was beside herself. The thought of having a child, her first precious angel, made her cheeks pull taught into a smile so bright, Santa Claus his own self would've hired her to guide the sleigh. Those were her words. She was smitten. Most mothers, if I might be so bold, were smitten with their unborn children. The difference in what those mothers knew versus what Hen knew was that they would continue to be smitten once the little mugwumps entered the world.

Her pregnancy was perfect. No morning sickness, no gas, none of the unpleasantness she'd read about. Just a healthy baby filling up her belly and pushing it out in front of her into a "bump" that people seemed to gravitate toward...as if she had grown so large, she had her own gravity. Hen was tall, a big girl from the beginning when she'd entered the world, and carrying the extra pounds was no problem for her. She glowed, as the saying goes and when the baby kicked and rolled inside her, she invited people to feel its progress.

She craved the attention, as no one had ever paid her any. Her parents treated her as a nuisance due to her height, her awkwardness, and a face more suited to a pig--or maybe a boxer with a losing record. She'd never had friends, and dates were things she learned about in history class. The bun in her oven was a mistake. A trick played on her by three rude college boys who had gotten her drunk and used her for *their* perverted pleasure on *her* eighteenth birthday.

"But I love you," one had said; the one with the coal-black hair and icy blue eyes. He was a smooth talker. Could've talked any girl out of her panties, but Hen, had he just asked, would've agreed. She wanted to be a momma more than anything in the world. She let it happen with all three of them. The handsome one, the funny one, and even the one that was a little chubby and ignorant. He looked at her like he really did like her, not like she was just an experiment in one human's ability to overtake another. He even smiled at her when it was over and said, "Thank you." A gentleman rapist to the end, it seemed.

She was fine with that...had learned to live with it, and even though she knew she would never see those boys again, she wanted that child. When the news came that she was pregnant, she celebrated. Hen preferred it that way. It was her baby, no matter which one the father was and there was to be no sharing.

Her own father was no consequence to her, especially since her mother had died. He drank his home-made mash and sat on the porch watching the world go by, and Hen got him to and from his bed and the bathroom when he needed it. He never spoke more than a grunt or a groan to her, and she kept things clinical as far as he was concerned. He never mentioned her belly or showed any interest in a grandchild. It didn't surprise Hen, as he didn't show much interest in his own child either.

The pregnancy being perfect didn't keep her from wondering about what happened after the birth. After the child came into the world and grew up and had to live life. That's where things went horribly wrong for her. She was a simple farm girl. She didn't need much. The baby, her son or daughter, might want more from life. He or she might want and be disappointed. He or she might be ugly, just like Hen. She couldn't take that thought. She would love the child beyond love, but what others did or said could not be prevented.

When she missed her second appointment with her doctor, he called her.

"Hen, what's going on? Are you feeling well?" he asked.

"Better'n ever," she said. And she meant it. Her smile was as wide and bright as ever.

"Good, good. It's just that you're entering your third trimester, dear, and we haven't seen you for a checkup in...well, in a while. Can you come in?"

"Nope. Doin' fine, doc. I'll call you if I need help."

After that statement, she hung up. He didn't call back. Hen was content, and she had a plan. Misguided as it may have been, her plan was to keep the baby, and to keep it inside her body forever. That way, she would keep the happy attention of strangers, the good feeling of growing her little miracle, and that little miracle would remain safe within his mother's womb. What safer place was there on God's green earth?

It took her several weeks to do the research and decide on the dosage of tocolytic meds to inject into her system. Living on the farm made it a bit easier to come by the Clenbuterol—something her father and the vet had used to calm the labor in one of their cows. The leftover container was out in the barn and was still within the use by date on the label. She figured a per-pound equation and applied it to her own weight. There was enough for several doses.

The baby grew at an alarming rate toward the end of the pregnancy, they all did. She'd named it Robert after her own father and began treating it as a boy. When the first contractions came, she shot up and out of bed and into her bathroom.

"Don't be too late," she said, sweating and fretting. Her face was drawn into a childish look of concern. She pulled the syringe from the cabinet and drew out the number of cc's she had calculated and shot herself with the Clenbuterol. It wasn't long before her body relaxed and she was able to go back to sleep.

"Bed rest for me," she said as she crawled into bed, rubbing her growing stomach.

It continued on that way for weeks. She developed a cocktail of vitamins and meds that she subjected herself to in order to keep little Robert healthy and tucked away where he belonged. She moved only when absolutely necessary, and as far as she knew, her father still went about his business of drinking himself to death on their front porch. He never once checked in on her.

In her thirteenth and fourteenth months of pregnancy, she started to wither. The child inside was growing and draining her of nutrients and she could no longer replace them fast enough. She stayed exhausted, dehydrated, and the meds were no longer helping. In month fifteen, even the Clenbuterol stopped working. She was running out either way, and the injection points on her body were bruising and infected. When the contractions hit, they were like being kicked from the inside by a mule.

"So strong," she said with a pained smile.

She rubbed her belly with love for her child, but her life was fading. The parasite in her body had taken its toll, had exceeded its welcome and was ready to come out. Hen died that evening of internal bleeding and of malnutrition.

Robert continued to kick, to punch, to roll. There was no way he would exit from the intended orifice. No way to survive inside the dead meat sack that was once his loving mother. His undulations became more violent.

It was Hen's father who called 911. He babbled something insane into the phone that the operator couldn't interpret. The poor woman sent a police cruiser and ambulance to the address that matched the phone number and told them she had no information about what to expect. What they found wouldn't have fit any sane description.

Hen's father was dead, his heart seized and he fell face first into the floor of Hen's bedroom. The floor was spattered with blood, and on the bed sat Robert, breathing on his own. He had busted through his mother's abdominal wall and gotten his upper body free, and he leaned there, cradled in the recess of her ribcage, helpless and covered in an unmentionable film of dried gruel. Hen's body lay in a bundle, propping the child into a sitting position, his legs still inside, and he wore her like a skirt.

Michael Faun
The Boy at Ruby Lester's

Dr. Tipton stared at Vera's gravid belly like someone watching a comet heading toward the crust of the earth. Vera, of course, didn't notice the female doctor's concerned face; not with all the painkillers she was under the influence of at the moment; mere minutes away from delivery. Only thing Vera saw, was candy-colored scenes of herself lying on a blanket in the park; holding her cooing baby up toward a sunny blue sky.

Dr. Tipton was walking back and forth, biting her long fingernails, when the door to the examination room suddenly swung open and a nurse entered.

"Is Sanchez ready yet?" the petite redhead nurse said while glancing at Vera's journal.

"No...Actually, I must call Doctor Marantz and get his opinion." Dr. Tipton noticed her hand was trembling as she picked up her phone from the pocket of her white uniform.

The redheaded nurse furrowed her brows. "Oh? Are there any complications—Dear Lord!" she stepped away from Vera; hands covering her pinkish mouth.

They exchanged concerned and slightly disgusted looks.

Dr. Tipton then started out of the room while the nurse stood frozen, watching Vera's naked belly. She could hear Dr. Tipton's strained orders from the corridor.

"Get Doctor Marantz and prepare for acute C-section. No, I don't know. Never seen anything like this before..."

The redheaded nurse staggered into the toilet and threw up.

Vera awoke to what felt like a nightmare. There were screams, sounding like several infants, and blood--Lots of blood. Through the blending white light from the huge lamp above her, she saw the green-clad surgeons surrounding her sides; homogeneous and anonymous; their narrowed eyes bristling with horror.

What is wrong? Vera thought. Or did she say it aloud?

"She's awake; someone put her back to sleep!" The surgeon's voice sounded stern and far away. In the corner of her eye, Vera noticed a dark shadow approaching her. A sudden sting and her consciousness dwindled away again.

The last thing she registered was how bloody flesh and matted hair was being pulled out of her womb.

One Year Post Birth

Vera's forced smile reminded of cracked porcelain. She was sitting in a bamboo rattan chair, smoking a menthol while watching her toddler Rex crawling around, drooling on the living room floor. The ashtray was brimming with menthols.

Rex had proved an unusual child already from the delivery. There had been complications, life threatening ones, which had forced them to stay quite a while at Saint Joseph Memorial. Actually, they had even gotten their own room; like a tiny apartment. Frank had abandoned them after only a month inside that bizarre place. Said he couldn't stand it anymore. Couldn't stand the tiny stove; couldn't stand the tiny painted fake windows; the tiny furniture or the tiny bathtub. But worst of all—he couldn't stand their own little Rex.

"Poor little Rex," Vera drove the menthol cigarette hard into the ashtray tower and picked him up; smelling his head. "At least it's you and me, and your little friend, what's her name again sweetie?" Vera giggled and muzzled him.

"Fnoghla," Rex bubbled.

He smelt so innocent and pure. Vera couldn't understand how people could be so mean; laughing at her as she took little Rex in the stroller to the park. Only to come back to find somebody had painted the words: Satan's Witch!!! over the house with red dripping paint. It was the three exclamations that hurt the most.

One should've done the job, Vera thought, and sadly glanced down at Rex, who was sleeping so peacefully in the stroller. Perhaps she was a witch after all. That would make Frank Satan, which made sense. On that note she went inside, feeling the neighbors gloat behind her back.

Vera had already made her decision. She only wondered how mental preparation she'd need for it.

Mirrors

Rex was born on a beautiful winter's day. It was a Tuesday, Vera recalled, and the first snow was covering the streets and treetops outside the frosted hospital window. Imprisoned with Rex, sitting in the bamboo rattan, building menthol pyramids had become her ritual while watching Rex play and develop. Lately, Rex only communicated with mirrors—Vera wondered if this behavior was healthy. Probably not.

Three years had passed since that Tuesday, and it had taken Vera three years to muster up enough courage to take the necessary actions. The harassment from the outside world had become quite unbearable. Grocery shopping had to be done after dark.

Vera was beginning to break. Her heart felt like nothing but a big black mollusk. Not long now, till everything should change; turn the blackness into something good.

Or, would it only pulverize everything to a pile of soot? Vera jumped as the doorbell rang.

Rex watched as his mother rose from her chair, her heels clicking as she paced toward the door. Just before opening it, she gave him a strange look. She reminded him of the flowers he used to see through the barred window. The wilted ones. Not like Finola, his best friend, who smiled at him each and every day, with that cute round face and big blue watery eyes that never blinked or strayed away. Finola who lived in the mirrors.

Mumblings sounded from the threshold. Dark and light voices whispering. The bright sun that was leaking through the shutters turned the furniture inside into inanimate twisted shadows. Then came a moving, looming one.

Rex's reptile brain picked up danger. Even Finola could sense the hostility that was growing; radiating from the black-booted, giant man that entered the door and came tramping toward them with arms outstretched; leaving muddy stains on the hard wood floor. Rex got on his feet and tried to run. But the sinister man, with a face covered in white furry hairs, managed to catch him with his large hands; snickering while holding him aloft and inspecting him. Finola tried to bite off the ear of the ugly man.

Thrashing about, Rex desperately called for his mom, who was nowhere in sight, as the hairy giant headed back and out through the door, with Rex in a steady lock under his meat-stinking arm. The last thing Rex smelled, saw, and heard, was a cloud of menthol incensed smoke pouring out from the yellow-red-striped kitchen door, which was ajar, and a sad sniffling sounding behind it...

Inside the cramped backstage room, Rex was getting ready. He could hear the drunken audience outside laughing and roaring as the three-legged woman was tap dancing and making a fool of herself to please the crowd. Rex had gotten used to it. He'd been working the night shows at Ruby Lester's for nearly two years now—since he was three. At least, Lester had told him so. Memories were vague from that time. He could recall large smoldering pyramids and gray surroundings. A smelly mouth, seldom smiling and a warm voice, flecked with sadness. That was all.

"You think I look old?" he whispered to Finola, who giggled in return.

Rex sipped on a fizzy lemon beverage from a straw and looked deeply into the cracked mirror in front of him. The lamps encircling it produced a strong glow, casting horrible shadows on the wall behind him. As if big round spiders were sitting there staring at him with vicious smirks.

"*And now, ladies and gentlemen!*" the announcer said outside and the crowd turned silent with expectation. The air was electric. Only seconds left now. Rex placed a hand on Finola's bulbous head, caressing the throbbing veins of her temples that were raging as they always did right before a show.

"It's show time now. Love you, see you on the other side." Rex kissed Finola and stood up. The smirking wall-spiders scuttled toward the ceiling.

Finola shed a single tear.

A drum roll started and then the announcer's ghastly voice continued, "*Let me present to you...Rex, The Boy With The Human-Shaped Face Tumor!*"

Rex wiped Finola's tear off his cheek and stepped into the dazzling lights onstage.

Essel Pratt
Immaculate Deception

Between the old dime store and new hipster café, a narrow alleyway muffled the helpless cries of an infant. Rain beat down on the dumpsters that lined the south side of the corridor, nearly drowning out the screams. Passersby were in too much of a hurry to listen to the shrieks, even if they heard them. Tanya was no different. As always, five o'clock came and the world around them disappeared from their peripheral sight as they rushed to get home and leave their jobs far behind them.

Tanya had not expected the chilly downpour and left her jacket and umbrella at home. The showers were an unexpected inconvenience on the fall afternoon and interrupted the early evening rush as the local businesses closed for the weekend. Her pace was much slower than the rest, as she walked the two blocks to the parking garage. She had no big plans for the weekend, but hoped the chilled rain didn't invite a cold into her otherwise healthy physique.

As she approached the alleyway, her left heel wedged in a sidewalk crack and snapped off. She stumbled, but caught herself on the cornice of the dime store. She cursed and broke the heel off of her right shoe by hitting it against the building. Slipping the shoe back on, cursed again, and shoved both broken heels into her large purse.

Before continuing on, she heard the cries from the alleyway. She had little experience with children and thought, at first, that it might have been a cat. She decided to check anyway. A broken wood fence, about waist high, created an unwelcome obstacle for her wiry frame. Hiking up her tight pencil skirt to miniskirt height, she straddled the planks and hoped that she would avoid a splinter to her nether regions. It took some wiggling, but she made it over unscathed.

The north to south facing corridor only allowed a little of the fading light to enter. Before searching for the source of the cries, Tanya allowed her eyes to adjust. Looking around, she found that a few forgotten dumpsters were accompanied by an array of weeds that had emerged from between the decaying red brick pavement.

She tried to pinpoint the location of the screams, finally settling on a dumpster toward the middle of the alley. Overgrown weeds stood diligently, guarding access the bin, showing no signs of a recent invasion by the person that heartlessly disposed of the helpless child.

The screams echoed within, making it impossible to pinpoint the child's exact whereabouts. Growing impatient, she rummaged through her purse for her smartphone. As always, it was buried at the bottom under the many unimportant items that she had stuffed in there. She turned on her flashlight app and pointed it into the dumpster. The bags of refuse within had obviously been there a while. Thick layers of dust covered most of the contents, however an incongruous burlap sack moved slightly within, revealing the hidden child.

Tanya pulled an old milk crate in front of the dumpster and used it to gain height so she could reach the child's forsaken confine. The unnatural contour of her broken shoes made it difficult to balance, but with some work she was able to grasp the sack and pull it free.

Tanya took shelter under an awning to shield her from the rain so she could focus on freeing the baby from the burlap sack. She struggled with the taught knot but her fingers were numb from the cold. Finally loosening the knot, she pulled open the sack to reveal the infant within. The baby boy didn't seem much older than a few days, although that was only a guess since she hadn't seen a newborn baby since her junior high sex education class. His skin was red from crying, and his eyes were bloodshot to match.

She held him tight to her chest, hoping to comfort his screams. It seemed to work as his little head rested gently upon her left breast, cooing to the sound of her beating heart. He seemed to doze off for a second, or two. She decided it would be best to get out to the street and find a warm spot inside the café. Maybe someone inside would have some formula to share until the police arrived. Of course, getting out would be no easy chore. She barely made it in by herself. Carrying a baby and trying to jump the small fence could be disastrous. Regardless, she felt that waiting for the rain to slow down a bit would be for the best.

Completely naked, the baby instinctively snuggled close to her chest for warmth. His hunger drew him toward her breast where he tried to suckle. Tanya was not comfortable with the child's advances, so she decided to rock him to sleep. She attempted to stand up and pace while she rocked him, but her broken heels slipped on the moist bricks, causing her to fall hard to the ground. Effervescent pains rushed through her head as it slammed against the bricks. The impact did not knock her unconscious, but she did see stars for a few seconds. Despite the hard hit, she held on tight to the infant and cradled him upon her stomach.

Tanya's head was dizzy, so she decided to remain in the lying position until it settled. It was no use endangering the infant any more than she had already. The baby cuddled tummy to tummy as she rubbed his back with her soft hands. He kneaded her belly like a cat does when it is trying to get comfortable; she smiled a little at the feeling and thought that she could get used to it.

The child's sharp fingernails dug into her toned belly; it was uncomfortable so she repositioned him to a more suitable position. He immediately began clawing at her stomach again. She tried to sit up, but vertigo took hold, forcing her to lie back down. Meanwhile, the child's assault on her abs was brutal. His fingernails clawed at her, despite further attempts to reposition him. His grasp upon her was becoming excruciating to the point that she could no longer bear it.

She called out for help, but no one on the empty street heard her. Using all her strength, she tried to push the child away from her exposed flesh but he held on tighter and dug in deeper. Her cries of agony did little to ease the pain as the infant tore open her flesh, ripping through the skin and muscle. When the hole was cavernous enough, the baby forced his way into the warmth of her exposed womb. The screams summoned by her reverse cesarean had rendered her voice nonexistent. Tanya soon passed out from the pain.

She awoke upon the moist ground with a horrible headache, feeling as though she spent the night out throwing back shots of tequila with strangers. The sun's rays did little to ease her discomfort; her stomach ached just as much as her head. Afraid to look at the mangled mess that the infant made of her gut, she opted to extend her arm down toward the scene of last night's attack. Flinging the burlap sack to the side, she did not feel the wounds or the dried blood that she had expected. Instead, her rounded stomach was as smooth as a baby's bottom.

She sat up carefully and stared at her noticeably pregnant belly, then shouted for help until her voice was raw.

But no answers came from the barren weekend streets.

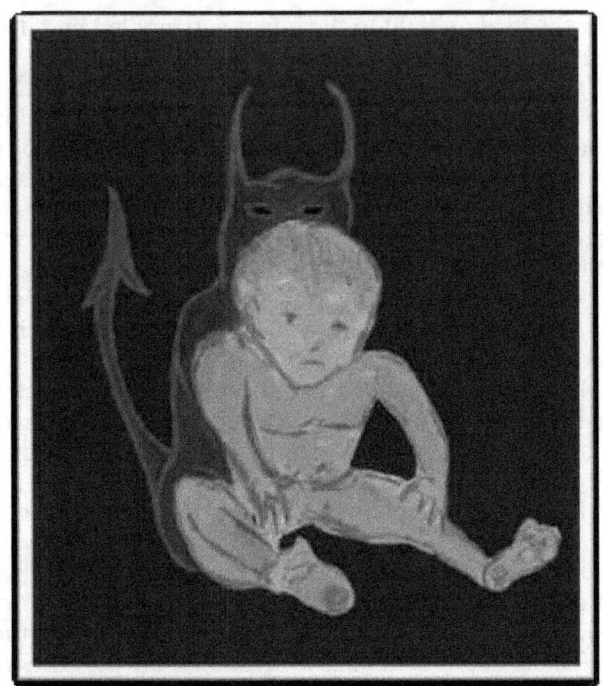

The Devil's Child by Essel Pratt

DJ Tyrer
The Swelling

The members of the Burgen family were all surprised to see Mary's belly swell in the manner of her namesake. Father had thought he'd kept a close eye on his youngest daughter and all her brothers disavowed any knowledge of a boyfriend, her sisters likewise. And, when confronted, the girl herself denied that any boy or man had had his way with her, even when Father promised to expunge her shame with a wedding at the point of a shotgun.

"I ain't done let any man have his way with me," she staunchly denied, again and again.

"Then, how's it yer pregnant, gal?" her Father demanded.

"The Spirit of the Lord done entered into me, Paw," she replied, to his disgust.

"Don't yer dare blaspheme, gal!"

"But, Paw, is true! Not the Lord as they teach about him in Church on Sunday, though, but the Lord of the Dark Cavern, in the hills."

"The dark cavern in the hills?" he asked, perplexed.

"Yer know, up the trail past the waterfall; the cave the Injuns done call the Womb of the Earth."

Realization dawned. He knew the place. The cavern was cursed, according to the pioneer lore passed down through the generations and said to be a haunt of witches and monsters. Nobody with any sense would approach it. Why had his daughter?

"I done went there with the Injun gal from the Reservation I met at school, Zita. She taught me the chants and the prayers that her people used to call upon the Lord of the Dark Cavern, the God who mated with the Earth and impregnated her womb with the ancestors of mankind.

"Blasphemy!" roared Father, but his daughter gazed back at him, unperturbed.

"Is not blasphemy, Paw, is truth! I made the prayers and chants and call up the Lord, all black and fluid, and let him enter into me and give me a baby."

Father didn't want to believe her crazy story, yet he could hardly deny the swelling of her belly, which continued to grow as the days lengthened through Summer then began to decline again; nor could he deny her sincerity: looking into his child's eyes, he could see that she believed what she said. He went to the Sheriff, of course, but didn't dare tell him such a wild story and, without suspects to suggest, there was little the Sheriff could do.

"I done talked to that Injun gal yer mentioned," he told Father, 'n' she denies ev'rything. She's the perfect picture of wide-eyed innocence."

That was the best he could get, leaving the Burgen patriarch and the rest of the family to accept that Mary was 'spectin' with no father for the child anywhere on the horizon. They kept her away from town to hide their shame and just hoped it would all soon be over. But, such a hope was a forlorn one, for her belly continued to swell, bloating to obscene proportions far beyond the usual human capacity, leading her Father to comment that she was "the size of a cow!"

It wasn't just her enormous size that shocked and revolted her family, though. What was worse was the way in which her belly would seem to pulse or throb in the manner of ripples in a watery custard, and the peculiar and nauseating manner in which lumps would push out for several inches from the mound of her belly as if the baby were attempting to reach out to observers.

"Oh—oh—oh—that is *not* right!" exclaimed her Father as the baby in her belly reached out toward him. "I think I'm gonna be sick!"

The birth itself was horrendous, an auto-caesarean ill-timed for a visit to the farm by the Pastor, who'd come to enquire regarding odd rumors that were circulating through the county. The child pressed with vigor against the flesh, eager to escape the womb, bursting forth in a fountain of blood and viscera that sent the Pastor, attracted by the terrified, pained shrieks, into an apoplectic fit from which he never fully recovered.

Freed from the confines, however generous, of Mary's womb, the baby perched upon the ragged ledge of her ribcage as she wheezed her final breath, spread its wings and let out a hacking cough of a cry.

"It's disgusting!" Father said, recoiling.

"Horrible!" Mother shrieked, vomiting.

Their grandchild was the color and texture of tar with a barely-featured face and wings a little like those of a bat. Ropey limbs reached out imploringly toward them as if seeking the comfort of a grandparent's loving hug, but found no such response in them. Instead, Mary's Father ran to his gun cabinet and returned with a shotgun that he used to blast the hideous little thing in a manner that surely would have had childcare experts reeling in shock, before dropping the gun as realization struck as to what he had

---

done. As violent as the discharge was, the pellets that tore through the tar baby had no more than a momentary effect, the strange plastic flesh just reforming behind them as if no shot had been fired. The baby seemed to give a shrug as if offended at the shot, spread its wings further still and took flight, smashing through a window and sweeping off into the night.

Silence fell and it was all over for a moment. Had it not been for Mary's shattered corpse and the gibbering Pastor, they might have imagined it had all been a bad dream. The cleaning up would be neither easy nor pleasant, and there would be many awkward questions for which the family would have to invent answers.

But, it didn't end there, for the family's cattle and the cattle of their neighbors began to be the subjects of vicious attacks that left them with ragged wounds marred with dabs of a black, tarry substance that soon evaporated away into nothing. The peculiar mutilations were the subject of much discussion and controversy locally, with a coven of Satanists receiving the bulk of the blame. Only Mr. Burgen understood what it meant, that his unnatural grandchild remained at large in the vicinity; it was his guess that it had found sanctuary in the place where it had been conceived.

Slowly, wearily, fearfully, the Burgen patriarch made his way up the trail past the waterfall to the cave known to the natives of the region as the Womb of the Earth. The cave was dark and dank with walls that were black with a liquid sheen to them that reminded him of tar. Somewhere in here roosted his prey, his very flesh.

At last, he saw it, dangling from the ceiling roof of the cave like a hybrid of roosting bat and pulled taffy, slick and alien in texture. He looked to his hand, which grasped a Molotov cocktail and fumbled for a lighter with which to light the wick. But, a certain compassion stayed his hand. This was his grandchild, after all, no matter how vile and disgusting and, yes, unnatural it seemed. He just couldn't bring himself to set it alight.

Hanging his head in shame, he tossed the bomb aside and turned and fled the cave with tears in his eyes, knowing that the horror would continue to haunt the area and torment cattle. But, no matter how great the evil and no matter how unnatural the form, there was no way in which he could harm it. It was his flesh and, after all, it was only a baby.

R.T. Tandy
Tender

Joe walked into the darkened hallway of his apartment and numbly closed the door. Placing his keys on the small table he made his way into the living room and sank down into a chair, his eyes staring unseeingly into the distance.

Reaching up to his throat he loosened the tie around his neck, grateful for the relief from the uncomfortable closeness of the fabric, before slipping it over his head and throwing it onto the seat beside him. Inside his jacket pocket his phone burst into life for what felt like the hundredth time that night but he ignored it, knowing that it was likely to be another friend checking on him or, even worse, congratulating him.

Suddenly he stood up and began pacing the small room, his mind too frenzied to allow him to sit still. He laughed bitterly to himself as he moved, convinced that he must be the first man in the world to feel terrible at being found not guilty by a jury. He walked into the kitchen, flicking on a light for the first time since coming home, and turned the coffee machine on. As it began to percolate he eased himself down onto the cold tiled floor, his back resting against the kitchen units.

At the time of accident he'd been only just graduated from college, and was working as a barman at a local pool hall while he saved enough money to go travelling. With his hand on the bible he'd recounted for the court how he'd been travelling home that night when the brakes on his elderly Camaro had failed as he'd approached the intersection. Frantically he'd tried to steer toward the ditch on the side of the road but the road surface had been slick with an earlier rainfall, and he'd been powerless to stop the car as it shot across the junction and ploughed side on into another vehicle.

When he'd finally come around a few days later he'd found himself in a hospital bed, severely bruised but otherwise fine. His parents had been there waiting for him, and such was their relief it was several minutes he had been able to ask about the other car. He could still recall the silence with which his father had greeted his question, and although he had to ask him several times before he would tell him the haunted look in his eyes had confirmed Joe's worse fears long before he finally spoke.

The passengers were a young family returning from visiting relatives up state. Of the three people in the car at the time only the mother survived, although she'd been rushed into the intensive care unit and her condition was still listed as critical. The father, who had been driving the car, died instantly along with the couple's three month old daughter. Once his father had finished speaking Joe had only just managed to turn his head over the side of the bed before he'd vomited, tears coursing down his bruised face.

The following weeks and months had passed him by like a blur, an accelerated film reel that seemed to flood his vision with colors and words he could not process. Hours of police interviews and meetings with lawyers had flown past in what felt like seconds, and it felt like scarcely days after he'd first woken in the hospital that he was being driven to the courthouse by his anxious parents.

As they filled into the court Joe was surveying the gallery when he caught her eye. She was sat at the back of the room, away from everyone else, and was dressed from head to toe in black, the only splash of color in her appearance the mane of red hair framing her drawn, pale face. He'd learn from news reports and conversation that her name was Maggie, but because of the trial he'd been forbidden from trying to make contact with her.

In the days and weeks since the accident he had longed to apologize to her and to let her know how truly sorry he was, but as their eyes met he knew that no condolence he could offer was ever going to be enough. Her eyes burned into his face with laser intensity, the waves of hatred emanating from her like heat from a log fire. Joe had held her gaze for a second before dropping his head, and he'd kept his eyes fixed on his hands as he'd taken his seat and waited for proceedings to start.

He'd all but known he wasn't going to prison, the evidence clearly in his favour and the expert testimony had soon put pay to any doubts the jury may have had. In fact, the only moment that may have tipped them against him was when Joe himself took to the witness stand.

As he had spoken Joe had longed to convey his own guilt for what had happened to Maggie's husband and little girl. Even though he'd knew there was nothing he could have done, that the accident was due to the tragic failure of a machine, the knowledge that there was the slightest chance he could have done something to avert the accident hung like a great weight around his neck. But his lawyer, a tall rangy man in a cheap suit whose kindly eyes had reminded Joe of a basset hound, had told him to simply stick to the facts.

So Joe followed his advice, his eyes facing downwards for fear of catching Maggie's furious gaze again, and recounted the events in a monotone before returning to his seat. The next day they returned to the court to hear the verdict, and while his family and friends had whooped and cheered as the not guilty decision was delivered Joe felt his heart drop down into his stomach, a remorse hardened ball that seemed to root him to the spot. He'd turned his head toward the back of the courtroom, but only caught a glimpse of black fabric as Maggie exited the room, her back turned to him.

Back in the present Joe reached up with the back of his hand and wiped the tears from his eyes. He'd declined the offer of both a ride home from his parents and a drink with his friends, preferring to walk back to the apartment alone. The idea of celebrating this day was abhorrent to him, and he'd left them staring after him in concern as he walked away.

Joe placed his hand to his mouth, stifling the cry that threatened to escape from his lips. He felt fresh tears form in the corner of his eyes and dropped his head to his chest. Regardless of what the courts said, he knew that it was his fault. That woman would never be able to see her daughter or husband again because of him, and the weight of this knowledge was tearing his soul in two.

Joe dropped his head into his chest and covered his face with his hand, his chest heaving as his sobs filled the otherwise empty house.

The next few weeks seemed to go on forever. He'd been replaced at his old job long before the trial, and although Cal had told him he could come back once he had recovered Joe knew that there was no way he could face the pity and potential anger of the bar's patrons. Even though he had been found not guilty the death of a child always bit deep, and Joe knew there were some who would always hold him responsible. This feeling was made worse by the fact that Joe was inclined to agree with them.

With no reason to leave the house Joe began to withdraw from the outside world. His mobile phone had broken not long after the conclusion of the trial and he hadn't bothered to replace it, seeing no reason to give people another line of communication that he would only ignore. The home phone was left off the hook, and with the curtains drawn and no one answering the door his friends soon began to fall by the wayside, many of them secretly glad they no longer had to socialise with someone who had become such a drag to be around.

Soon Joe had almost completely isolated himself from everyone, his only contact coming from the occasional visit from his parents. Their concern that he was cutting himself off from everyone was valid, but he had no interest in listening to their pleas that he talk to someone. As far as Joe was concerned he deserved to be alone, isolated from the world with only his guilt for company.

It was hard to remember exactly when the nightmares started but from that first night of waking up in a cold panic Joe couldn't remember a day when they weren't present. Each night he was tormented by the vision of the young man and his daughter at the window of his car, their faces horribly scarred and coated with blood. They clawed at the windows and cried out, hideous shrieks that would haunt him even in his waking hours, until they eventually broke through the glass and begin to crawl into the car, their gnarled and twisted hands reaching out toward him. Each time Joe would wake up as the girl placed her tiny hand on his leg, and he would fall from the bed screaming in terror.

As the weeks turned into months the lack of sleep and human contact began to take its toll on Joe. He began to gain weight, despite the fact he did not have an appetite and rarely ate, and had difficulty concentrating on anything for more than a few minutes. Bright light hurt his eyes and made his head ache, forcing him to spend long periods led in the darkness, and he began to suffer from serious bouts of nausea.

It was after one such visit to the toilet that Joe first saw the figure. He had been pulled from his now familiar nightmare by a sudden wave of sickness so intense that he barely made it to the bathroom in time. When he emerged a few minutes later, pale and sweating, he made his way down the stairs to fetch a glass of water. But as walked through the living room and into the kitchen he paused as a cold chill ran down the back of his neck like droplets of ice water. He stopped in the kitchen doorway and turned slowly around, his eyes straining in the darkness.

The figure was stood in the far corner of the room, its back to Joe. At first he wasn't sure if it even was a figure; there was very little light coming from outside and the darkness seemed to hang on every surface. But as his eyes adjusted he was able to distinguish the figure's outline, and with his gaze still fixed on his uninvited guest he reached over and clicked the light switch. But the light did not blink into life.

Slowly the figure began to turn, and try as he might Joe could not muster the strength to do anything other than remain on the spot. Fear rooted him to the floor as the figure began to walk slowly toward him, its slow, gliding gait terrifying him even more than its unexpected presence. As the figure made its way across the room Joe noticed that it was holding something in its arms, and his sense of dread worsened.

As it got within a few feet Joe was able to make out certain details. The figure appeared to be female and was wearing a cloak of some kind, with a full hood that obscured her face and hair. The bundle in her arms appeared to be made of white blankets that had been stained dark in places, although Joe could not tell what had caused this.

Joe stood stock still, his eyes wide with fear, as she stopped in front of him. Slowly she adjusted her grip on the bundle of blankets and reached one hand out toward his face, a gentle movement that looked almost like a caress. But as her fingers touched his cheek Joe let out a scream as his head was filled with a hideous, unrelenting cry of pain. The noise cut across his eardrums like a saw, but even as he grasps his hands to his ears he knew that this wouldn't help, that the sound was somehow being placed into his head by the figure in front of him. As the pain grew Joe felt himself slipping out of consciousness, and the last thing he saw before he passed out was the woman, watching him silently.

When Joe awoke the next morning the figure was gone, and there was no trace that anyone else had been with him that night. The doors and windows were all locked and undamaged, and there was no other way another person could have gotten into the house. In the cold light of day Joe felt his fear ebbing away and dismissed the figure as a particularly vivid nightmare, an extension of the guilt ridden dreams that plagued him each night.

From that moment onwards, however, the woman began to appear with alarming regularity. Unlike their first meeting she never made contact with him but would simply appear, often standing unmoving in the corner of the room for a while before fading away. To begin with she would only ever appear at night, allowing Joe to convince himself that she was still an extension of his dreams as he would stir awake to find her silently watching him from the foot of his bed. But soon she was appearing at all hours, and Joe began to dread that creeping feeling on the back of his neck that would announce her arrival. After a few weeks Joe could not stand it any longer and decided that he needed to seek professional help, arranging an appointment with the psychologist that his mother and father had begged him to speak to all those months ago.

As he sat in the doctor's office later that day and recounted the visions that had plagued him for so long Joe felt certain that there could be some explanation for these strange occurrences. But the psychiatrist, a thin, pinch faced woman, told him that the visions and dreams were nothing more than projections of his own guilt over the accident. She wrote Joe a description for anti-depressants and scheduled him in for a weekly appointment, hoping to help him get to the route of his problems. Joe took the medication but declined to return.

By the time the one year anniversary of the accident had rolled around Joe was almost unrecognizable from the young man who had been driving the car that night. Still plagued by the dreams and the visions of the spectral women he had not been able to sleep more than a couple of hours a night for weeks, and the dark shadows under his eyes combined with his greyish, sun deprived pallor to make him look more undead than human. While the rest of his body had wasted away to skin and bones his stomach had become bloated and bulging, and while he hardly ever felt hungry the constant stabbing pains made it difficult to get comfortable in any position.

That night had been spent like most of the others, with Joe led on his now filthy sofa, too exhausted to do anything but stare into space. The pain in his stomach had been particularly bad for the past week or so, and he had been swallowing pills every hour or so in a vain attempt to keep the agony at a manageable level. When combined with the anti-depressants it was a wonder that he could even lift his head from the pillow each morning and make his way downstairs.

Unusually he managed to drift off to sleep at some stage during the evening, awaking around midnight with the sort of sudden start that usually precluded a visit from the mysterious woman. But as he came around and scanned the darkened room she was nowhere to be seen, and it was only as his heart rate began to slow back down to normal that the sound of movement toward the door behind him made Joe turn around.

The woman stood in the doorway, framed against the light from the hallway. As before she was staring intently at him, but Joe knew instinctively that this figure was different from the one that had been plaguing him. She was more solid and substantial, and when she started moving toward him she did not glide but strode purposefully.

Joe tried to turn and move toward the other end of the sofa but a sudden burst of pain in his stomach caused him to double over in agony. Immobile, he watched through tears of pain as she advanced toward him, noticing that she was reaching into the folds of the cloak as she approached.

When she reached the sofa her hand withdrew, now clasped around the handle of a thin, black handled knife. Joe half rose from the sofa and tried to lift his hands as a shield but another ripple of pain tore through his abdomen, almost causing him to pass out with the intensity as he fell back into the fetal position. The figure reached out with her free hand and pushed his head back roughly, forcing him back flat onto the sofa. As she positioned herself in front of him, she began to speak, a low, unbroken string of words in a language Joe had never heard before. She removed his hands from and held them to one side, and in one swift motion brought the blade down toward his stomach.

But instead of stabbing him the figure hooked the knife onto his stained t-shirt and swiftly pulled it downwards, partially splitting the shirt down the front. Releasing his hands she moved quickly, grasping the two pieces of fabric and pulling until the shirt came apart. She stepped back as Joe looked down at his now exposed torso, his mind ablaze with pain and confusion. What he saw caused him to cry out once again, only this time it was in fear rather than pain.

The skin of his bloated stomach had darkened to a deep angry red, which appeared almost black in the dim light of the room. As he stared, open mouthed, at his alien flesh another wave of pain crashed over him and Joe brought his hands back on his stomach. However he quickly removed them when he felt his skin shift beneath his fingertips, as if something inside him had pushed to get out.

Near delirious with pain and terror Joe turned his head toward the woman, who had been stood watching him. As he stared back up at her she lifted her hands up to the hood of the cloak and pulled it down, a mass of flame red hair cascading around her shoulders. It took Joe a few seconds before he realized who it was, as the only time he had seen Maggie before this was at the trial. The scar on her cheek had faded, and as she stared down at him her eyes seemed to glow red in the twilight of the room. An amulet in the shape of an inverted triangle hung from her neck, and even in his pain Joe was terrified to see that it appeared to be made from three bones bound together with what looked like human hair.

He opened his mouth to speak, to ask her what was happening to him, but before he could speak he was struck by the most intense pain he had ever experienced. The words died where they formed and were replaced by a scream of agony that tore at his throat. He looked down at his stomach again, and to his horror found that the skin across the top appeared to be splitting, unleashing a stream of dark blood that ran down either side of his bloated gut.

He reached his hands down to try and stop the bleeding, but Maggie moved faster than he could and grabbed both his wrists. She moved the end of the sofa behind him and held his hands above his head, staring down at his anguish etched face with a blank expression. He tried to fight against it but the combination of muscle wastage and pain had rendered him weak and helpless.

As he struggled the pain seemed to intensify, and he looked down toward his stomach again. The tear now stretched right across the bump, and beneath the gore Joe could see what looked like a transparent sack, although the contents were obscured by the blood. As he watched the sack began to lift, as if being pushed upwards by some invisible force. The pain of this was too much for Joe, and he blacked out for a few seconds.

When he came to his hands were no longer held, although he did not have the strength to move them. He looked down to see Maggie stood over him, her hands bloodied to the wrists. She reached forward, placed her hands either side of the wound and pushed outwards, widening it even more. She reached into his stomach and removed the sack, pausing only to use the knife to cut the tether between Joe and the mass. Another thick spray of blood arched out of the severed flesh as the blade bit through, painting the wall and immediate area around the sofa a deep crimson.

He watched as she took the knife again and gently cut into the surface of the sack. A wave of liquid came rushing out, along with the sound of crying. Maggie reached into the sack and removed the occupant; a human baby.

Maggie tenderly wiped the liquid from the child's head and unwounded a blanket that had been wrapped around her waist under the robe. She wrapped the child up tightly and adjusted her grip, making sure its head was supported. As she shifted the child in her arms Joe caught a glimpse of its face, noting even in his agony that it was quite beautiful. Maggie seemed to think the same thing, and it was only when she looked down at Joe that the look of adoration slipped away, replaced by the same callous hatred that she had worn on the day of the trial.

She took a step toward him and leaned forward, her face nearly inches from his own. She stared down at him for a long moment before moving her lips to his ears. When she spoke it was barely a whisper, her voice a harsh rasp, but Joe heard every word as if she had screamed them.

"Now we are even."

With that she turned and left the room, the silent little bundle still held in her arms.

Joe watched her leave, his vision starting to dim. He stared back down at his near eviscerated torso, his body too far into shock to feel any pain or confusion, and felt an odd smile break across his face. However it had happened, be it by magic or some other unholy means, Maggie had once again become a mother to a child.

As the darkness closed in around him he let out a final, shuddering breath, the guilt that had weighted him down for so long replaced by a perverse sense of peace. Somehow, against all odds, he had atoned for his sins. Somehow, he had made it right.

Patrick Lacey Bad Egg

"So what you're saying," Laura told the doctor, "is that my eggs are spoiled."

He'd stopped speaking for a moment, looked down to the floor, then continued on with his jargon, throwing out terms that all came down to the same thing.

She was broken.

It was quicker to head straight on Washington, but she didn't much feel like getting home in a hurry right now. All of the baby gear she'd bought, the rattles and the blocks, would call out to her the moment she walked in the door.

You are broken.

And the nursery door would be open. She made a note to convert it back to an office this weekend.

The air chilled her skin. She pulled her collar up and crossed the street. The park was on her left and her mother's voice came into her head, warning her to never set foot in there after dark. But tonight she felt like not much more could go wrong.

Her phone rang. She let it go to voicemail. It was probably Stephan. She'd been seeing him for a few months now and he was the only man in the last year that hadn't been scared away by her wanting a child so late in life. He'd been good through all this, but right now she couldn't take his voice, no matter how soothing.

Right now, she'd rather walk the city alone until the baby names stopped floating through her head.

To her right, a homeless man lay face down on a bench, his pants hanging so that his ass was exposed. She walked a little faster.

The wind picked up, blowing branches. A few specks of dirt flew into her eyes. They felt razor sharp against her lids and for a moment she was blinded. She stopped, took off her glasses, and rubbed until her eyes started to water. She suspected the tears weren't just from irritation.

She also suspected that something was watching her.

It came at her with no warning, just a realization.

You are not alone here and it is not the passed out bum that's got his eyes on you.

She turned back around. The man seemed to be snoring away.

The street would be a few minutes' walk in either direction. Her mother's words echoed through her mind again.

Something rustled nearby, a bush trembling. ... A raccoon or a stray mutt.

The surrounding bushes began to shake as well.

Laura picked up her pace. The light to her left flickered and went out. Overhead she could see the stars and on any other night they would have been beautiful.

Something growled.

She whipped around and saw that a shadow had crawled from the bushes and onto the path. It was too dark to make out, but her pulse sped with a warning.

She ran.

Her stomach started to churn, a combination of pre-natal vitamins and fear. Her pursuer was gaining. It grunted. She managed to unzip her bag and grab the pepper spray.

The thing grabbed her legs from under her and her face collided with the ground. Pain shot through her forehead and something salty dripped into her mouth.

She turned over and pressed down on the spray. A stream shot forward, hitting it in the eyes. It howled and brought hands to its face. It looked horribly deformed.

She tried to slide away but it grabbed onto her legs, pulling her closer.

"Please," she said, but it covered her mouth. She tried to bite the flesh but it was too hard, like scales.

This close, the moon cast enough light to reveal its face. It was not a street crazy and it was not a man.

Laura screamed but it went unheard. The thing ripped her blouse open and with a slimy tongue, it explored her skin, moving downward until it tore her skirt open. With one hand covering her mouth, it used the other to pull down her panties.

She managed to tear one of her arms free and claw at its face. Its skin was rough like granite and one of her nails tore off. It roared, saliva dripping from its teeth, and pushed her head to the ground.

The world turned a thousand shades of red and she woke several times to find it grunting on top of her.

I am a broken woman, she thought wildly. I am a broken woman and there is no coming back from this.

Before she blacked out, a name appeared: Joshua. If it had been a boy, she was going to name it Joshua.

The thing noticed her eyes were open again and brought a scaly fist down.

"Are you all right?" Stephan asked.

Joshua was going to have a dimple in his chin. His hair was going to be a shade of red she'd once seen on a man in the subway. His smile would be her father's, only he wouldn't have his cynicism. He would grow up to do whatever it was he wanted and he would make his mother proud.

She'd seen him in her dreams for days, each time just a little bit older, until he began to seem real enough to reach out and embrace.

Until the doctor had told her she was broken and the thing from the park had broken her even further.

"Laura?"

When she went home that night, the water in the tub had turned red.

"Laura?"

She'd crawled into bed and cried herself to sleep, wincing whenever the blankets brushed the bite marks.

"Laura, you're scaring me."

And that thing's face. It came to her whenever she dozed off.

Laura shook her head and she was back at the restaurant. The spaghetti in front of her looked too much like slimy tendrils, and the sauce was a familiar shade of red.

Her stomach churned but not just from nausea. It began to spasm, as if her insides were actually moving on their own. This was not the first time. It had been like this off and on for two weeks, since the night in the park. The doctors said there were no internal injuries, just scrapes and scratches.

She held herself and willed the pain away but it seemed to latch onto her like a leech.

Stephan put a hand forward but she pushed him away. "I'm fine, really."

"You certainly don't look fine. God, I hope they find that son of a bitch. Actually, no, I hope they don't. I hope I find him first."

She looked up through the haze of pain and wanted to tell him that despite his attempts at being supportive, she just wanted him to shut up. Instead she smiled and excused herself to the ladies room.

Inside there was a woman putting on eyeliner, looking at herself in the mirror like she was God's gift to the world.

Laura stepped into the last stall and waited until she heard the door shut. In the silence, her stomach growled like a beast and she let loose. Vomit filled the toilet bowl. *You're infected,* she thought. *Infected by that thing.*

But she still wasn't sure of what she'd seen. It had been dark and she badly wanted to believe that it had just been a scarred man, a leper perhaps.

He hadn't felt like a man, though. He'd felt...foreign, like something out of a nightmare. Just thinking of the flesh, rock hard and oozing with something, sent her stomach into another spasm. She lost what little she'd eaten.

"I'd like to go home now," she said when she was back at the table. "I'm sorry. I'm just not good company these days."

"Of course." Stephan stood and handed grabbed her jacket. "No need to be sorry. I understand. You've been through a lot." He told her things would get better as if he knew all about what she was going through, as if she could just shrug it all off.

They took a taxi to her place and he walked her to her apartment.

"Are you sure you don't want me to come in?"

She held her stomach and shook her head. "I'll be fine."

He kissed her on the cheek, lingered for a bit, and headed down the hall.

Inside she headed straight for the bathroom and let loose again. She wiped at her lips with the back of her hand and stumbled into the nursery. There was a crib, the most expensive she'd been able to find, and a baby monitor sitting atop a bureau. The walls were aqua, gender-neutral.

Laura fell to her knees when the pain became too much, like something had crawled inside her and wanted out again. She screeched and rocked back and forth, tears coming on when she remembered this was going to be her baby's room. She'd been sure of it this time. She was going to have a baby boy named Joshua and he was going to have eyes that matched hers. She was going to be a single mother at forty despite what anyone said.

Her panties felt warm suddenly and she was sure it was internal bleeding. That thing had torn her through and through. Some hidden wound had not closed properly and it was opening back up. She took off her pants and underwear to check.

There was blood everywhere. It leaked from her and the pressure in her midsection doubled so that she fell on her back from the intensity. When she opened her eyes she expected to see it, hovering over her, watching her suffer, but there were only the glow-in-the-dark stars she'd stuck on the ceiling, stars that looked too much like those above the park that night.

The feeling of wetness grew and she bit her hand at the oncoming pain, somehow worse now, like her body was getting ready to burst. And just when her death felt imminent, something gave.

Through a sweaty haze, she tried to make sense of it. The pain was still there, but it had lessened. She struggled onto her elbows to investigate.

When she saw it, she didn't scream. She'd done enough of that already. And she didn't vomit either. She didn't black out and she didn't cry.

Laura sat there with her jaw hanging open, numb, as she stared at the baseball-sized egg that stood a few feet away.

She wiped the blood from her groin and left in a hurry.

She went shopping, bought a new fur coat she had no plans of wearing, and a handful of tea lights she just had to try, all of them with a hint of cinnamon.

She went about her night as if everything in the world were normal, because the alternative was too much to even consider.

Something just came out of you. It was not a tumor and it looked an awful lot like an egg.

A bus sped by and she shook her head. She dialed her sister's number.

"Hello?" Chrissy answered.

"Hey, it's me. Can I come over?" The signal buzzed and she began to cross the street.

"Laura, it's almost nine. Is everything okay?"

She opened her mouth, shut it quickly and sighed. "Everything's fine. I just wanted to stop by."

Matthew giggled in the background, making nonsense sounds. "I'll put the coffee on," Chrissy said.

When she arrived, there were two steaming cups on top of the kitchen table. Matthew, going on six months, sat at his high chair. Laura kneeled down and gave him a raspberry on his neck. He howled and squirmed and she gave him a kiss on his chubby little cheek.

"You don't look so good," her sister said, handing her the cream.

Laura picked the carton up and for a moment the liquid inside was thick and membranous, like the coating of a newborn. She put the cap back on and drank it black. "I feel like shit."

"They'll catch him. And when they do, he's going to rot in a cell. Makes me rethink my stance on the death penalty."

"He's starting to look like his mother." Laura nodded toward Matthew, a wide grin on his face, a teething rattle in his mouth.

"As long as he doesn't look like his father, wherever he is." Chrissy sipped her coffee and pushed aside a strand of greasy hair. Her eyelids looked as though they hadn't closed in days.

"How did you know you wanted children?" She hadn't told Chrissy about any of her attempts at being a mother.

"I'm still not so sure I do." She laughed. "I don't know. I woke up one morning and I guess I felt like I wanted more, you know? Like I wanted to leave my mark on the world after I was gone. Sounds morbid but it's the truth."

Laura smiled and bit the inside of her mouth. She did know. She knew what it felt like to wake one morning and feel an emptiness, a hole you could try your hardest to fill, but in the end it stayed there, gaping.

"What about you?" Chrissy asked, looking at Matthew, who was starting to nod off. "You ought to settle down and try for one yourself. It's not too late."

Laura looked down at her cup. "No, I suppose it isn't."

She opened her kitchen drawer and rummaged until she found the hammer. The nursery door was open a crack but the light was off. An image came to her, making her bladder feel weak. He was in there. The father was inside, sitting on the rocker and swaying back and forth, his little creation in his lap.

After a long moment, she charged forward, threw the door open all the way, and turned on the light.

Part of her was glad to find she was not crazy. It lay there on the floor, staining the carpet red. The shell was thick and dark green with ridges running down the sides like inverted veins.

The other part of her trembled, because if she was not crazy, then everything that had happened was real, and somehow that was much worse.

Laura fell to her knees and brought the hammer back. It seemed to stay there, frozen, her arms too stiff to bring it back down.

She caught her breath and readied herself.

And stopped at the last moment, because it moved. The egg moved, just enough to notice. A quick tremor and that was it.

Something inside breathed.

She put the hammer on the floor and watched it for a long time.

"Is this the largest one you carry?"

The man with the mustache looked up from his magazine, his brow wrinkled. "I could look through our catalogue, but as far as I know that's the biggest one."

She looked at the dimensions on the side of the box. "I'll take it."

He nodded and rang her up. "What kind of lizard is it?"

She stopped rummaging through her purse. "I'm sorry?"

The man tapped the box. "What kind lizard you got?"

She shook her head and smiled. "To tell you the truth, I'm not entirely sure."

Laura thanked him and carried the heating lamp outside.

There was a knock at the door but she didn't notice at first. She was too busy humming along to the classical music. The stuff had always put her to sleep before, but now it made her feel so alive. There was something about the strings, how they all collided at one moment and went their separate ways the next.

Plus it was good for brain development.

"I'll be right there," she said when the knock came again, turning the volume down. She shut the nursery door and locked it behind her, putting the key in her back pocket.

She opened the door and Stephan was standing in the hall. His hair was a mess and his eyes looked glazed over.

"About time. I've been standing here forever."

"I was in the shower."

"Your hair doesn't look wet."

"What do you want?"

He tried to come inside but she blocked his way. Before she could sidestep, he zigzagged, pushed past her and entered the living room. "Jesus, Laura. I've been calling you all week. What the hell's going on?" His words, she noticed, were just a bit sloppy. By the sound of them, he had a good buzz going.

"I'm sorry if I've been a little preoccupied, Stephan." She walked to the sink and washed her hands. There was residue on her palms, from running her hands over the shell.

He came up behind her. "Look, I get it. Honestly, I do. You need your space and you need to come to terms with all this, but you don't have to shut me out. I've been nothing but supportive."

She turned around and looked at him. There was something so sad in his face, like a child who had been denied dessert. She put a hand on his cheek. "No one here thinks otherwise. But really, I've got too much on my mind right now."

"It's going to get better. You'll see." He wrapped his arms around her and although she wanted to push him away, she allowed the embrace. "And maybe when you're ready, you can look into adoption."

She cocked her head. "How do you mean?"

"I mean since you can't. You know."

"I'm not adopting, Stephan. We've been through this a hundred times, and I'm still not sure why you think you'd have a say anyway."

"I just want to see you happy, and you're not going to be happy until you come to terms with this, Laura. It's not just the assault. You're in denial."

"The doctors says they've seen plenty of women in my scenario conceive. It just takes time."

"That's what I mean," he said, stepping back and rubbing the back of his neck. "You're delusional. Just accept it. It's not the end of the world if you can't have children. Just say it."

She shook her head. "I'd like you to leave."

"Come on. Trust me. Say it."

"Stephan, I'm serious. Please leave."

He stepped closer and there was something different in his eyes now, no longer the sloppiness of the buzz, something like anger. And she would have reached for the knife drawer if it weren't for the sound.

A faint sound, something like a muffled cry. They both turned their heads toward the nursery. There was silence for a moment but the sound came again, louder this time. Stephan looked back at her. "Is someone else here with you?"

She opened her mouth to answer but he cut her off.

"I get it now. Why you've been so distant, why you haven't answered your phone. There's someone else, isn't there? You're fucking someone else."

She slammed her hands on the kitchen table. "Yes, because sex has been the biggest thing on my mind these days. You're a selfish and weak man, you know that? I want you out of my apartment now."

Stephan snorted, a smile distorting his face. It made her shiver. "I'm not going anywhere." He walked over to the nursery door.

Her heart thundered and she began to feel light-headed. It was happening, she thought.

Stephan tried the door and swore. "Where's the key?"

It was happening. That's all she could think. She wasn't crazy because it was really happening. "Stephan, please leave. We can talk about this later. I've got work to do." Without thinking, she grabbed the key from her back pocket and Stephan's eyes caught the movement.

He came at her, grabbing her wrists. She managed to smack and scratch one of his cheeks, a bead of blood forming, but he took the key from her and pushed her against the cabinet. Pain flared in her midsection, still sensitive from the other night.

From the birth.

"You'd better hope I find an empty nursery in there." He stopped once and turned around. "And you ought to turn it back into an office." He put the key in the lock and turned the doorknob.

And screamed.

Laura sped to the door and lost her breath. The egg lay in the crib, shifting back and forth. It was happening, all right. The heating lamp gave off a warm glow, like a crackling fire. The classical music was still on, playing softly, background noise.

And the beast stood at the window, a pile of shattered glass at his feet. This close, she noticed his skin was greener than she remembered, and his nose came to a strange point, not unlike a crocodile. Jagged teeth lined scaly lips. He resembled something that had walked the length of sewers for years, sleeping deep within the city's bowels.

A few drops of urine ran down her legs but they went unnoticed.

"What the fuck?" Stephan screamed over and over, a symphony that somehow coincided with the music. *Whatthefuck. Whatthefuck. Whatthefuck.*

She wondered for a moment what this must look like to him, an egg the size of a football (it had doubled in size the last few days), an indescribable thing growling, dark saliva dripping down its chin, and in the middle of it all was Laura, the woman he'd been so supportive of.

But that had been a lie, hadn't it? He'd been just like the rest of them, unable or not willing to understand that there was a hole in her very being, a hole that was supposed to be filled with Joshua.

Laura fought the fear and walked forward. She pushed Stephan toward the father. He stumbled and fell to the floor, crying like an infant now. How ironic.

The beast stepped down from his perch and took hold of Stephan's shoulders. It brought him toward its mouth, lifting Stephan's body like it was just a candy bar and nothing more. It took his entire head into it mouth and crunched. She closed her eyes. The bones sounded brittle as they snapped.

When she finally opened them again, there was nothing left of Stephan beside his suit, torn and soaked. The beast kneeled down and lapped up the blood like a dog at dinnertime.

When every last drop was gone, their eyes met. He broke the stare to look toward the egg.

"Please," she said. "Don't."

It roared, the sound loud enough to make her bite her lip, but it stopped suddenly.

The shell broke in one place, a small chip in the side. A tiny finger reached out, then a hand, then an arm. Until the shell broke apart completely and the tiny thing crept out, a miniature version of its father but with faint traces of its mother too, a vaguely human-like face. It wailed, waiting for its mother's milk.

She hadn't realized she was crying until now.

The father turned around and leapt back outside. She ran to the window and saw that he stood at the foot of the drive, waiting.

She picked up the creature and brought it to her, putting its head in the crook of her neck. Its skin was softer than its father, scaly but somehow smooth at the same time. She checked its sex and smiled. Though he didn't have red hair, his eyes did match her father's.

She walked outside to where the beast waited—the thing that had given her what she could not give herself—and followed it into the night.

Joshua lay in her arms, sleeping soundly.

Ugly Babies

Andrew Freudenberg
Meat Sweets

Moses allowed himself a smile as he surveyed the room. Business was booming. There was an inexhaustible hunger for his 'specialist' meat products that he would never have imagined possible. Prices were through the roof, and he had wasted no time in building a brand new barn. There was now room for twenty-five beds and they were all occupied. Of course it hadn't been easy. Since Gideon had died, he had to shoulder all the hard work himself and fertile young women didn't simply grow on trees. He must have driven a good thousand miles in his quest for hitchhikers who fit the bill. When he wasn't out hunting, he was stoking up the furnace to dispose of unwanted males and when he wasn't doing that, he had a thousand other things to consider.

After Marylyn caught him taking personal care of the spermatising and had given him a solid beating, it became necessary to sit down and rethink that part of the process. At first he'd tried using a couple of drifters that he'd caught camping down in the bottom field, but quite frankly, their performance had been disappointing. If he was honest with himself, he found them a little distasteful; and so he had gone the mechanical route. Moses wasn't an educated man, but he had found himself enjoying the long evenings reading up on the fine art of insemination. The names of the drugs rolled off his tongue in a satisfying manner and he found himself repeating them as he went about his rounds. Sometimes he even sang them to himself.

"Cystorelin, Estrumate, Lutalyse. Cystorelin, Estrumate, Lutalyse."

These were just the bovine medicines that his friendly veterinarian, a faithful customer, was happy to provide in quantity. From there he had moved onto clomiphene and gonadotropins. These substances were so sacred that they were actually meant for human consumption. The fat medical tomes that he laid out on the kitchen table were full of possibilities. Marylyn would bring him tidbits and sweet meats to chew on while he traced each line with his stubby fingers.

He kept all of these substances in a refrigerated cabinet that was his pride and joy. Always polished to perfection, it sat humming happily next to his collection of applicators and syringes. Marylyn had bought him one of those white coats that scientists wore, and she was happy to keep it crisp and clean for him. Wearing it gave him an almost religious sense of purpose. He considered himself an expert, and when his wife jokingly called him "Doctor Moses" over breakfast one morning, it had put a smile on his face that lasted all day.

Now it simply wasn't enough for things to work as nature intended. That might have been sufficient for any other un-ambitious baby farmer, but not for this man. No. There was a lot of scope for improvement. Gestation was a bottleneck that he was determined to defeat. Nine months was far too long to wait for every crop. It was time to experiment. He immersed himself in articles about fertility and childbirth. He read so much that at night he would dream that laughing fetuses were dancing around his bed crooning his praises.

His first attempts had been unfortunate. Several of his best breeders had died at his hands and there had been a fair amount of unpleasantness to deal with. Moses was an incredibly stubborn man though, and he pushed on with his work. Although actual genetic modification was far beyond his remit, he still mixed his sperm samples together and doused them in chemical cocktails. This unprofessional approach had yielded few results, but now he was sure that his hard work was about to bear fruit. He could feel it in his water.

May had been with him the longest. He had a particular soft spot for her and so far had resisted meddling with her pregnancies. She'd churned out eight delicious little infants for him over the years and her milk was legendary. However, this was precisely why he had made the hard decision to get her involved. May was like a lucky charm and he needed all the good fortune he could get.

A faint clanging sound rose above the room's piped music and brought him back to reality. It was Marylyn ringing the breakfast bell. As he walked back to the house, the smell of bacon reached him and his stomach rumbled in anticipation. He'd slaughtered one of the porkers the day before and was eager to taste her. She had grown huge in captivity, and he expected her to be some good eating. He'd spent a good half an hour selecting a fine blade for the slaughter and the actual act had naturally been a great pleasure. It was the circle of life, or whatever it was that cartoon lion had called it. For a split second she had seemed to remember her former life as a legal secretary, but it had been fleeting. As he cut her throat, she had been pure pig, squealing like the animal she was.

"Morning darlin'," he said as he sat down at the kitchen table.

Ugly Babies

"Darling?" his wife returned, blocking out the light as she loomed over him. "Someone's in a good mood today."

He stuffed a fork full of food into his mouth. A stream of grease ran down his chin as he chewed happily.

"You know what? I am in a good mood. I think today's the day."

"Well ain't that nice."

Marylyn was very proud of Moses. Not only was he an excellent provider, but he had also turned out to be such a clever man. In her mind's eye, she liked to imagine him receiving a prize for what she imagined to be his groundbreaking research. That'd show all those know nothings who had made her childhood hell. She'd have loved to see all their stupid faces then.

"I was thinking we might keep the little 'un for ourselves this time. What's ten thousand dollars compared to some good eating? We're going to do ourselves some celebrating."

Overcome by emotion, Marylyn leant in behind Moses and hugged him with arms like ham hocks. He patted her hand and then swatted her away.

"Come on honey, I'm eating here."

She smiled and disappeared out of the room. When she returned, she was hiding something behind her back.

"Now, I was saving this for Christmas—but all things considered, I don't think Jesus would mind if I gave it you early." She held out a gleaming stethoscope.

"I think you'd look real nice wearing this."

Moses swallowed the last of his breakfast and threw down his cutlery. After wiping his mouth with his sleeve, he turned and gazed up at her. There was a small tear in the corner of his left eye.

"Oh, you're such a sweet little thing."

He got to his feet and embraced her before planting a moist kiss on the top of her head. Releasing her, he took the gift and put it round his neck.

"How do I look?"

"Like George Clooney on E.R." He laughed and slapped his thigh.

"You're too much sometimes, honey. Right, this man has work to do. Wish me luck."

There was a spring in his step as he crossed the yard humming to himself.

"Cystorelin, Estrumate, Lutalyse. Cystorelin, Estrumate, Lutalyse."

He unlocked the door and stepped inside. After slipping his lab coat over his checked shirt, he straightened the stethoscope and rubbed his hands together. A muzak version of Ted Nugent's "Weekend Warrior" was droning over the sound system. He felt good.

As he walked along the row of cubicles, he inspected the other girls. He'd already done so earlier, but he'd learnt that attention to detail hurt nobody. Many years ago one of his captives had escaped and he'd had a hell of a time tracking her down. Fortunately for him, she'd fallen in a ditch and broken her ankle before she could get off his land. Of course he'd had no choice but to euthanize her there and then, but it had left a bad taste in his mouth. Now each girl was securely chained down and he was generous with sedation. Lesson learnt.

He peered in at his latest acquisition, a pretty girl by the name of Jackie. Miraculously, she had already had a bun in the oven when he found her standing beside her broken down SUV. She had been looking a little green recently and he was concerned about her. She seemed to be doing all right now, though. Her eyelids fluttered slightly as he got closer to listen to her breathing. It was shallow but regular.

May was snoring when he reached her. Her hands were resting on her swollen belly. She was only six months gone, but looked more than ready to pop. He walked over to his fridge and pulled out a small bottle marked "Misoprostol". Moses had been looking forwards to using this. After reading an article in the New Scientist, he had moved heaven and earth to get hold of it. He unwrapped a fresh syringe and pierced the lid. Once it was loaded with double the recommended dose, he returned to May.

"Here we go."

The substance took effect immediately. May's chains clattered as she started to shake and emitted a guttural howl. Moses frowned. According to the books, it should have taken some time to work.

"Come on, now. Daddy's here. Ain't nothing to worry about."

A ripple of activity crossed over her belly. Something was moving beneath the surface. She gripped the side of her bed and howled again. He bit his lip and watched as she instinctively pushed in parallel with the muscle spasms that the drug was inducing.

"Good girl. Keep it coming."

Moses took a glimpse "down under", as Marylyn liked to say. Apart from an ominous twitching, there was no sign of the child. He ran his tongue over his teeth, not quite sure what to do next.

Waiting was not one of his strengths. Realizing that he had forgotten to wear sterile gloves, he walked off to retrieve a pair. Once he'd pulled them on he returned to May.

At first he missed the tiny fingers gripping the sides of her most intimate parts. When he saw them he did a double take. It made no sense. As he puzzled over this, her lower lips were suddenly torn asunder. May's body shook in violent spasm for a few seconds and then fell still. Flesh ripped and a gaping wound was created between her thighs. From this newly expanded orifice a head appeared. In essence, it was that of a baby—at least it was roughly the correct shape—but Moses' knees buckled at the sight of it. The skin was rough and blackened as if burnt. The eyes, yellow and feral, stared at him with an intensity that put the fear of God into him. It was without lips so that its jagged teeth were permanently on display. When it saw the farmer staring at him, the mouth opened and a bowel splitting screech filled the air.

Moses instinctively looked around for a weapon, but there was none. He watched in horror as the child pulled itself free from its mother's body. A wave of putrid black liquid gushed onto the bed. The smell was hideous, and he gagged as the stink washed over him. Around them, the other inhabitants of the room began to groan and writhe and rattle their chains.

The ugly baby crouched on all fours and leapt at Moses. As it struck his chest it bounced back, restricted by the still attached umbilical cord. It hit the edge of the bed and fell onto the floor. The chord was still holding firm, but after a few tugs it came free and brought the placenta with it. The child skittered across the cold concrete and disappeared under a bed. A dark trail was smeared across the floor where it had been.

Moses looked down. As he did so, his stethoscope fell apart and the pieces rained down onto his feet. His coat was smeared with filth. He looked at the eviscerated remains of May and slowly shook his head.

"You're going to regret this, little man. It. Is. On."

It took him about thirty seconds to run out and retrieve his shotgun and a pocketful of cartridges from the cab of his pickup. When he returned, the wailing and screaming had intensified. But it didn't seem like the child, or thing, had moved.

"Come out of there."

Nothing. Cautiously, he edged over and pushed the bed aside. The child rushed off, trailing its glutinous package behind it. Moses got off a shot. The placenta exploded, but the baby was unharmed. It veered toward Jackie's bed. Moses swung the gun round and fired again. This time the shot went wild and put a large hole in the girl's side.

"Hell fire!"

The child kept moving and Moses reloaded. His next attempt shattered the glass on the front of his beloved drugs cooler.

"You're going to pay for that in spades, boy."

More shots rang out and more carnage ensued. Two more girls were given a bloody release from their ongoing torment. One poor innocent lost her head and the little thing leapt onto the bed and basked in the arterial fountain. It stuck its tongue out and lapped up the salty plasma as it fell.

Moses saw red and charged, his shotgun now reversed and held out like a club. He swung it, but before it could connect he lost his footing on the slippery floor. There was a crack as his head hit the concrete. Darkness swamped his consciousness and he blacked out. When he came round, he wasn't sure how long it had been. The little one was gone. A trail led to the door. It didn't go straight there, though. Looking around, he could see that while he was asleep the thing had been to every bed in the room. His skull throbbed as he went from girl to girl. Their throats had all been torn out.

With a wail of frustration and fury, he hobbled out of the new barn and crossed the yard over to the old one. This was where he kept his sharp items. A wall of gleaming pain potential greeted him as he entered. He selected a large machete and an orbitoclast. The latter was essentially a surgical ice pick intended for use in lobotomies. Marylyn had given it to him for his birthday. It had come in a beautiful presentation box.

Back in the yard he could see a bloody trail leading to the house.

"If you've done anything to that woman..."

Gripping his weapons, he cautiously approached the front porch. His heart hammered at his rib cage as he imagined the damage he was going to do to that little bastard. Inside, old Uncle Vern stared down at him from the cracked portrait that dominated the hallway.

"What the hell you doing, boy?" it seemed to shout.

"Shut up. I'm getting payback," whispered Moses as he deftly avoided the floorboards that creaked the most.

Marylyn wasn't in the kitchen. That made him nervous. She was always in there cooking something up or bolting something down. The dead porker's head lay on a baking dish on the table surrounded by onions and peppers. Its hair had been shaved off and there were small cuts in the cheek where chopped garlic had been inserted. Its sightless eyes stared up at the ceiling. Marylyn had been making Cabeza, one of his favorite dishes. Damn, how he loved that woman.

A soft cooing from the front room caught his attention. He readied himself for action and followed the sound. The curtains were still drawn and it took his eyes a couple of seconds to adjust to the darkness.

"Marylyn?"

When his wife turned to face him, he saw that the top half of her dress was torn away and left her bosom exposed. Her eyes were wide and she had a half smile on her face.

"Moses?"

A shiver colder than a penguin's pecker ran down his spine as he realized that the baby was attached to her. It was feeding. That made no sense, though. Marylyn's milk had run dry decades ago.

"What...?"

There was a wet sound as the child detached itself and turned its head toward him. It hissed and bared its blood stained teeth before turning back to bury itself in her flesh once more. Marylyn's eyelids fluttered as she spoke her last words.

"Ain't he just the sweetest thing?"

Lolly by Ashley Scarlet

Michael C. Schutz-Ryan
Brother

Courtney's pregnant belly felt caught in a vise. Lying in her bed—tawny hair clinging to her sweating forehead in long strands—she struggled to remember her breathing.

She screamed, her wail like that of a gothic heroine. "Gaaahhhd."

There was no one else in the house to hear. Her husband, David, was in Atlanta for a conference. He'd only been gone a day and was due back tomorrow. Such a short window, why was this happening to her right now?

Courtney's own father had gone to buy a used Mustang one Saturday when she was three. He'd never returned. Only one birthday card had ever come from the deadbeat, two years later, the bottom edge ringed from the butt of a beer bottle.

Was that what she could expect from David?

Don't be stupid, she told herself. He's gone for two days. For work. And you insisted he go.

A wrenching cramp gripped her bottom like a brutal urge to defecate. The pain made time both drag out and accelerate. It was as elastic and terrifying as her recurring dreams of running desperately away from an unseen horror, while her legs were stiff as granite and the horizon never came any closer.

The metal teeth of that invisible vise bit deep within her. This was nothing like the Braxton Hicks which twice had sent her to the hospital.

Is this the real thing?

She wasn't sure.

There was a second pain—call this knives—underneath that vise squeezing her. No, not underneath. Inside the contraction pain. Like stainless steel kitchen knives plunging into her stomach.

Not my stomach.

Into her unborn boy.

God, the knives were . . .

Slicing.

She gritted her teeth against another contraction. This one definitely a contraction. Different from that secondary, unworldly (ungodly) pain. She remembered this well enough from 3 AMs in the Emergency Room, the blue-scrubbed and white-jacketed medical staff shaking their heads sympathetically.

Dueling levels of pain, only one natural.

She was due next week, so this could be the real thing. But it didn't feel right. It felt like...well, it seemed that these furious cramps were coming from her baby.

Her panicked mind conjured up the horror of a still birth. How would she go on after that final tragedy? Her son already had a nursery, and clothes, and a name.

Gabriel. Like the angel.

She had already lost one; Michael, the other angel.

Fetal reabsorption, Dr. Salinger's rational voice echoed in her head. That efficient little man should have had a German accent, but didn't. He had spoken these quickly paced words after her second ultrasound. There is only one detectable heartbeat. The other fetus must have miscarried. It's not that uncommon. One in every eight multi-fetus pregnancies results in a vanishing twin.

Vanishing Twin. Quite a trick. Now you see him—Michael—now you don't.

Courtney gathered the courage to send probing fingers between her thighs. She brought her fingertips up to examine them. No blood. That was good. She couldn't lose Gabriel, too.

"David, where are you?" she asked the ceiling, tears streaming down her flushed face.

David was in a buffet line. Laughing it up with other conference attendees wearing cute My Name Is stickers on their sweaters.

Courtney was here. Alone.

No, not alone. There was no blood. She still had Gabriel.

A contraction gripped her abdomen. Sudden warm wetness poured out of her and ran down her inner thighs and legs. She cringed, thinking that she'd peed herself. As the cresting cramp tightened her body along the pelvis and her tailbone, she realized that her water had broken. Gabriel was coming.

But Gabriel was in danger.

At first she had doubted she was ready to be a mother. Lately, she'd marveled at how she ever could have doubted. Mother and son were simpatico. Her cravings for sardines and saltines now seemed intrinsically linked with Gabriel's fits of kicking. She knew the son who had grown inside her. She knew—right now, sweating and panting and contracting in her sodden bed—that Gabriel didn't just want out. He needed out to save himself.

I've gone batshit crazy.

Courtney recognized the need for an ambulance, but her phone was dead. She'd accidentally pulled the charger out of the wall socket last night, and she was too big and pregnant to bend down to plug it back in.

The next contraction seized her. It couldn't come close to taking over the shredding feeling deep inside of her, but the contraction hit and she gasped and bit her lip, wincing. She dug her hands into the soaked sheet and tried to pull her legs up closer to her. For a few seconds she chugged breath in and out like the leggy Lamaze instructor had drilled into her.

I need hot water and towels...

This wasn't the voice of Kimberly the breathing expert. This was simple logic—all the movies said home births required hot water and towels. Courtney hadn't a clue what to do with them even if she could get out of bed and prepare them herself.

No husband. No ambulance. No boiled water and rags.

Utterly alone.

But for Gabriel.

And the pain.

Her stomach tightened, and she shrieked through her breaths. She pushed. She couldn't help it. Her bowels let loose a little, and the baby inside her moved closer to his freedom.

The knifing pain moved with him.

Again, she sought out her most private of places, which had once been for sex and pleasure but now had transformed for a whole other purpose. Her fingers couldn't decipher how dilated she was, but that was academic. It didn't matter how ready she was. Gabriel needed out, and he was coming.

"Dear God..." she began, but found no words to finish her prayer.

Bright dots blinded her sight. She took longer, soothing breaths; she couldn't faint.

She was tearing and stretching. In her mind, she saw Gabriel crowning—his tiny, slick head a battering ram going the wrong way. The under-pain diminished. Gabriel was carrying that with him. The final contraction was agony enough. She felt her son slide out of her, but the final eruption of pain in her abdomen climaxed and she passed out.

Warm sticky blood and fluid covered the sheets when Courtney came to with a gasp and a cry.

First she noticed that the vise in her belly had subsided to the dull remembrance of a great pain. Next she became aware of Gabriel, a wet, squirming thing between her legs.

She reached down and found her son. Courtney wrapped her hands around him and brought him up to her. The umbilical cord trailed after, but she would deal with that later. Gabriel was red and wrinkled and ugly—the most beautiful thing she had ever seen. His tiny face contorted in a bursting scream. His little fists clutched in miniature frustration. It was music. She laid him on her chest where he could feel the familiar reassurance of her heartbeat.

Gabriel rolled over onto his back. Courtney thought he was wriggling to find a breast. But he stayed on his back. In a moment, his little belly swelled.

Courtney assumed he was passing gas. She didn't know.

It was not so much a swelling as a pushing out. Gabriel's stomach distended in a mimic of Courtney's own pregnant belly. And then the swell moved, lazily extending downward to Gabriel's tiny abdomen.

His tender skin bumped up, as if a finger poked from the inside.

Four more eruptions from his small belly.

The umbilical cord, wet and cold, slid its slimy length against Courtney's leg, a wounded snake. Gabriel twisted, and a small cry came from his pink lips.

It's inside my baby.

All of her pain had evaporated to a distant memory during that minute after Gabriel's birth. But now she remembered it all. Not the contractions, but the under-pain. Those skewering knives truly had been apart from her. Her instinct had been right—it had come from inside Gabriel.

He's giving birth. Oh my God, he's giving birth.

The thought tripped hysterically through her head. Too exhausted to cry out anymore, her ravished body shook with a seizure of horror.

Gabriel's tiny body quivered as if in response to Courtney's. He wailed a piercing cry. Courtney's heart hammered in panic and empathy.

The bulge in Gabriel's belly undulated lower, down past his tiny red penis. Gabriel shrieked, his soft pelvic bones warping.

The parasite inside her baby rolled back up to Gabriel's belly. Courtney's mind gibbered. She could actually sense the resentment of the thing when it found no exit through a birth canal.

A ripple a couple inches long ridged Gabriel's stomach. Courtney flashed to the scene in The Exorcist when Reagan reached out for help by scribbling words from inside her possessed body.

Like a caesarian scar of proud flesh, the ridge of skin lightened and distended. Gabriel slipped down onto her stomach; she tried to hold on to him but he was so slick with after-birth.

The thing inside her son pushed up and outward. Gabriel's skin tore in small vertical fissures. Tiny drops of blood pooled, as if Gabriel had been pricked a dozen times with a wide gauge needle.

The fissures grew wider and the blood drops ran like narrow rivers from the larger horizontal gash breaking through Gabriel's belly.

Those narrow rivers became a single torrent and raged down Gabriel's twitching body. His belly burst open. Flanges of ragged flesh hung raw like ratty carpeting. Gabriel laid still and silent on Courtney's chest.

A tiny, unmistakably human head emerged from the tatters of her son.

Courtney thoughts babbled. The vanishing twin reappears!

For this was Michael, not absorbed into the healthy fetus that became Gabriel, but existing inside his twin brother as a perverse mimicry of pregnancy.

Michael's bald head was slick with the dripping tissue and blood from his twin brother Gabriel. Michael's tiny arms reached out from the hole that was Gabriel's stomach. Miniature hands pushed down on the ragged infant corpse, slipping once in the blood but finally finding traction. Michael—a child within a child—pushed himself out of the human hole.

Not even a quarter-size of a natural newborn, Michael crawled out of Gabriel. He stumbled. His puny arms and legs scrambled for purchase.

Courtney, only barely holding onto sanity, prayed for him to fall off of Gabriel—off of her, off the bed—and fall to the floor. Hopefully to crush his skull and die. Such a monstrosity of nature should not be allowed to live.

But Michael went to his hands and knees, steadying himself. He crawled over the body of his brother.

As his cold, wet hands touched Courtney's stomach, she shrieked. She thought to bat him away, to shove him off, but the thought wouldn't translate into motion. It was as if her body—if not her mind—claimed this aberration as her surviving twin son.

Michael gurgled. To Courtney, the sound was a garbled voice crying, "Mommy."

Soaked in gore and only the size of the runt of a puppy litter, Michael crawled up her chest.

Wet bubbles of breath seemed to say, "Hungry."

Beseeching fingers wiggled over Courtney's flesh. She sobbed. Her body shook with revulsion.

Michael found her breast. His fingers played and squeezed with the areole and worked down over the round flesh full with nourishment. His mouth seized her nipple. It felt like a blind, suffering rodent suckling on her in a terrifying nightmare from which she would never wake.

Courtney screamed at the soft sucking sounds.

But she didn't grab his mutant body and fling him to the ground. She closed her eyes and breathed out a ragged and disgusted sigh. She lifted her arms. Her hands sought the wrinkled body of the almost alien thing she was nursing.

He wasn't alien.

The body was too small to hold in two hands. She rested one hand on his back, and after a moment she began to gently caress.

He was Michael.

He was her son.

Her nipple popped out of his mouth. She thought he was done. But he cried fussily, unsatisfied. His tiny mouth clamped back down on her breast.

Michael already had teeth. He bit into her, making Courtney yelp. Wetness poured from her breast and she looked down, expecting to see her own breast milk. Instead, blood streamed from the fusion of Michael's mouth and her flesh.

The disgust she had held in check resurfaced, and she pulled Michael away. Her nipple came off. Bitten through, it hung from Michael's imperceptible lips. A moment later it dropped with a soft plopping sound back onto Courtney's chest.

Courtney's motherly affection for this affront to nature had entirely gone. Disgust, fear, and hatred reclaimed their rightful places.

Michael wriggled, slippery, out of her hands. Breast abandoned, he crawled farther up. His fetal-sized body slithered to her neck.

Dizzily, Courtney feared that Michael was coming in for a kiss. She imagined the paper-thin and bloody infantile lips brushing hers. She gagged.

But Michael buried his head under her chin.

The faint voice of motherhood chirruped one last time: He's cuddling.

With miniscule but sharp teeth, Michael tore into his mother's neck.

Courtney gagged. She tried to cry out, but produced only a thick gargling. She felt Michael waggle his head back and forth. Chomping and ripping through her throat, he thrust his little head into her, a devil's suckling.

Great gouts of blood pumped from Courtney's throat. The sudden loss of so much blood quickly brought her to the point of passing out. She knew that once she passed out, she would never wake up. Weakly, she battered at Michael's bottom. Her feeble blows had no effect. She closed her eyes to the wet lapping sounds.

Michael continued to feed for several minutes. Hunger temporarily sated, he dislodged himself from his mother's neck. He clumsily sat back and gurgled...

...and waited for his father to come home.

about the authors and artists

Ed Ahern resumed writing after forty odd years in foreign intelligence and international sales. He has his original wife, but after 45 years advises that they are both out of warranty.

Devoted to the practice since 1985, **Daniel Ari** writes and publishes extensively. He has recently placed creative work in *Writer's Digest, McSweeney's, 42 Magazine, Defenestration, Wisdom Crieth Without* and *Conscious Dancer*. His quatern, "The Artists' Honeymoon," will appear in the 2014 edition of *Poet's Market*. He also leads poetry events and performances throughout the Pacific Northwest. His blogs are imunuri.blogspot.com and fightswithpoems.blogspot.com.

Ben Arzate once spilled an inkwell that flooded the whole world. He now lives in Des Moines, IA. He blogs at dripdropdripdropdripdrop.blogspot.com/.

Neil Baker is currently dabbling in writing, and has had stories and artwork accepted into the upcoming Chaosium anthology, *Atomic Age Cthulhu* as well as *Cellar Door: Words of Beauty, Tales of Terror Volume Two*. He is a filmmaker and animator, focused on traditional styles, and at the moment he's wrapping up a research project film for the University of Waterloo, before turning his attention to a stop-mo version of Lovecraft's Dagon that he has in mind. He is married with two small children, and this story is all true.*
*Editor's Note: This might be a slight lie.

Carly Berg is a dark cloud hovering over sunny Houston. Her flash stories appear in several dozen journals and anthologies, and she welcomes visitors to her site: http://carlyberg.weebly.com/

Stephen Cooney is from the UK. He studied art at Exeter Art School before becoming a freelance illustrator for a number of computer games companies. He provides artwork for the science fiction and fantasy company Games Workshop. He left painting and became a tattoo artist, but after a few years he took up the brushes again and has recently had work published in both the UK and the US. He loves to paint horror, sci-fi, and murder mysteries...and some friends also say he has a messed up mind. Stephen and his wife Amanda have two children, Hayley and Steven Jr.

Dusty Davis has had poetry published in *Timeless Voices* from the International Library of Poetry, and his short story "The Beast" was published in the Jan/Feb/Mar 2013 edition of *The Story Teller Magazine*.

Dan Dillard is the author of the short story collections *Demons and Other Inconveniences, Lunacy* and *How to Eat a Human Being* as well as the novel *Giving Up the Ghost*. He also writes flash fiction for his blog, and has written in collaboration with many other talented writers for William Castle's Scare it Forward, and an upcoming secret project that might scare the cotton candy out of you. His work has been included in numerous anthologies and horror magazines with more on the way. He lives in the Midwest with his wife Stephanie. She is the navigator. They have two children, who provide the lessons and entertainment. When he isn't writing, he has a boring desk job that leads to daydreaming, which leads to evil thoughts, which become stories. The cycle is vicious and wonderful...but mostly vicious.

Residing in North-Western Ontario with his wonderful wife and four kids, **Dave Dormer** spends most of his time outdoors either fishing, camping, or hunting. In one form or another, he's been a horror/fantasy enthusiast since grade school.
*Editor's Note: Dave also provided the editor with her favorite new moniker, "The Den Mother of Horror". The editor can also confirm that he is the **real** Dave Dormer.

David Eccles writes the tales that prevent him from sleeping night after night. He feels they have a life of their own and deserve a full and long life, which is why he releases them onto the page. His stories are often tinged with sadness and a typically British sense of humor. His first collection of flash fiction and short stories, *Darke Times and Other Stories,* is well reviewed and available in all popular e-book formats. He has been previously featured on various blogs and websites, including BOOKSoftheDEADPRESS.com. His work can be read in other

James Ward Kirk's anthologies, including *Sex, Drugs & Horror*, *Serial Killers Tres Tria*, and *Bones*.

Michael Faun has written two short story collections; *First Harvest* (Fanatic Fabrications 2011), *Six Pack o' Strange Tales* (Sigill Forlag 2013) and has fifteen flash fiction stories featuring in the pulp anthology *Feverish Fiction vol#1* (Hyperpyrexia Press 2012). He lives with his wife and daughter in the East coast of Sweden, and enjoys everything trash culture: books, comics and movies. He also dabbles in spicy vodouesque cooking and, rumor has it, he was once nearly blinded by ghost pepper chili.

Dona Fox's short stories and poetry has appeared in *Eldritch Tales, Haunts, Thin Ice, Cemetery Dance (Issue #1), Beyond*, and *New Blood*. She also has work forthcoming in Volume Two of *Cellar Door: Word of Beauty, Tales of Terror*.

Timothy Frasier is a novelist, short story writer, and poet. His work appears in several James Ward Kirk anthologies, Static Movement anthologies, the soon to be released *Zombies Gone Wild Volume 2*, Dark Media, and a few literary magazines.
Frasier lives in Western Kentucky with his wife, Lisa, and their German shepherd, Chief.

Andrew Freudenberg is a creator of dark fiction. He has always loved words. He returned to writing seriously after a long period of musical distraction. As well as running his own label, making records and playing live, he also promoted club nights including London's notorious "Club Alien". Although his DJ appearances were few he did once play for Russian gangsters in Moscow. He'd never admit it though. His short stories can currently be found haunting the pages of numerous anthologies, including *Kizuna: Fiction for Japan* and releases from KnightWatch, MayDecember Publications, RainStorm and Angelic Knight Press. He is also busy creating "longer stuff". He lives in the South-West of England and is working on a variety of projects as well as raising three young sons. "Milkshake", another tale of Moses and Marylyn, can be found in the JWK Publishing release *Barnyard Horror*.

David Greske grew up in rural Wisconsin and ever since he can remember has had a fascination with the horror genre. He spent his Saturdays watching the afternoon creature features when he should've been doing chores. Writing horror stories since the age of seven, one of his first literary endeavors was a rip-off of a Dark Shadows episode. Since then his works have appeared in several magazines and anthologies including Black Ink Horror, Thirteen, Back Roads, and Dark Moon Digest. To date he has published four novels, ANATHEMA, NIGHT WHISPERS, RETRIBUTION and BLOOD RIVER. All are available at amazon.com. He co-wrote the screenplay to his latest novel. BLOOD RIVER, which has been made into a feature film by ForbesFilm. He currently lives in Minneapolis, Minnesota and may be contacted through Facebook.

Erik Gustafson holds master's degree in psychology and is a veteran of the United States Air Force. He is the author of two novels and many short stories. His first novel "Fall Leaves and the Black Dragon", is self-published and his second novel is out seeking a publisher. His has also been previously published in *The Horror Zine, Death Throes Ezone* and by Visionary Press, The Horror Society, and other anthologies. He is currently working on his third novel, *The Carousel in the Sky*. To learn more, please visit his blog at www.erikgustafson.wordpress.com.

Gary Hewitt is a raconteur who lives in a quaint little village in Kent. He has written two novels which are currently being edited. His writing does tend to veer away from what you might expect. He has had several short stories published as well as the occasional poem. He enjoys both writing prose and poetry. His style of writing tends to feature edgy characters and can be extremely dark. Some of his influences are James Herbert, Stephen King, Bulgakov, and Tolkein to name but a few. He is also a proud member of the Hazlitt Arts Centre Writers group in Maidstone which features an eclectic group of very talented writers. He has a website featuring his published works here: http://ghwt9996.wix.com/tales#!.

Justin Hunter is an emerging author and freelance writer. He writes primarily on the human condition, wrestling with idealism and dignity in poverty. Sometimes he writes a bit of horror, but it keeps him up at night. He is an early childhood educator, husband and adoptive father of two beautiful boys.

J.D. Isip's academic writings, poetry, plays, and short stories have appeared (or will appear) in a number of publications including *The Louisville Review, Changing English, Revista Aetenea, St. John's Humanities Review, Teaching American Literature, The Citron Review, Poetry*

Quarterly, Scholars & Rogues, Mused, and *The Copperfield Review.* I am a doctoral student in English at Texas A&M University-Commerce.

Mathias Jansson is a Swedish art critic and poet. He has been published in magazines as The Horror Zine Magazine, Dark Eclipse, Schlock, The Sirens Call and The Poetry Box. He has also contributed to several anthologies from Horrified Press and James Ward Kirk Fiction, including *Suffer Eternal Anthology Volume 1-3, Hell Whore Anthology Volume 1-3, Barnyard Horror,* and *Serial Killers Tres Tria.*
Homepage: http://mathiasjansson72.blogspot.se/.

Tom Johnstone lives and works in Brighton, on the South coast of England, where he works in the City Parks department, and occasionally mows and strims around tomb stones. Recently he even saw inside an ancient, unmarked, open grave with a skull in! His short fiction has appeared in Dark Tales(Vols. 12 and 13), Holiday of the Dead (Wild Wolf Publications), the 9th Black Book of *Horror* (Mortbury Press). At the time of writing, other stories are awaiting publication in the *10th Black Book of Horror* (Mortbury Press), *Cellar Door* (JWK Fiction) and *Brighton - the Graphic Novel*(Queen Spark Press). He is also co-editing *Horror Uncut - Tales of Austerity*, with Joel Lane for Gray Friar Press.

Caroline Kepnes lives in Los Angeles and returns home to Cape Cod every chance she gets. This summer, her short stories have appeared in *Fried Chicken and Coffee, Necessary Fiction, The Subterranean Quarterly* and *Two Serious Ladies.* She is contracted to write a novel for Alloy Entertainment and covers television for Yahoo! TV.

Matt Kurtz is a lover of all things horror. When not writing twisted tales, he enjoys watching a frightening flick or reading a terrifying tome. His fiction can be found in anthologies from Evil Jester Press, Blood Bound Books, Comet Press and *Necrotic Tissue Magazine.*

Patrick Lacey is an Editorial Assistant in the healthcare industry. When he's not reading about blood clots and infectious diseases, he writes about things that make the general public uncomfortable. He lives in Massachusetts with his wife, his

Pomeranian, and his muse, whom he's pretty sure is trying to kill him. Follow him on Twitter (@Patlacey).

Ken MacGregor's work has appeared in several speculative fiction anthologies from Siren's Call Publications, Hazardous Press, Bloodbound Books, Dark Opus Press and more; his work has appeared in magazines and podcasts. Ken is a member in good standing of The Great Lakes Association of Horror Writers. Ken writes horror, fantasy and the occasional children's story. Ken will sometimes reread a piece he wrote and shudder in revulsion or glee (often both). He lives in Ypsilanti, Michigan with his wife, Liz and their children Gabriel and Maggie. He can be found on Facebook (Ken MacGregor - Author), Amazon and Goodreads. His story "Disaster Blanket" originally appeared in *Erie Tales, Volume V* by GLAHW.

Carrick McCleary is the pseudonym of a man with many personalities. He is Legion. A tech geek, an actor (working under his true name and Richard Strychnine), and a writer who has had many articles, a smattering of short stories, and poetry published over the years. He writes constantly; his work bends, shifts, and weaves its way through multiple genres. He doesn't write because he wants to as much as because he must. Carrick enjoys tinkering with the accepted conventions of media and multimedia, trying to reach beyond those conventions to something greater. Something more. In recent years, Carrick has been published in the Necon Flash Anthology a few times (under his true name, Sean R. Padlo), but mostly he experiments with whatever media a project draws him toward... among other things.

Angela Meadon is an author of fiction and non-fiction work. Her stories can be found in the Pill Hill Press anthologies *Rotting Tales, Leather, Denim & Silver,* and *The Trigger Reflex.* Angela's novel about the zombie apocalypse with a dash of psychological terror and a sprinkling of guilt, *A Taste of You* (Amazon), was published in December 2012 by Damnation Books.
Angela lives in Johannesburg, South Africa with her two sons, three cats and a husband who rick-rolled her at the altar on their wedding day.

Angelin Miller represents the natural world through painting, drawing and textiles.

Maria Mitchell has had poems published in the *Innsmouth Free Press Gothic* horror anthology, *Candle in the Attic Window*, issue #80 of Sage Woman, *Yester Year Fiction* and *The Absent Willow Review*. She is currently the horror film soundtrack columnist at Innsmouth Free Press. She authored the short stories "Second Coming" at Dead Man's Tome, "The Mermaid Promise" at Flashes in the Dark, "Song of the Catherine Clark" in Cthulhurotica and "The Kadath Angle" in Future Lovecraft. She has one unfinished serial at Fried Fiction called *Kadaxia* and wrote Monster Bytes at Innsmouth Free Press. She is an affiliate member of HWA.

K.Z. Morano is a registered nurse with experience in the pediatric field, a freelance writer, and a blogger who lives in the Philippines. She recently won the *Popcorn Horror Presents 100 Words or Less Horror Stories* competition and got her story published in the anthology. She's currently working on a high fantasy novel.

Believe it or not, M.C. O'Neill is most known for the young adult saga *The Ancients and the Angels*. Even though this genre may be his forte, he also enjoys delving into his love for Bizarro and Horror. Having numerous publications with editors such as James Ward Kirk, Ksenia Anske, James Roy Daley and Danielle Tauscher, O'Neill is no stranger to the dark and the occult. His influences include Manly Wade Wellman, J.G. Ballard, Robert Anton Wilson, Paul Laffoley, and P.K. Dick.
Although, to wit, no such radio host as Tommy Westwood exists; O'Neill has appeared on New Zealand's premiere conspiracy news production, *The Vinny Eastwood Show*.

Niall Parkinson is an Irish artist specialising in the origination of dark, surrealist, conceptual and spiritual hand drawn illustration from which he explores the darker regions of the human heart and experience. His background is in the realm of graphic design and he had spent over 20 years working in this capacity within the printing industry. Niall has also had success in the music industry designing cd covers and booklets for European metal bands.
His real interest now lies in pursuing his illustration service DARK AGE DESIGN from which he hopes to work in the realm of specialist areas such as magazine, book illustration and cover

design with perhaps some comic work which incorporates horror and nightmarish themes and concepts

Niall is also available to work within more conventional areas of design including signage, logo design, crest and typography development and other areas of design and layout. Niall's work can be seen at http://neonangelus68.wix.com/dark-age-design and www.artwanted.com/parky68. Niall can be contacted via email at: neonangelus68@hotmail.com.

Joseph J. Patchen's publication credits include Dark Waters Press, Your Title Here, Schlock! Webzine, Microhorror, Flashes In The Dark, The Carnage Conservatory, High Tide, Three Minute Plastic, Terribly Good Stuff, Surreal Grotesque, FeatherTales, Night to Dawn and Slit Your Wrists. His anthology credits include: Rigorous Mortis, 31 More Nights of Halloween, Tales for the Toilet, You Can't Kill Me, I'm Already Dead: A Vampire Anthology, Aliens, Sex and Sociopaths: The Best of Surreal Grotesque and the soon to be published Tortured Souls Volume 2. His own dollar dreadful titled "Corpses Don't Bleed" published by BizarrEBooks is available on Amazon.com. Joseph's website is josephjpatchen.weebly.com and blog is "Wide Awakes Redux". He is also the resident literary critic for Lurid-lit.com.

David S. Pointer has new work included in *Indiana Crime Anthology 2013*, *Bones*, and other James Ward Kirk Fiction titles. David can be reached at dspointer@hotmail.com.

Married with three kids, Essel Pratt lives a busy life in his hometown of Mishawaka, IN. Essel is a daily contributor for Nerdzy.com and Infendo.com, in which he writes about video game news and other nerdy stories. You can follow Essel's other writings on facebook.com/esselprattwiting.

Bruce L. Priddy is a weird fiction writer living in Louisville, KY. His work has appeared in the Lovecraft eZine, *Grave Robbers* from James Ward Kirk publishing and in the upcoming *Edge of Sundown* anthology from Chaosium.

Ryan Rice is a part-time freelance artist and full-time graphic designer who lies and works in the Pittsburgh area.

Randy D. Rubin resides in Portsmouth, Virginia, with his lovely wife Lisa, and his uglybaby dog, Eva La Rue. He is an honorably retired Navy veteran and enjoys writing horror, reading, watching horror and sci-fi movies, and an eclectic mix of music. He is a grandfather of three, father of four and devoted husband of one. That's all he can afford, for God's sake! He cooks, gardens, and metal detects. He's a wee bit cuckoo for cocoa nuts.

Suzy Saylor is a freelance writer outside Philadelphia, Pennsylvania. She is currently a stay at home mother of two children, neither of which is named Lucy, despite what she often tells people. She is currently working on her first novel with plans for more to follow.

Never judge a book by its cover. **Ashley Scarlet** likes to keep things dark and mysterious, yet the other side of her feels compelled to bring out the naive child-like beauty in her art. Growing up in the Midwest, Scarlet broke the rules of Society and hides inside a house made of candy, painting to her macabre delight.

Michael C. Schutz-Ryan was born and raised in the frozen tundra of Wisconsin. He attended the UW-Stevens Point and graduated with an English degree from the Madison campus. A lifelong diet of Ray Bradbury and Stephen King whet his appetite for the macabre. A lover of all things horror, he likes to plumb the depths of Netflix in search of decent scary movies. His short story, "Autumn Trees" was published in *Expanded Horizons*. Currently, he's finishing his first novel. He lives and writes in San Jose, CA.

Mark Slade has appeared in *The Rusty Nail, Hell Whore, Diabolic Tales III*, and *Flash Fiction Offensive*. Horrified Press will be publishing his novella, *A Six Gun and the Queen of Light*. Mark runs the podcasts Dark Dreams and Blackout City. He lives in Williamsburg, Virginia with his wife and daughter.

John Stanton is a writer/photographic artist living in Indianapolis, Indiana. For the past eight years, John has provided hundreds of images to the small press, electronic and print editions as well as book covers, earning Top Ten Finisher in the annual Predator and Editor polls, as well as three mentions in Ellen Datlow's "Best of" collections. His "Subtractive Illusion" is featured on Corel.com, along with an interview. Currently, his artwork can be seen in *Not One of Us Issue #49*, the *Indiana*

Horror 2012 and *Indiana Crime 2013* anthologies, as well as www.3AMBlue.com and http://johndstanton.blogspot.com/.

James Suriano grew up in Upstate NY, where he always imagined forces working behind the curtain of what he saw in the world. When he got to the Philippines in 2005 for a work assignment, his suspicions were confirmed and he was compelled to write his first book to chronicle the horror of what was lurking there. The passion of telling stories never left him, and he continues to create novels and short stories monthly. James lives in Washington, DC with his husband and son, has a Master's Degree from Johns Hopkins University and is the Director of Internal Audit.

Jeff Swenson graduated from The Art Institute of Seattle and jumped into a variety of projects; some admirable, some questionable. He has worked on *Glyph*, a brief tabloid run of free comics distributed in Seattle, animatics and promotional flash animation for the movie *Heart of The Beholder*, parody animation to promote the website AmazingKarma.com, and artwork for the *Joovia* comic strip series for Unicorn Multimedia. His personal comic strip runs include *The Cynic, Frenetic Funnies, Halloween Funnies* and *Freethunk—* collections can be found on Amazon.com. He has also done some animations for the web in poor taste, but you'll have to find those on your own.

R. T. Tandy is a fiction writer currently working in both traditional literature and graphic novels. His short fiction has previously appeared in *Another 100 Horrors, Dear Santa,* and the *E4 Frightfest* magazine. He currently lives in Cardiff, Wales, with his fiancée Sarah.

DJ Tyrer is the person behind Atlantean Publishing and has had numerous poems and stories published in the small presses of the UK, USA and elsewhere, as well as online. DJ Tyrer is the author of the novella *The Yellow House* and the critically-acclaimed poetry sequence *Our Story*. Most recently, he contributed three vignettes to *Sorcery & Sanctity: A Homage to Arthur Machen* from Hieroglyphic Press.

M.E. VonBindig's short stories "Small Country" and "Sirens" will soon be featured in the upcoming *Chilling Whispers* from the DailyNightmare.com: Volume One. A neurotic Basset Hound resides with the author in the wilds of northern Michigan and stands guard against the ghoul and rabid raccoons that lurk in the forest behind their home. M.E. is a member of the Great Lakes Association of Horror Writers and is currently working on several projects when not hoarding printed books to read for the impending apocalypse!

Matthew Wilson, 30, is a UK resident who has been writing since small. Recently these stories have appeared in *Horror Zine*, *Star*Line*, and *Sorcerers Signal*. He is currently editing his first novel and can be contacted on twitter @matthew94544267.

Stephanie M. Wytovich is an Alum of Seton Hill University where she was a double major in English Literature and Art History. Wytovich is published in over 40 literary magazines and HYSTERIA is her first collection. She is currently attending graduate school to pursue her MFA in Writing Popular Fiction, and is working on a novel. She is the Poetry Editor for Raw Dog Screaming Press and a book reviewer for S.T. Joshi, Jason V. Brock and William F. Nolan's Nameless Magazine. She plans to continue in academia to get her doctorate in Gothic Literature.

www.ingramcontent.com/pod-product-compliance
Lightning Source LLC
Chambersburg PA
CBHW070923180626
46817CB00003B/1176